G000160363

LUCIENNE BOYCE has always been
Era. In 2006 she gained an MA
Open University specialising i
She has been a member of the
shortly after its foundation. She is a member of the steering
committee of the West of England and South Wales Women's
History Network. The first Dan Foster Mystery, *Bloodie Bones*,
was joint winner of the 2016 Historical Novel Society Indie
Award, and was also a semi-finalist in the M M Bennetts Award
for Historical Fiction 2016.

Want to know more?
Find Lucienne Boyce on Twitter: @LucienneWrite
You can also stay up-to-date by visiting her website
lucienneboyce.com

# THE BUTCHER'S BLOCK

## LUCIENNE BOYCE

**SilverWood**

Published in 2017 by SilverWood Books

SilverWood Books Ltd
14 Small Street, Bristol, BS1 1DE, United Kingdom
www.silverwoodbooks.co.uk

ISBN 978-1-78132-676-3 (paperback)
ISBN 978-1-78132-677-0 (ebook)

British Library Cataloguing in Publication Data
A CIP catalogue record for this book is available from
the British Library

Page design and typesetting by SilverWood Books
Printed on responsibly sourced paper

# THE BUTCHER'S BLOCK

# Chapter One

Dan Foster took the pistol stamped with the words "Bow Street" out of his coat pocket and placed it on the desk. Perkins, the night clerk, picked up the weapon. He held it close to his long, thin face, which was grotesquely up-lit by the lamp on the desk. "It hasn't been fired?"

"Didn't need it," Dan said, putting the powder flask and cartouche of shot next to the gun.

Perkins laughed and winked at the blood-soaked handkerchief tied around the knuckles of Dan's right hand. "Wish I'd been there to see you."

Dan grunted. The night clerk would not have been too pleased if his wish had been granted. Earlier that evening Dan had been called to a burglary in King Street. An elderly couple had been tied, gagged and beaten. All for the pleasure of it: they had not resisted. The old man had handed over the key to his money chest at first demand.

It was that sheer, pointless brutality that had given Dan the clue to who had committed the crime. A few foul taverns and quaking informants later his hunch had been confirmed: a known low-life was back in town and as mean as ever. Dan had tracked his quarry down to the Old Alehouse in Chick Lane, on the edge of St Andrew's Parish, one of the most dangerous streets in London. The Old Alehouse was its foul heart, the place where all its wickedness concentrated, the haunt of the most vicious thieves, murderers and prostitutes.

Not a place a lone principal officer of Bow Street could safely venture into. Dan had waited for the man to leave, staggering arm in arm with a woman, and followed them to a little-frequented, stinking alley before making his move. When the fighting had started the female had abandoned her companion and stumbled away. Dan had been thinking of the old woman's lined, fragile face, a mass of blood and bruises, as he drove his fist into the burglar's jaw.

Now her assailant was locked up in the cell which the landlord of the Brown Bear, the tavern across the road from Bow Street Magistrates' Office, provided for the use of the principal officers. He would be brought before the magistrate when the daily session opened at eleven in the morning, be in Newgate awaiting trial by the end of the day, and swinging before the year was out.

Perkins took a bunch of keys from the hook on his belt, unlocked the gun cupboard and placed Dan's service-issue weapon inside. Dan yawned and glanced down at the young patrolman who sat on one of the office chairs, hunched over a bucket swilling with the sour-smelling contents of his stomach.

"What's up with him?"

"Jones?" Perkins locked the cupboard and replaced the bunch of keys on his belt. "Had a bit of a nasty surprise." He jerked his head at the large laundry basket which stood on the floor by the desk.

"What's inside it?"

Perkins grinned. "Take a look."

Dan frowned at the clerk. It was nearly midnight, he was tired, he had no patience for stupid games. He clicked his tongue and lifted the lid.

At first he thought he was looking at a limp doll or huddled marionette, its face pale and chiselled, its half-lidded eyes exposing a line of white. It lay on a darkly stained cloth, and there were what looked like two little animals curled up on either side of it. It took Dan a minute to realise that he was looking at a human head and hands.

"Jones here and Captain Ellis stopped a pair of suspicious-looking fellows carrying this basket on Holborn

Hill, close to St Andrew's churchyard," Perkins said. "Turns out they'd bagged a couple of resurrection men on their way to St Bartholomew's dissection room. Ellis's locking them up now." He sniggered. "He's put 'em in the basement with the darkness and the rats."

A measure of how detested body snatchers were. Dan's burglar was better off. He at least had a bed, though he was chained to it.

"Did they find any grave goods on them?"

"Unfortunately, no," Perkins said.

Sometimes, Dan thought, the law he was expected to uphold was exceedingly stupid. According to the learned justices, no one owned a dead body so it could not be stolen. It was only if the resurrectionists took something else from the grave, such as a shroud, keepsake or even the coffin itself, that they could be charged with theft. The obvious result was that most body snatchers took care to leave all but the corpse behind, knowing that if caught, the most they would get was a few weeks in Bridewell for vagrancy.

There was no need to voice his opinion: Perkins was doing it for him. "Now, I says, it's the family as owns the corpse, and it's the family as suffers when a loved relation is dug up and snatched away, and so it ought to be treated as a theft like any other. Even worse nor any other. Don't you say so, Mr Foster?"

Dan gazed down at the remains, not listening. He was about to replace the lid when something caught his eye. He snatched up the lamp and held it over the basket, stooping so low that his own head was almost inside with the grisly remains. Perkins's voice was a muffled drone somewhere above him.

"I do wish the captain would hurry up. I'm ready for my bed." The night clerk had apartments at the top of the house so that he was on call in case of emergencies. He chuckled. "Might have a bit of supper first. Pigs' trotters, perhaps. Or a bit of tripe and onions."

Jones retched and released a stream of stringy vomit into

the bucket. Dan straightened up, the lamp shaking in his hand. Perkins winked at him. But Dan was not interested in his clowning.

"Hell," he said. "It's Officer Kean."

# Chapter Two

Captain Sam Ellis appeared in the doorway rattling a bunch of keys and chuckling to himself.

"Dan, how are you? Got a couple of –"

"Give me the keys."

"Here they are. But –"

Dan snatched the key ring out of Ellis's grasp and sprinted down the stairs. Behind him he heard Perkins's husky voice, "He says it's Officer Kean…" and Jones's wavering, "How can he be sure in this light?" Dan did not hear what Ellis said in reply.

It was dark in the passageway, smelt of damp, drains, and rats. He should have brought a light; he had run down here without thinking. But there was no need to go back: Ellis was not one to waste time standing around exclaiming. A yellow glow appeared at the foot of the stairs, the patrolman's bulk behind it. It was enough for Dan to find the lock and insert the key by. He swung open the door, by which time Ellis was at his back shining the light into the cell. The prisoners sat on the floor, one with his head sunk on his knees, whimpering. The other scrambled to his feet. He was a tall, sinewy man with an aura of dung about him.

"About bleedin' time," he said. "You ain't got no right to leave us down 'ere like this."

Dan charged into the cell and grabbed him by the throat. "Where's the rest of the body, you whoreson?"

"Dan! Dan! Let him go, for Christ's sake. You're throttling him," Ellis cried.

The man's eyes bulged, spittle oozed from his slack mouth. His cries of pain and protest were no more than a desperate gurgling, and his hands flapped uselessly at his sides.

More footsteps, more voices, the light danced crazily over the shining walls. Perkins grabbed Dan's right arm and tried to pull him off. "Stop, Mr Foster, stop!"

Ellis thrust the lantern into Jones's hand, moved to Dan's left. His low voice penetrated Dan's understanding as Perkins's frenzied yelling did not. "We'll never find Kean if you don't let go."

Breathing heavily, Dan stepped back, pushed the body snatcher away from him. The man pressed his back against the wall and sidled away, his eyes rolling, head lolling.

"He belongs in Bedlam! Keep him off me!"

"Shut your noise, Reynolds," Ellis said.

The patrol captain pressed one hand flat against Dan's chest to prevent him going for Reynolds again. Dan wiped his hand across his face. The makeshift bandage had gone and his knuckles had started to bleed afresh. He prowled back and forth, clenching and unclenching his fists, pivoting around Ellis's arm as the captain shadowed his pacing, holding him at bay. Dan flung back his head, flexed his shoulders, glared at the body snatcher who shrivelled into his corner. But by now Dan was in control. The threatening attitude was deliberate: the pre-fight poise of a man in the boxing ring. Ellis sensed this and relaxed his arm. Dan nodded at him: *It's all right.* Ellis stepped out of his way.

"I'll ask one more time," Dan said. "Where is the rest of the body?"

"How should I know? I never seen it," Reynolds answered.

"Do you know who he is, the man in your basket?"

Reynolds shook his head, winced at the pain. "It's just a Thing. We was going to sell it, that's all."

"He's a Bow Street officer."

Reynolds sucked in his breath. The man on the floor flung his hands protectively over his head and rocked back and forth, wailing.

Dan glanced down at him. "Get up."

"No...no...leave me alone...I never done nothing."

Ellis reached down and hauled him up by one arm. "My friend's not in a very good mood, Wallace. I'd do as he tells you, if I was you."

Wallace was bigger and stronger than Reynolds, but he hadn't a fraction of the other's bravado. Didn't look like he had a fraction of the other's sense either. He reeked of the gin that had half-rotted his brain and guts, his little eyes were dim, and his speech and movements were slow and lumbering.

"Which of you killed him?" Dan demanded.

Wallace shrieked, "It wasn't us! We just had the Thing in the basket. We had no idea he was one of your lot or else we'd never have touched it."

"So if you didn't kill him, where did you get the remains?"

"Off a man in a tavern," Wallace answered eagerly. "Said he's a porter at Guy's Hospital, said they had some parts left over, said if we wanted 'em we could have 'em."

"What's his name?"

"He never said."

"What tavern?"

"The Black Raven."

"In Chick Lane?" Chick Lane again: the corruption at the centre of the metropolis. "When was this?"

Wallace's face puckered with the strain of trying to remember. "Not yesterday. Could have been the day before."

"It was last night," Reynolds said. "We paid ten shillings, could have got a guinea. Heads always bring a good..." He saw the dangerous look in Dan's eye and his voice trailed away.

"So this man you'd never met before came up to you on Saturday night and offered you some body parts."

"That's right." Reynolds again.

"Doesn't sound like much of a story to me."

"But it's true," Reynolds insisted. "I swear on my mother's grave." He licked his lips, realising how foolish the oath sounded coming from him.

"What did he look like?"

Reynolds shrugged. "Ordinary."

"I said, what did he look like?"

"He wasn't much to look at," Reynolds said. "Medium height, brown hair, wore a blue coat."

"A white cravat," Wallace put in.

"What else?"

"That's it."

"Was he young? Old?"

"No. I mean, he wasn't one or the other," Reynolds said.

"What did he sound like?"

"Sound like?"

"Was he from London? Was he a Welshman, an Irishman, a Yorkshireman, the man in the moon?"

"I don't know. He spoke ordinary."

Dan turned to Ellis. "Anything you want to ask?"

"I think you've covered everything."

Jones cleared his throat.

"What?" Dan asked.

"Where did they pick up the...the basket?"

"Good question. Go on, answer Patrolman Jones."

Reynolds did so. "From off the back of a cart in Liquorpond Street."

A street of breweries not far from Holborn Hill, where a laden cart would not attract much attention.

"And the driver?" Dan did not expect the answer to be anything other than what it was.

"All wrapped up. Never saw him."

"I'm done," Dan said to Perkins. "You can lock them up again now."

The police officers filed out of the room, taking the lamp with them. Perkins shut and locked the door.

"Hey!" Reynolds bawled. "Leave us a light!"

As they walked away, Dan heard Reynolds snarl, "Shut your blubbing!" at his cellmate.

Upstairs, Ellis glanced apprehensively at the basket. "You really think it's George Kean?"

"I know it is. There's a scar by his left eye. I was with him when he got it. We were in the Lord Rodney's Head in Chequers Alley after a couple of street robbers. They put up a fight and Kean got hit with a broken chair."

Perkins, meanwhile, had gone into the chief clerk's tiny room where they could hear him opening a cupboard and moving bottle and glasses. He came back to the main office carrying a tray on which there were four brimming glasses of brandy. He offered one to Dan, who gave him a withering look. As if Perkins did not know he never drank spirits. He had never got into the habit; he had seen what drink did to other men, how it turned their muscles slack, blurred their vision, slowed their reactions. He had seen what it did to a marriage too, but that was something he buried deep when he was working.

The clerk shrugged: more for him. Ellis and Jones helped themselves.

"So what now?" Ellis asked.

"I'll go to Guy's first thing in the morning," Dan answered. "See if I can track down their porter. And I don't think we should tell anyone else about this until the chief magistrate's been informed. I'll be back here before Sir William gets in."

"You don't think I should send for him now?" Perkins asked.

"No point. There's nothing to be done till the morning. Which isn't that far off." To Ellis and Jones he said, "You two better be ready to give your statements."

Silence fell between the four men, each busy with his own thoughts, none wanting to look at the basket, none able to forget it was there. It was Perkins who spoke first.

"What shall I do with…?"

"Put the basket downstairs, where it's cool," said Dan. "We'll need a doctor to examine the remains in the morning."

"Someone will have to help me lift it."

Ellis and Jones exchanged appalled glances.

"I'll do it," Dan said. "And then I'm going to get a couple of hours' sleep."

The patrolmen put their glasses on the tray and rose to their feet. They shuffled towards the door, glad to be going, but ashamed of themselves for being so. Dan caught hold of one of the rope handles and signalled to Perkins to do the same. The basket creaked and sagged as they took its dreadful weight.

# Chapter Three

It took Dan only a few minutes to walk to his home in Russell Street. Already he could hear the clatter of carts and babble of voices from the marketplace in Covent Garden Piazza as the first of the day's traders began to arrive from the outlying market gardens. He let himself into the dark house and stood in the hall to listen for a moment, imagining he would catch the sound of Eleanor's soft breathing. All he heard was his mother-in-law's snoring. No sound came from the bedroom which he shared with his wife Caroline, Eleanor's sister.

Telling himself he would only disturb Caroline if he went upstairs, he went instead into the kitchen and settled in an armchair by the hearth, which still gave out a residual warmth from a heap of grey ash. He pulled off his boots and sank back into the seat. Kean had been a police officer some years. He had been in the Army before that. He knew how to take care of himself. So how, Dan wondered, had he let this happen? To what trick or ambush or savagery had he fallen victim?

Dan shut his eyes and saw Kean's face staring up at him from the depths of the basket, the half-open eyelids exposing the whites of his eyes, the mouth gaping as if in a last cry of rage and despair. There would be no sleep for Dan while that spectre haunted him…

He was woken by a flood of daylight and the bang of the window shutters over the sink. He sat up.

Mrs Harper, his mother-in-law, turned round. "Dan, I didn't see you there. We never heard you come in. You must have been very late. What time was it? Let me get that fire going and I'll make some tea."

"Don't worry about the tea. I'll have something at the gym."

"Are you sure? I can do you a bit of breakfast. Won't take many minutes."

"No, thanks. Have I got a clean shirt to take with me?"

"Of course you have. They'll be upstairs in your room."

"Could you look for me? I don't want to wake Caroline. You're lighter on your feet than me."

This was not true. Mrs Harper was a noisy, bustling woman, but she took him at his word and went upstairs. He put on his boots and was ready to leave when she came back.

"She didn't stir," she said, handing him the shirt. "What time shall I tell her you'll be back?"

He bundled the clean linen under his arm. "I don't know. Late. There's a new case. Don't wait up."

He walked down to the Strand and came out by Exeter Exchange. Cafés and restaurants were serving breakfast to men and women on their way to work, cab- and chairmen on their way home, dazed travellers who had been deposited at some nearby inn after a comfortless night's journey. Coaches pulled in and out of yards thronging with stable lads, ostlers, porters, maids selling pies and drinks. None of the shops or other attractions were open yet, but the animals in Pidcock's Menagerie on the top floor of the Exchange were restless as always. Here lions and elephants, tigers and zebras, apes and exotic birds, defeated in their attempts to pace or flutter around tiny cages, snarled, roared and grunted. When there was not much traffic, their bellows of rage and frustration would often be heard in the street.

Dan turned in the direction of Charing Cross and passed the area known as the Savoy with its jumble of houses, barracks, churches and coal wharves. A few steps later he turned into Cecil Street and walked down towards the river. Halfway along he went in through an unlocked door squeezed between a lodging house and the steam baths. He ran up a flight of wooden stairs and opened the door at the top into a long room. Though it was early, the gymnasium was full of snarling, grunting men whose half-naked bodies gave off the familiar smell of sweat and liniment.

It was sixteen years since boxing trainer Noah Foster had watched a wild street brat fight with a bigger opponent amongst the crowds assembled for the Oliver v Johnson match at Blackheath. Dan and his adversary had been there to take advantage of the spectators' distraction to dive into a few pockets. The other boy had claimed the territory as his own and given the outsider a beating. A thief Dan might have been, but Noah had seen that he had the courage, speed and bearing of a born athlete. So Noah had given the boy a home, found the decency in him, and turned him into a disciplined pugilist.

Dan returned the greetings of several of the athletes, some sparring with their fists muffled in leather gloves, others punching sacks, some lifting weights. He had trained with many of them, and some he had also defeated in gymnasium competitions. At the far end of the room, Noah Foster's assistant, Paul, shouted instructions to a young novice who had not progressed beyond aiming enthusiastic punches at the air.

Dan went through a curtained doorway into the living rooms. Noah looked up from his newspaper. "Hallo, son," he said, folding the journal and placing it on the table beside his half-full coffee cup. "Can I get you something?"

"I'll have some coffee."

Dan lowered himself into a seat opposite Noah's. The old man busied himself at the fireplace with the coffee jug, placed a cup of dark liquid in front of Dan and topped up his own.

"What have you done to your hand?"

Dan spread out his fingers and looked down at his swollen knuckle. "You should see the other man."

The attempt at lightness failed. Noah looked at Dan for a moment, then rose and reached a box of bandages, oils and balms down from a shelf. He poured some hot water from the kettle into a bowl, which he took back to the table, then he sat down and washed Dan's wound with a clean cloth.

"So what's happened?" he asked as he worked.

"There's an officer dead. Kean."

A guarded look came into Noah's face. Dan knew what he was trying to hide: his fear of one day hearing the same news of Dan, who had been nobody's child until Noah Foster took him in and brought him up as his own.

"It's a nasty one, Dad." Briefly, Dan described last night's find.

Noah listened without interrupting. He tied the ends of the bandage, wrung out the bloody cloth and threw it on the fire where it sizzled and steamed on the coals. "Was he a friend of yours?"

"We worked together sometimes. He was a good officer." Dan stood up. "I'll go and get changed."

"As to that, no hitting with that hand. Stick to lifting some weights and a bit of leg work. I'll come and have a look at you by and by."

Though he had not had much sleep, Dan pushed himself through his exercises and felt more energetic by the time he had finished. He went to the steam baths to shower, shave and dress, left his dirty clothes at Noah's to go out with the laundry and set off for Guy's Hospital.

He crossed the river by Blackfriars Bridge, which was jammed with foot and wheeled traffic. The river was crowded with barges and boats. Further down, beyond London Bridge, ocean-going vessels moored in the centre of the stream towered over smaller craft darting around them. Strung along the shores was an irregular network of quays and warehouses, some old and sagging, others new and solid. Watermen and passengers jostled around the numerous flights of steps down to the water. The yeasty smell of breweries, the putrid smell of tanneries, the sickly, burnt smell of sugar refineries, and the smoke of innumerable chimneys, furnaces and forges filled the air.

He passed through the iron gates into the courtyard of Guy's Hospital. A group of students loafed noisily, heedless of the crowd of herniated, injured and abscessed poor who waited for the outpatients' room to open. Dan crossed the court, ran up a flight of stone steps and passed through a door in an archway which brought him into a long corridor. None of the nurses and dressers who hurried between the male and female wards took any notice of him, but the top half of the door in the porters' lodge just inside the entrance shot open and a craggy face under a shiny hat thrust itself out.

"Not open yet. Join the queue."

Dan reached into his pocket for his staff of office. "I'm from Bow Street. I need to speak to the head porter."

The man regarded the wooden tipstaff with its gilt crown with an unimpressed air then said, "Come in, then."

He shut and secured the top half of the door before sliding back bolts top and bottom and swinging the whole door open. Dan entered a cluttered den with a table and four chairs arranged around a small fireplace over which hung an ancient and smoke-stained kettle. All the signs pointed to the seriousness with which the porters took their comfort when they were not doing their rounds, delivering messages or running errands for the surgeons. The wooden chairs were softened with worn, flattened cushions, and the table was covered with cake, bread, cheese, biscuits, jugs: enough supplies to ensure that hardly an hour need go by without something to drink and nibble on.

"Are you the head porter?" Dan asked.

The porter planted his feet wide apart and rested his hands magisterially on his round stomach. "I am. Mr Rummage at your service. And you are?"

"Foster, Principal Officer, Bow Street. I'm looking for one of your men. An ordinary looking sort of fellow, middle-aged, wears a blue coat and white cravat."

"No one like that here. Most of my lot are older men. Ex-Army or Navy, many of 'em."

"So you don't know anyone who's got a line in selling bits of bodies left over from the dissecting room?"

Rummage's eyes narrowed, deepening the lines around

them. "So that's what you're here about, is it? Pinning it on the working folk when nine times out of ten when a body goes missing it's the young gentlemen you ought to be looking at."

"The students, you mean? Why would they steal from their own dissecting room?"

"We haven't got a dissecting room. They go to St Thomas's for their anatomy classes. But we have got a mortuary."

"Are you saying that the students take bodies from the mortuary to dissect at St Thomas's?"

"They can't cut 'em up here."

"They could dismember them in the mortuary, though? To make it easy to carry them, for instance. Or to make a profit by selling the separate parts to other medical schools."

"I suppose they could do that. They'd have to clear up after themselves."

"Do all the bodies in the mortuary come from the wards here?"

"They don't walk in off the street."

"So is there any way of finding out if a man called Kean was admitted over the weekend?"

Rummage rubbed a fat finger down the side of his ruby nose. "The answer would be, he wasn't. Taking-in day is Thursday."

It seemed unlikely that Kean had been missing since Thursday without anyone noticing. Even so. "I might as well check while I'm here."

"You'd have to look at the surgeon's books."

"How do I do that?"

"You could ask the dressers."

"I'll do that. Do any of the students match the description I gave you?"

"I couldn't say. There's seventy or eighty of 'em at any one time. They come one year, they go another. All look the same to me."

"Very well, Mr Rummage. Now, take me to see the dressers."

"Now?"

"Yes, now."

"They'll be busy getting ready for outpatients."

"And I'm busy serving the magistrate of Bow Street."

Rummage fetched a deep sigh, adjusted his hat, made a great to-do of lifting a bunch of keys from a hook by the door and locking the door when they were on the other side of it. He led Dan down the corridor past the wards, where most of the patients lay in miserable silence, either waiting for their treatment, or having already received it. Dan followed Rummage into a large room with a bare wooden floor and wooden benches around the walls. Leading off from it was a room filled with chests and cabinets, from which a couple of women gathered lint, ointments and bandages and packed them in the dressers' portable tin boxes lined along the counter.

Rummage stalked past without deigning to notice the women, ahemed and knocked loudly on the open door of the consulting room. Inside, a harassed-looking man in his shirtsleeves and wearing a stained linen apron was setting out lotions, blisters and plasters on a trolley next to a high, narrow wooden bed. On the desk, between a pile of paperwork and a stack of ledgers, black leeches writhed in a glass jar.

"This is Mr Forrester of Bow Street Magistrates," Rummage said. "Wants to look at the admission lists."

"Oh, yes," the other replied, looking about him as if he expected the lists to appear out of the air. "They're here somewhere. Will it take long?"

"Thank you, Mr Rummage," Dan said. "I'll find my own way out."

The porter sniffed, jangled his keys, and walked off.

"The name's Foster," Dan said, walking into the room.

"Oh, yes, Foster, yes. I'm – ah – Evans. Dresser, yes, dresser. Was it the admission lists you wanted to see?" Evans dithered around the desk, shifting things from one spot to another and then back again.

"Is it one of those?" Dan asked, pointing at the ledgers.

"One of those? Ah yes, it is. Here we are. Admissions."

Dan cleared a space for the book on the edge of the desk and, stooping over the neatly ruled lines of text, ran his fingers slowly down the columns labelled name, age, sex and reason for admission. It was a parade of horrible diseases or ghastly injuries: scalding; fell from scaffolding; run over by a cart...

He tapped one of last Thursday's entries with his forefinger. "It says here gunshot wound to abdomen. Man called Noakes. Do you remember it?"

Evans looked at the page. "Ah, yes. Patient died a few hours later."

"Was he conscious when he came in?"

"Was he –? Yes."

"If someone was brought in unconscious, you wouldn't know their name unless there was someone with them who could tell you?"

"Or something amongst his – ah – effects, if any."

"But you are sure this man was conscious and gave his own name?"

"Yes, oh, yes. If the patient is unconscious we make – ah – make a note of it in the book."

So it could not have been Kean. None of the other entries looked as promising. There was no trace of the dead man having been at Guy's.

# Chapter Four

When Dan turned into Bow Street he saw that a crowd had gathered around the Magistrates' Office. Newspaper men, porters, idlers, market traders, hawkers, women with children in tow, and other representatives of London's street life pressed around the front of the building. The door that was usually open to the public was shut and guarded by two patrolmen. Seeing Dan pushing his way through the mob, one of them banged on the door. Someone inside turned the key.

"What's happening? Why won't they let us in?" one of the reporters bawled.

"Why haven't today's sessions started?" demanded another.

"Is it true there's been an attempt to assassinate the King?"

The clamorous throng surged after Dan. The guards pushed them back while he squeezed through the door. Inside, Lavender, the chief clerk, re-locked it.

"Sir William's waiting for you, Foster," he said. "The surgeon is with him."

The sound of voices came from the main room where the gaolers, clerks and messengers had collected, their duties ignored. Dan glanced in as he passed along the corridor and spotted a number of fellow-Bow Street principal officers. They clustered around Perkins, the night clerk, bombarding him with questions. *Why had Kean been murdered? Where had Mr Foster gone – did he know who'd done it? When would Sir William examine Wallace and Reynolds?* Since Perkins did not have the answers, the interrogation only increased their frustration.

Putting in a rare appearance at the office was John Townsend, holding court to an admiring circle of attendants.

He rapped his cane on the floor to emphasise his utterances, which sounded authoritative enough, except that he knew nothing about Kean's murder. For the last few years, Townsend had been employed as bodyguard to the royal family, in particular the Prince of Wales. That meant the races, boxing, gambling: a flash lifestyle Townsend had taken to with relish. A short, big-bellied man in his late thirties, he swaggered about town in a garish yellow waistcoat and a broad-brimmed hat like that worn by the Prince.

Though no official announcement had yet been made about Kean's death, the news had already begun to spread through the force. A few principal officers from other magistrates' offices had come in to show their solidarity with their colleagues. So too had many local constables and watchmen.

The housekeeper, the only woman amongst them, pressed a handkerchief to her eyes and sobbed, "He was always such a gentleman." Dan wondered how she made that out. Kean had struck him as a man who lacked the most basic social graces.

They caught sight of Dan and flowed towards him, shouting questions. He shook them off, loped up the stairs and knocked on Sir William's door. The murmur of voices within broke off and Sir William called, "Come in!"

The chief magistrate stood behind his desk. In one hand he held a glass of brandy; the other fidgeted with his watch chain. The surgeon had his back to the door and was bending over a metal tray on the desk between them. He had removed his hat and dark blue, high-collared coat, revealing a buttoned-up, vertically striped waistcoat over fawn breeches and black boots.

"Ah, Foster," Sir William said. "We were just about to begin. This is Mr Charlton of St Bartholomew's Hospital."

Dan shut the door and advanced towards the desk, his stomach churning. The lidless basket stood on the floor by the surgeon's feet. Dan forced himself to look at the tray where Kean's remains lay.

"If you will, Mr Charlton," Sir William said.

Sir William fortified himself with frequent swigs of brandy, while Dan was surprised at how his own stomach settled itself under the influence of Charlton's cool professionalism. When the doctor had finished assessing Kean's partial cadaver, he took a sip from his own glass and beckoned Sir William and Dan to draw close.

"As you can see," he said, turning the head to and fro to illustrate his points, "we have here the head and hands of a male in his late thirties or early forties. He appears well-nourished, so we can rule out death by starvation. As to what caused the death, it is impossible to say except that it was not from a blow to the head as there are no head wounds, and neither was it drowning. There are no defensive wounds on the hands, so it is likely that death did not occur during a fight or struggle. You see, incidentally, this pale band on his finger, which indicates that he wore a ring. The neck, so far as we have it, shows no signs of a ligature or knife entry."

"So he may have been shot or stabbed," Dan said.

"Or suffocated, poisoned or struck by lightning for all we can tell. It is difficult to place the time of death. Rigor begins within a few hours of death and affects the head first, but the whole body is not affected until approximately twelve hours have passed. Here of course we do not have the whole body. In what we do have, rigor has passed: you see the jaw is loose. However, much depends on the temperature and we do not know how the remains were stored before being delivered to the body snatchers. All I can suggest is that he met his end during the last two or three days."

"That would fit with what I have ascertained of his movements," Sir William said. "Mr Lavender tells me Kean came into the office late on Friday afternoon."

"Death could very well have occurred on Friday," Charlton answered. "These severance wounds were done by someone who knows his business. You say that the men you apprehended claim that these items came from a porter at Guy's, and they were going to offer them to St Bartholomew's?"

"That's their story," Sir William answered.

"And it doesn't hold up," Dan said. "There's no porter matching Reynolds's description at Guy's. No record of Kean ever having been there either. However he died, and wherever he was cut up, it wasn't at the hospital."

Charlton took his hat and coat from the sagging chair where he had left them. "If I can be of any further assistance, please do not hesitate to ask."

He gave a lingering look at the remains that had so nearly ended up on his dissecting slab, shook hands with Sir William, and left.

"For heaven's sake, cover it up," Sir William said. He refilled his glass while Dan looked about for a cloth, and eventually had to settle for the one from the basket. "You're sure about the porter?"

"Yes, sir."

"Then let's get Wallace's and Reynolds's depositions over with. After that, I have to go and tell Kean's widow that this is all she's got left to bury."

He emptied his glass and put it on the desk. Dan stepped aside to let him go first and followed him downstairs. Two new arrivals stood in the passageway, hats in hands. The younger of the two stood over a crate with a loosely-nailed lid. He kept a respectful silence while Lavender and his master conferred, standing close to one another in order to make themselves heard over the noise from the street.

"Sir William, this is the undertaker," Lavender said. "May I send him up?"

"You may. And mind, the casket is to be lead-lined oak. And make sure it is sealed before his family sees it. Send the bill to me; the office will settle it."

"I understand," the undertaker answered with professional sympathy. "The coffin will be impregnable. Your fallen comrade will not be disturbed in his final resting place." He shook hands with the clerk, beckoned to his assistant to follow with the crate, and started towards the stairs with soft, self-effacing steps. The effect was spoiled by the ostentatious creaking of his shoes.

"Foster, have the prisoners brought up," Sir William said. "And, Lavender, let the reporters in."

Sir William continued along the passage and out into the court leading to the courtroom. Lavender moved off towards the front door. Dan drew him back.

"Were you here when Kean came in Friday?"

"I was."

"Did he say anything about where he was going on Friday night?"

"Not to me."

"What was he working on?"

"Nothing out of the routine as far as I know. But then none of you officers tell me everything you're up to."

Lavender opened the door and ushered the reporters through the building to the courtroom while Dan went into the clerks' room and located the gaoler.

"Bring 'em up."

An angry hush fell. The gaoler and his assistant clumped downstairs. The jangle of keys and clink of handcuffs drifted up after them. The cellar door opened and closed, stumbling footsteps approached the stairs. A few moments later Reynolds and Wallace, blinking in the daylight, appeared in the doorway to face a storm of hisses. Reynolds, his hands shackled, halted in alarm. Wallace licked his lips with his thick tongue, his heavy face quivering with fear. The gaoler shoved them forward. The Bow Street staff parted to let them through, their silence more menacing than any uttered threat.

Sir William was already seated at the table on the raised platform at the top of the courtroom, Lavender at his side setting out pens and paper. The gaolers hustled the prisoners into the dock in front of the magistrate, where they stood gripping the rail and looking timidly about them. Wallace flinched when the gaoler knocked his hat off his head.

Dan, as one of the deponents, took his place on the

benches behind Sir William, next to Captain Ellis and Jones. The young patrolman still looked pale. The remaining space on the dais quickly filled up with Bow Street personnel. Dan spotted a flash of Townsend's yellow waistcoat.

In the pit below the dais three reporters, pressed in by the mass of spectators, jostled for elbow room at the railing separating the dock from the audience. Usually the hearings attracted only a few members of the public. Most of the visitors to the courtroom were lawyers and their clients, people waiting to give evidence, or men and women about to face their accusers. They came and went without taking any notice of the magistrate and the prisoners, gossiping or conducting their business, sometimes their flirtations. Today there was a mass of ghoulish faces turned towards the court, eager for sensational revelations. The courtyard was packed with those who could not get in.

Captain Ellis and Patrolman Jones gave their evidence. The reporters' pencils raced across their notebooks. In an atmosphere thick with heat and unpleasant smells, Dan outlined his part in events, including his investigations at Guy's Hospital.

"So you are perfectly satisfied that Officer Kean was never in Guy's Hospital?" Sir William asked. "And that there is no employee matching the description given by the prisoners?"

"I am."

"Thank you, Officer Foster."

Dan went back to his seat and Sir William consulted briefly with Lavender. An excited hubbub broke out, which the beadle quickly dealt with. When silence had been restored, the magistrate addressed Reynolds and Wallace.

"You both insist that you purchased the remains of Officer Kean from a man previously unknown to you who claimed to be a porter at Guy's Hospital?"

Wallace's mouth hung open and his wide eyes were fixed uncomprehendingly on the magistrate.

"We do, as it's true," Reynolds answered for both of them.

"You do not wish to take this opportunity to change your story in any way? To add some details about how and when Kean was killed?"

"We don't, as we don't know anything about it," Reynolds said.

"You refuse to reveal the whereabouts of the remainder of the corpse?"

"We never seen more than them bits in the basket."

"You have heard Officer Foster's evidence. Taking that and all the circumstances of the case into consideration, and in particular the fact that you were found with the victim's remains in your possession, I have heard nothing to suggest that there is anyone other than yourselves who had any connection with his death. That being so, I have no hesitation in remanding you both in custody pending trial on the charge of murdering Principal Officer George Kean."

Wallace plucked at Reynolds's sleeve. "What's he saying? What's he mean?"

Reynolds shook him off and struggled to make himself heard above the cheers, whistles and applause. "But we never done him in! It was like we told you – we just bought the body parts."

"Take them down," Sir William ordered.

The gaolers dragged the pair from the dock, Reynolds protesting, Wallace still bleating, "What's he mean?" They were jostled, jabbed and kicked as they passed through the press of police officers and clerks.

John Townsend grabbed Reynolds's arm and hissed into his ear, "Think you'll be safe in Newgate? Think again." Reynolds tore himself free, and he and Wallace made their torturous way along the packed corridor, cringing beneath further blows, threats and spittle.

Dan, who had stood up to watch them go, felt someone slap his shoulder. He turned to see a grinning Ellis behind him.

"Well done, Dan. If it hadn't been for you being so quick off the mark, we'd never have got that scum charged this fast."

"But there's no why or where or when to it," Dan said. "What are you talking about? Where are you going?" The captain was already talking to the noisome air.

# Chapter Five

Outside, Dan stood breathing in the cooler air and thinking. He had a couple of options. He could go to the Black Raven, the Chick Lane tavern where Reynolds and Wallace claimed to have bought Kean's remains, and see if anyone knew anything about the man who sold them – or whether they would tell him if they did. Which was unlikely. But there was another source of information he could try, one that might be more fruitful.

A commotion from the office doorway announced the spilling forth of John Townsend and the other officers in a noisy, triumphant gaggle. They swept across the road to the Brown Bear. They would be drinking to Kean's memory and celebrating the arrest of his killers for the next several hours, unless Sir William sent them out on a job, or some robbed or battered victim came in to ask for help. And woe betide any law-breakers who crossed their path in their current mood.

Dan's King Street burglar was still locked up in the Brown Bear waiting to be brought up before Sir William. He would have to wait until the evening sessions. Dan straightened his hat and strode away.

The Falcon in Clerkenwell stood in a gloomy street flanked on either side by filth-filled gutters. Ragged children played around the doors of lodging houses so old they were thatched with straw, their walls bulged and window frames had rotted away. Men and women loitered about on the lookout for the sort of money that could be made on the streets by begging, stealing, selling themselves. None held his or her hand out to Dan as he strode down the road, his boots ringing on the cobblestones, his hands in his coat pockets hinting at the presence of the pistol. A pockmarked young man slouching against a wall hiked himself upright and sidled away into the shadows in front of Dan.

Dan stepped over a puddle of horse piss, unlatched the alehouse door and flung it wide open. Every face turned towards him. He paused on the threshold, letting his eyes adjust to the dimness, smoke, and fug of stale ale, stale food, stale bodies. The Falcon was a flash house, as well known to the Bow Street officers as the officers were known to its habitués, who represented a fine cross-section of London's burglars, footpads, coiners and sharpers. One or two had already slipped out the back way by the time Dan stepped down into the room.

The pock-fretten youth from the street was at the bar guzzling a glass of ale, his reward for running ahead to warn the company they had an unwelcome visitor. Three men stood next to him. The trio were better dressed than most in the room, the one in the middle showy in buff waistcoat and plum-coloured jacket. The man on his right opened his coat and drew a short bludgeon from an inside pocket, the one on his left snatched a bottle from the counter.

Dan stepped down onto a floor that had rarely seen water or mop. Now everyone could see that he had come on his own, a murmur of astonishment passed around the room. Some laughed; others exchanged delighted glances. A toothless old bundle of vermin-ridden skirts hissed, "Fucking pig!" Behind him one of the drinkers crept from his chair and fastened the door.

Dan reached the bar and looked down at the fat landlord, who stood trembling and sweating behind a wall of dirty glasses. From upstairs came the sound of hasty footsteps, the dragging of cases, the opening and closing of a door. Someone was trying to shift a cache of stolen goods.

"I'll have a ginger beer," Dan said into the tense silence.

One or two people guffawed. The landlord licked his lips,

reached for a bottle from underneath the bar, uncorked it and lifted down a glass. The drink spilled over the rim of the glass, but Dan made no complaint and handed over his coins. He took a sip of his drink.

"I'm looking for Ben Hardyman."

"Think you've come to the wrong place," said the man in the buff waistcoat before the quivering landlord could answer. "And this ain't no molly house neither."

His henchmen sniggered. Dan ignored them and asked the landlord, "Is Hardyman here?"

"Oi, Puss," Buff Waistcoat said. "I'm talking to you. If you're going to stand drinking next to me, you'd better have a man's drink. Otherwise I'll think you're trying to proposition me, which I wouldn't like."

"I'm all right with this," Dan said. "But I thank you for the offer."

Anger flashed across the man's large, flat-nosed face. He snapped at the landlord, "A glass of brandy for the young lady. Make it a pint."

"Right you are, Mr Packer." The landlord reached for a pint mug, filled it with the cheapest brandy he had and pushed it across the counter.

"Here you are, miss," said Packer. "Drink it up, or I'll take it unfriendly-like."

Dan took another pull at his ginger beer. "Never touch the stuff."

"Now, I consider that a right real insult," Packer said. "Looks like the madge ain't got no manners. And someone with no manners don't belong in an establishment like this, where all is friendly and manly."

The man at his right elbow grinned and tapped the palm of his hand with his bludgeon. "Do you think me and Shipley ought to teach him some?"

"I do, Taylor, I do."

There were jeers and cries of, "Give it to him, Packer."

Dan put his glass down on the counter, turned and

faced Packer. "I don't want any trouble. All I want is to talk to Hardyman."

Packer rubbed his right hand across his nose, his head bent, as if thinking. The pose did not fool Dan, and when he jerked his head up and drove his fist towards Dan's chin, he was ready to parry the blow with his left, put his own right into Packer's face.

Packer staggered back. Shipley broke the neck of his bottle on the bar and jabbed at Dan with the jagged edge. Dan dodged him and landed a fist in Taylor's stomach. Taylor doubled over and Dan grabbed him by his hair and the waistband of his breeches and swung him at Shipley. The pair tumbled to the floor. Taylor rolled away, scrabbling for the bludgeon which had fallen from his fingers. Dan stamped on his wrist. Taylor clutched it with his other hand, screaming in pain.

By this time Packer had recovered his balance. He came at Dan puffing and wheezing, blood bubbling out of a nose that had been broken so many times one more punch had almost turned it to a pulp. He did not come empty-handed. There was a knife in his hand.

Dan skipped back, avoiding the blade. Still the big man came on, stabbing at him, driving him against the bar. The onlookers yelled and cheered. Out of the corner of his eye, Dan saw that Taylor and Shipley were on their feet and closing in on him. He lunged to the right, grabbed a chair and flung it at them. As the chair bounced to the ground and Taylor and Shipley went down in a tangle, the shouting died away.

"What's going on here?"

Packer whirled round to face the speaker. The newcomer, almost as tall as he was broad, stood on massive, muscular legs. Heavy gold rings glinted from his huge, fight-scarred hands. A thick gold watch chain hung from his silk waistcoat, and his shirt was ruffled lawn.

"It's a Runner, Mr Hardyman," Packer said. "And he ain't welcome here."

"No more is he," agreed Hardyman. "Where's the rest of them?"

"I've come alone," Dan said. "I don't need a mob to back me up – and I can remember the days when Ben Hardyman fought his own battles too."

Hardyman's little eyes narrowed. "Is that so?"

"Shall we finish him off?" Packer demanded.

"Go on," Dan said. "There's just the three of you. Four if Hardyman joins in. Or do you just watch other men fighting for you these days, Ben?"

"Think you could have a go, do you?" Hardyman said.

Taylor laughed. "The last man who thought that shits into clouts now."

Packer reached for the pint of brandy that still stood on the counter. "I asked you to have a drink with me. You two, hold him down."

Dan backed against the counter and threw up his fists. Something flapped in front of his eyes. Before he could move, a twisted cloth tightened around his neck and his head was dragged back by the landlord's considerable weight. Dan scrabbled at the noose but could not shift it. Taylor and Shipley forced his hands down and grasped his arms. Packer advanced with the tankard. Someone slapped his palm on a table and cried, "Drink! Drink! Drink!" The company took up the chant, accompanied it with stamping feet and drumming tankards.

"Wait!" Hardyman's voice cut through the din. He stripped off his jacket. "Leave him to me."

The room erupted into enthusiastic applause.

"Go it, Mr Hardyman!"

"Lay him out, Ben!"

"Crush him! Kill him! Break him!" screeched a young girl.

"Clear a space here," Hardyman commanded.

The landlord loosed the cloth from Dan's neck. The drinkers dragged the furniture aside and formed a circle. Dan wrenched himself free of Shipley and Taylor and moved into the middle of the room.

"I've come to talk," Dan said. "That's all."

Hardyman made a fist. "And all I've got to say to you is here."

This, thought Dan, is one of those times when walking away might be a good option. But he did not rate his chances of getting out unscathed. He could face Hardyman one on one, or he could refuse and have the whole lot of them give him a kicking.

Hardyman ordered a glass of brandy, took a mouthful, swilled it around his mouth and swallowed. He handed the glass to Packer and turned to face Dan, certainty of victory written in his face. Dan understood Hardyman's thinking: his opponent was a lightweight; he could not last five minutes against the once-legendary fists of Ben Hardyman – especially when those fists were loaded with metal. One punch from those ringed fingers with the power of Hardyman's shoulders behind it would reduce his face to a mush of broken bone and flesh.

Dan let Hardyman move towards him, mirroring his advance with his own retreat. The big man sneered and went on the throw, but before he could let fly with his first punch, Dan ducked, charged and brought his right fist up beneath Hardyman's chin. The bruiser's head bounced back, and his body staggered after it. Without giving him time to recover, Dan drove his left fist into his stomach. Hardyman's head wobbled forward and Dan's right met the jaw again, then the left, the right, the left...

Dan could hear the people screaming their hatred at him, urging Hardyman to finish him off, but the big man's eyes were already glazing over. Dan skipped back to avoid his loose swing – and fell over Taylor's outstretched foot.

Instantly Packer and his men were all over him, kicking and punching. He tried to get his hands up over his head but he could not move his arms. He flailed out with his legs, landing blows where he could, noted with satisfaction that he had got Taylor in the bollocks.

"That's enough!" Hardyman roared. "Leave him be, you dolt-heads."

The men climbed off him. Dan rolled on to his side, and sat up. He spat a gob of blood. "Never thought I'd see the day when Ben Hardyman couldn't stand up in the ring on his own."

"And you ain't seen the day yet," Hardyman said. "Get up."

Dan sprang to his feet and raised his fists.

Hardyman clicked his fingers at the man who held his jacket. He handed it over. Hardyman put it on, twitched it straight and smoothed down his hair.

"Another glass of ginger beer for the officer," he said to the landlord. "And half and half for me." He jerked his thumb at a couple of men who sat at one of the tables and they scuttled away. Hardyman sat down in one of the vacated places and swept their glasses and pipes onto the floor. "Have a seat," he said to Dan.

Dan sat down opposite Hardyman. They eyed one another while the landlord served the drinks. A few people muttered their disappointment, but Hardyman's mean little eyes quelled them. The company went back to its drinking, its conversation falsely casual, none daring to cast curious eyes or ears on Hardyman and the Runner. The landlord, with the help of Hardyman's crew, straightened the furniture and cleared up the broken glass.

"You're Dan Foster, right?" Hardyman said. "The boxing nabman. Trained by your dad, I've heard. Good man, Noah Foster. If he'd been my trainer, who knows where I might not have ended up?"

"He doesn't train dirty fighters."

For a few seconds Hardyman teetered between taking offence and being amused. He laughed. "You ain't so clean yourself. Going for a man before we've even started."

"I didn't notice anyone agreeing Broughton's Rules."

"True enough. Well, you've got my attention now. What do you want?"

"Information."

"About?"

"Body snatching."

Hardyman took a swig of his rum and water. "What makes you think I know anything about that?"

"You run the biggest grave robbing gang in London. There isn't a parish your men haven't raided. Looks to be a good business too. Pays for your smart duds."

Hardyman smiled and twisted one of his gold rings around his finger. "So what do you want to know?"

"An officer's been murdered. Murdered and cut up for sale to the anatomy schools. It was a professional quartering. I want to know who has the skill to do that."

Hardyman rubbed his hand across his chin, wincing over the developing bruises. "A surgeon."

"Or someone who's seen them at work. Like you."

"Yes, I portered at Guy's for a few years, until they sacked me for trying to make a little money on the side."

"Selling corpses to other hospitals."

"The surgeons don't like the idea of anyone but them profiting from the business, see. Students pay well for their nattomy lessons. But it wasn't me who cut up your Runner."

"We've arrested two men. Reynolds and Wallace."

"Don't know them. And even if I did, I ain't no snitch."

"But you're a businessman. Another gang trespassing on your territory is bad for business. You find out who they are, and maybe we dispose of them for you."

Hardyman considered this, his knitted brows giving his face an apelike appearance. Yet there was a shrewd brain at work behind the brutish face.

"Fact is, I don't know who your Reynolds and Wallace are with. But I've heard talk of a new gang muscling in. People have tried before." Hardyman spread his hands on the table and contemplated his loaded fists. "Never got very far."

"Can you find out who they were working for?"

"Very well, I'll do what you ask." He spat on his palm and held out his hand.

"There's to be no shaking on it."

Hardyman frowned. "You're a dab with your fists, Foster,

40

but don't push me too far. Next time you come in here you might not get such a friendly welcome."

Dan stood up and put on his hat. "Just get me that information, or next time I'll come in with the militia and close this place down."

"Son of a bitch," Hardyman said.

"I'll give you till the end of the week. You'd better have something for me by then."

Dan winked at Packer and his friends. "Gentlemen," he said, and sauntered out into the alley.

# Chapter Six

It was late by the time Dan got home, his burglar safely stowed in Newgate. He opened the front door to the sound of voices from the kitchen, Captain Ellis's amongst them. Reminding himself that he had no right to stop Ellis calling on Eleanor, he forced his jealous scowl into a smile and went in.

Caroline and Mrs Harper sat at the table which they had scattered with ribbons, beads, buttons, thread, needles and scissors. Eleanor sat by the fire, her hands busy with some mending, looking up now and again to join in the conversation. Ellis, a glass of beer in his hand, sat comfortably by the hearth, gazing at her when she was not looking, smiling when she was, hanging on her every word when she spoke.

"So you're in one piece, then," said Caroline.

Eleanor gave a sharp intake of breath. Even Ellis, as charmed as he was by his situation, was taken aback. He remembered his manners and jumped to his feet.

"Am I in your chair, Dan?"

"No, no, it's all right, Sam," Dan answered. "I can sit here." He pulled out a chair at the end of the table.

Mrs Harper fussed around him. "What a dreadful thing, Dan! Captain Ellis has been telling us all about it. That poor Officer Kean. The captain says he had a wife too. But you've caught the wretches who did it, and a good thing too."

"We think we've caught them," Dan said.

Ellis, who had resumed his seat, said, "Do you think there's any doubt?"

Dan hesitated, decided it was better to say nothing and muttered, "No, there's no doubt."

Ellis gave him a puzzled look, but seeing Dan was not in the mood to pursue the subject let it drop.

"Will you have something to drink, lovey?" his mother-in-law asked him.

"A soda water." He glanced along the table, caught sight of the beer jug and Caroline's glass a few inches away from it. He raised his eyes and met hers, fixed on him with a mocking glint.

"Why, Dan, do you think it wrong to send out for some refreshment when a friend comes calling?"

"No, I don't," he said, taking his bottle and glass from Mrs Harper with a nod of thanks.

"Just because you want to drink seltzer water doesn't mean everyone else has to."

"I said I didn't mind."

"Big of you." She drained her glass and resumed the conversation that had been going on when he came in. "So, it's settled then. We'll go to the theatre on Saturday. Captain Ellis," she explained to Dan, "has offered to take us all."

"I have managed to secure tickets for one of the boxes at the Haymarket," Ellis said. "Thought it would be a nice change for us to be inside a theatre instead of outside looking for pickpockets."

"Isn't that kind of the captain?" Caroline said. "I can't remember the last time anyone took me to the theatre. Or to any entertainment, for that matter. I'm retrimming this hat in honour of the occasion."

"It's going to look lovely," Mrs Harper said.

Caroline sighed. "I suppose so."

Ellis must be truly besotted, Dan thought. A box at the theatre must have cost him a fortune. It was a pity Eleanor seemed more embarrassed than pleased by the gesture.

"It's very generous of you, Ellis," he said. "What's the play?"

Ellis looked blank.

"*The Italian Monk*," Caroline said.

"Nell, Captain Ellis's glass is empty," Mrs Harper said.

"No, I won't have any more, thank you," Ellis said, adding

regretfully, "I'd better be getting along. Until Saturday, then."

"I'll have some more." Caroline reached for the jug.

Dan saw Ellis out. The captain paused on the doorstep. "Do you have doubts about the men arrested for Kean's murder?"

"I think there are some details yet to be filled in."

"But you think the right men are in gaol?"

"I think that's where they deserve to be."

Ellis smiled. "I get the hint, Dan. You won't say anything until you've got something to say. But if you should need any help, let me know."

"I will...goodnight."

Dan watched Ellis's lithe, active figure disappear into the gloom and head towards the light and noise of the Piazza. He shut and locked the door and returned to the kitchen. Eleanor was rinsing the jug and glasses, Mrs Harper gathering up Caroline's things. Caroline's glass had been refilled. She held a bunch of ribbons, but her hands were idle, her eyes downcast.

Dan drew out his purse. "Here," he said, placing some guineas on the table. "Buy yourself a new hat. Should be enough for all of you there."

She let the ribbons fall, leapt out of her seat, flung her arms around his neck and gave him a beery kiss.

"Oh, Dan, thank you! Look, Mother, what Dan's given me! Now I can get the hat we saw today."

"Well, isn't that lovely?" Mrs Harper said. "We'll all go to the Exchange tomorrow, eh, Nell?"

"But I don't need anything –" Eleanor began.

"Nonsense, lovey!" her mother interrupted. "A handsome man like Captain Ellis deserves to have a smartly dressed girl on his arm."

Caroline put her hand through Dan's arm and looked up at him. "And so does a handsome husband."

Dan had a couple of warrants to serve the next day, pocketing a shilling fee for each one. The money was not in his pocket for long. The clerks were collecting for a subscription for Kean's family. Not that Dan or any other officer begrudged their contributions. Who could be sure that it would not be for his own kin one day?

That done, Dan went to call on Mrs Kean in the rooms she had shared with her husband in a courtyard off Long Acre. No one at the office knew where Kean had been going on Friday, but perhaps he had said something to his wife. His widow.

When Dan knocked on the door, it opened to present two red eyes and a puffy white face. He started to introduce himself, but she turned her back on him and shuffled away, not caring whom she let in. She moved like a woman much older than her years, which he put at twenty-four or five.

He took off his hat and followed her. She was on her own, but the table was covered in cups, glasses and crumb-ridden plates left behind by recent company. She sat down in front of the hearth, where a small fire spluttered its last gasps.

Dan looked about until he located a pail of coal inside a tiny scullery off the main room. He carried it in and started to busy himself with kindling and coal.

"You don't have to do that," she said dully after a few moments. "Mrs Martin will be coming in soon."

"Who's that?" he asked, while he drew the flames back into life with a sheet of old newspaper. "A neighbour of yours?"

"Yes. They've all been very kind."

"Have you any family nearby?"

"They're in Kent."

He went into the scullery and washed his hands. When he came back she was gazing into the flames, her chin on her hand. "Can I get you anything to drink?" she asked, without looking at him. "There's brandy, I think. Tea. I think."

"No, I'm fine, thanks. Do you mind if I sit down?"

She fluttered her fingers, which he took as an invitation to go ahead.

"I worked with your husband. He was a good officer." Dan paused. "I am sorry to bother you at a time like this, but there are a few details we need to sort out. It's just routine, but I expect you know that it's important to get everything settled as quickly as possible."

"I thought you had the men who did it," she murmured into the flames.

"As I say, it's just a few details…Kean wore a ring, didn't he? Can you tell me what it looked like?"

"Does it matter?"

"If we find it, we can return it to you."

"It was gold, had a red stone – jasper, I think – squarish, with his initials on. His father's. They were the same. GK. George Kean."

Dan took out his writing tablet and made a note of the description. "Did he tell you anything about the cases he was working on?"

"Yes." A thought struck her and she looked up. "No. He usually did. We'd talk it all over, sometimes he'd tell me he was at a dead end so I'd tell him what I thought. Then he'd say I was as good as any man in the force. But lately if I asked him about work, he'd get angry, tell me to talk about something else."

"So you don't know where he was going last Friday?"

"No. He wouldn't tell me. He just said he'd be away all night, maybe the next night too. A Runner's wife has to be used to that. When he didn't come back on Sunday I was going to call into the office on Monday morning. But Sir William called first."

Many of the felons Kean arrested could testify to how rough and ruthless he could be. His wife had shed an unexpected light on a softer side to him: the side that sought her advice and judgement. Dan tried to imagine what life would be like if Caroline had ever shown any interest in his work, but she had never liked discussing what she considered to be a grubby business. As, sometimes, it was. Her feelings would have been different if he had pursued the career she wanted him to choose: a professional pugilist, rich, fêted by the aristocracy, adored by the mob. He had it in him, according to Noah, but he had never wanted to go professional, to be flattered by the Fancy while he won; dropped and left to go to the devil if he lost.

He put the thoughts aside, refocussed on the matter in hand. "Did he keep any notes or papers here?"

"A few, in that desk over there."

Dan glanced over at the bureau with its pigeonholes and drawers. "Can I have a look?"

She shrugged. He crossed the room and sat down at the desk. On the wall above it was a pair of crossed tomahawks. Souvenirs from Kean's Army days, Dan guessed, when he had served in America. Kean had always been proud of his service to King and Country, though he rarely talked about it. Rarely talked about anything.

The papers were domestic stuff mostly, family correspondence and bills – all paid, Dan was glad for the widow's sake to see, except for one or two recent arrivals. He discovered that Kean had a sister in Leicester. There were a few financial documents; it seemed Kean had started to dabble in investments in a small way. Dan wondered if he should consider doing the same. Probably wasn't earning enough yet; better just to keep saving as much as he could.

He opened the bottom drawer and took out a small notebook. It was a household expenses book containing neat rows of figures and calculations. There was nothing unusual in that: there was one like it in his own house, only it wasn't his wife who kept it up to date but Eleanor and her mother. Every now and again they would bring it to Dan to have a look at, the theory being that as head of the household he should sign off on the household accounts. It was rare for him to question anything: Mrs Harper and Eleanor were as meticulous and accurate as the housewife to whom this book belonged. There were a few annotations and additions in another handwriting: Kean's, no doubt.

Dan leafed through the pages. The sheets at the back were empty, all save the last one which bore a few characters in the husband's writing. Not that he could make out what they meant – the number "14" circled round, followed by "B&C 1/9". He puzzled over the letters. The last part might be a date: 1 September, the day Kean left home for the last time. Of the others, Dan could make no sense.

There was a knock on the door. The bereft woman roused herself and shuffled off to open it, admitting the aroma of meat pie. A stout woman with a relentless voice came in after it.

"Now then, Mrs Kean, I've brought you a bite of supper and a drop of something to help you sleep, and I'm going to sit here and watch you eat it. Tut! Look at the mess on the table. I'll clear that out of the way and then we'll tuck in. Who's this?"

Dan, who had taken advantage of the commotion to rip out the page and put it in his pocket, rose to greet the woman he presumed was Mrs Martin.

"I was just going," he said, taking up his hat. "Good day, Mrs Kean. Ma'am."

"One of your husband's friends? Eh, poor dear, he was a popular man and he'll be very much missed. There, dearie, don't take on. He wouldn't want that, now, would he?"

Dan closed the door and left the house.

# Chapter Seven

On Friday Kean was buried in St George's Burial Ground behind the Foundling Hospital, as St Paul's, Covent Garden's parish church on the Piazza, was still being rebuilt after the fire which had gutted it a couple of years ago. All of Bow Street's principal officers and many from the other police offices, along with magistrates, constables and watchmen from all over London, crowded the graveyard. The family was represented by Kean's brother-in-law, a draper from Leicester.

As Sir William had directed, the undertaker had provided a full-sized coffin so that a comforting – or at least less upsetting – pretence was maintained for the sake of Kean's wife. Afterwards they went back to Bow Street, the officers to gather in the Brown Bear for gin and beer, the magistrates in the house across the road for sherry and Madeira.

The following day the deadline Dan had given Ben Hardyman expired and he was back at the Falcon by early evening. The tap room was deserted, but Dan traced the racket of cheering and shouting to the yard at the back of the tavern where a cock fight was in progress. Dan took no pleasure in sports involving creatures who had no say in whether or not they fought, and went back into the bar. He sent the pot boy out to tell Hardyman he had arrived. While he waited, he ordered himself a drink.

"I'll get this." A hand weighted with chunks of gold pushed his coins back along the bar. "And bring over a jug of brandy and water." With the row from outside, Dan had not heard Hardyman and Packer approach. Dan was gratified to see that

Packer's nose was still red and swollen.

The Falcon's fat landlord hurriedly attended to the order. Dan picked up his glass and followed the others to a table against the far wall. The landlord placed a glass, jug and spoon in front of Hardyman and lumbered away.

Dan took a sip of his ginger beer. "Delicious. Want some, Packer?"

Packer scowled. "You shit sack." A look from Hardyman silenced him.

"What have you got for me?" asked Dan.

Hardyman splashed a small drop of hot water into his brandy and swigged a mouthful.

"No one in the business has ever heard of the men you arrested – Reynolds and Wallace. But I was right about a new gang. It's being run by Tom Dawson out of Southwark. Dawson used to work in the dissecting room at Josh Brookes's nattomy school in Blenheim Street. He's been supplying Brookes with cheap Things. Looks like he had some surplus to dispose of."

So Reynolds and Wallace were just a couple of flats who had been taken in by a stranger offering them dubious means to make money. A score of such transactions were made every day in the Black Raven; it was a veritable exchange for petty criminals. The so-called porter who had entangled them must be a member of Dawson's gang.

Hardyman took another mouthful of spirit. "Reckon we'd better send the good surgeon a little token reminding him of our agreement. Something nice and ripe."

"Be better still if it had the smallpox," Packer said.

Leaving putrid bodies outside the premises of anatomists who had bought corpses from a competitor was an old trick of the resurrection men. Brookes would get a nasty message, but Dan had no pity to spare for men like him who encouraged the plunder of graves, to the distress of the deceased's relatives and friends.

"Did Dawson kill Kean?"

Hardyman swilled the dregs of his drink around the glass.

"Dawson's not a killer, but he'd know all about how to dispose of – or preserve, if you had a mind to it – a corpse."

"So where can I find him?"

"He has a store house back of St John's on Horsleydown, next to the cooper's yard. And that's all I know and all you're to know from me. In return, you said you'd get rid of him for me."

"I said maybe. If what you've given me is useful he won't be left alone, and that's as much as I'll say." Dan stood up and walked to the door.

Hardyman called after him, "If you don't get rid of Dawson, I'll cross the river and do it myself."

Dan turned back. "You'll keep out of my way, Hardyman."

"Or what?"

"Or I'll see you at the rope's end."

Hardyman met Dan's eye. The resurrectionist's gaze slewed away and he laughed.

"You want to watch your back, Foster. Wouldn't want any harm to come to you one of these dark nights."

"Sentiment's the same here," Dan said cheerfully.

Dan crouched behind one of the headstones in St John's churchyard on Horsleydown. He felt the reassuring shape of the pistol in his right pocket and the bit of candle and flint in the left. A black shape like an upright coffin stood amidst the graves. The rumbling snores of the dozing sentry came from within the narrow box. It was not much of a deterrent to a determined resurrection man.

The moon, two nights past the full, hung bright in the sky. It was not a good night for grave robbers, even ones with a warehouse so conveniently close to a graveyard as Dawson's. Not a good night for a Bow Street officer who did not want to be seen either, and Dan took care to keep to the shadows. Luckily those shadows rarely lifted from Southwark's filthy streets and alleys.

The cooper's yard was opposite the church, identifiable by the stacks of barrels that towered above its wide wooden gates, which had been fastened for the night. A faint red glow marked the presence of the night watchman's brazier, but no footsteps sounded to suggest that the man was doing his rounds. He was most likely huddled over his fire with a tot of something to keep out the damp.

Dawson's warehouse next to it was surrounded by a high wall. When Dan had waited about a quarter of an hour and all remained still, he judged it was safe to go in. Stooping between the headstones, he picked his way across the graveyard and vaulted down into the street. He checked the roadway was empty before he ran across to the warehouse gate. From the cooper's he heard a dog's chain clink.

To avoid disturbing the animal, he followed the brick perimeter round to the side away from the cooper's. A narrow strip of wasteland that had once been a garden flanked the warehouse. A derelict house stood amongst the weeds. Its roof had collapsed, bringing down the floors and rendering the ruin fit shelter only for rats and prowling cats.

He found a crate amongst the heaps of litter and used it to give himself a lift up. At the top of the wall he lay flat, listening and looking. Satisfied there was no one inside, he dropped down onto an outhouse roof, and from there into the muddy yard.

He circled the warehouse building. High and narrow, it had two floors. The main door was wide enough to admit wagons, but it and the wicket door were both secured and there were no windows on the ground floor. Windows at the back were too high to reach and too small to climb through.

Drawing near to where he had started, he came to a flight of wooden stairs at the side of the building. They led up to a door that opened on to the upstairs offices. This too was securely locked. Dan did not dare kick it in and set the guard dog barking, but he noticed a warped, filthy window beside it which no longer fastened. Presumably Dawson had not bothered to have it repaired, thinking a man would have to fly to be able to get to it. It was not wings Dan needed, but he did have to lean out from the stairs at a perilous angle to reach the window. He hung on to the rail with one hand and struggled to work the rotten sash up with the other. His shoulder ached by the time the window shot open with a squeal of surrender.

He pulled himself back onto the stairs and knelt by the railing. The unseen dog growled and uttered a half-hearted bark, which was silenced by the night watchman's curses. Dan waited until the pair had settled down again before leaning over to grab the windowsill and swing himself across. It was hard work to pull himself up and through the window; would have been impossible were it not for the pull-ups he practised on the bar in the gymnasium. Even so, he lay on the floor inside for a few minutes to get his breath back and let his muscles recover from the effort. He pulled the window down in case someone should see it was open, but stopped it short by a couple of inches, wide enough to get his fingers under and quickly pull it up.

By the time he stood up, his eyes had grown accustomed to the gloom. Not so his nostrils to the smell. The place smelt like an abattoir, a latrine and a distillery rolled into one. There was nothing in the room but balls of dust. He stepped into the corridor, pushed open doors as he walked along it. The other rooms were empty except for odd bits of furniture: a chair and table in one; an empty chest with a broken lock in another.

Dan went back to the staircase in the middle of the corridor and looked down into the darkness beneath. A few moonbeams slanted feebly across the warehouse floor, casting pools of darkness around stacks of empty crates. He fished in his pocket for the candle. The flint took a while to strike, but at last he had it going.

The flame flickered in the draught of his descent. He followed a broad gangway which ran between the crates from the main warehouse door. The floor was scuffed and covered in muddy boot-marks. There were signs that something heavy had been dragged along: the twin trails of what could have been a pair of heels.

The trail ended at a door fastened by a large wooden bar between staples. Dan slid it back and swung the door open, releasing a concentration of foul smells. He pulled his scarf up around his nose and stepped into a long, windowless room. In the middle stood a butcher's block over a drain which was the source of the worst of the odours. He crossed to the block and examined its surface by the candlelight. It was much scored and stained, the wood damp and faintly greasy to the touch.

He moved away and groped forward a few steps until the faint beam from his candle met bare wall. He followed the wall round, running his hand along the rough brickwork to guide his steps on the uneven stone floor. In one corner he came upon a pile of sacks, shovels and ropes: the tools of the grave digger's trade. A large wooden box stood upon a nearby table. Inside was a collection of grave goods: small keepsakes such as a locket, a watch, a mould-stained Bible. Dan flipped open the locket, could just make out a miniature of a pale, nondescript youth. There was no ring matching the description of the one taken from Kean.

He replaced the trinkets and continued his circuit of the room until he felt wood beneath his fingertips. Another door, presumably opening into a closet or storeroom, but this one was locked. He reached into his pocket for his pick locks, but as he did so the outer warehouse door opened and he heard footsteps and voices.

He scrambled out of the room, closed the door and pushed the bar back into place. He snuffed his candle and dived behind a pile of crates as the first glow of a lantern reached him. Two men approached: a short, bulky one who carried the lantern and lit the way for a swaggering figure in a caped coat. The short man unbarred the door and held it open for his companion. The light shone on his face, revealing a broad, flat nose, little deep-set eyes, and a dark wart above his thick lips.

Leaving the door ajar, he lit the candles on the table and brought them over to the butcher's block while the other man stood by, his hat pushed back to reveal carroty hair shining red in the light. He had a narrow face; a thin, almost lipless mouth; pale eyes. He lounged against the block, took a flask from his pocket and swigged the contents.

The other, meanwhile, unlocked the inner chamber door and disappeared from Dan's sight. After crashing around for a minute or two, he emerged carrying a bucket which he lifted onto the block. Whatever was inside it rattled like nails. The red-haired man pocketed his flask and drew out a small canvas bag. He dipped his hand into the bucket, examined the objects he brought up on his open palm, and transferred them to the bag. He drew up another handful, picked something out, threw it on the floor and ground it with the heel of his boot.

"Rotten," he said. He drew tight the drawstring. "That'll do. We don't want to make Broomhall suspicious."

"How much do you think they'll fetch, Mr Dawson?"

Dawson shrugged. "Half a guinea apiece. Should keep you in cunny for a while, Capper."

The other grinned and carried the bucket back into the inner room. He locked the door, extinguished the candles, and after a last look round, the two men left. Dan waited until he heard the distant sound of the warehouse door being locked and bolted before leaving his hiding place. He relit his candle, went back into the room and knelt by the inner door, the candle on the floor beside him. He worked at the lock: a simple old-fashioned one, easy to pick. He opened the door and a gust of foul air streamed out, setting the candle's flame trembling.

It was another windowless chamber, but much smaller than the outer room. The air seemed to thicken and swirl as he moved inside. In the faint circle of light, he made out a line of pale shapes on the floor. Six bodies, one a child's. Beside them stood Capper's bucket, full of teeth. It was common practice for resurrection men to extract teeth from the corpses they stole and sell them separately to dentists, who turned them into false sets for those rich enough to afford them, and insensitive enough not to mind wearing a dead man's dentures.

Dawson and his friend had been dipping into the gang's profits.

So, what did it all mean? Dan asked himself later, when he was sitting in one of Covent Garden's all-night coffee houses, ignoring the well-dressed drunks around him and sipping a surprisingly good coffee. There was not much more peace to be had at home. Caroline had been waiting up for him when he got back from Horsleydown. She had been bitter on the subject of having to play duenna to Ellis and Eleanor when Dan had not turned up at the theatre. It had been no use reminding her that his job often called him away at unsociable hours. He knew he was in the wrong; he could have gone to the warehouse after the play, or tomorrow night, or any other night.

The truth was that he had forgotten about their theatre outing. All he could do was promise to go with her another evening, and throw in a supper beforehand at some expensive restaurant of her choice. When she eventually stopped crying and went to bed, his guilt drove him out of the house.

He brought his mind to bear on the problem in hand. Dawson certainly had the facilities to dispose of Kean's body, and it was likely that the warehouse was where it had been turned into a saleable commodity. But how had Kean fallen foul of the body snatcher and his crew? According to Hardyman, Dawson was no killer. So, he must have been disposing of the body for someone else. It would be a lucrative sideline.

Or perhaps the killer had been in a position to order him to do it. That Dawson and his crony had been stealing from other members of the gang was not surprising. Such treachery was common enough amongst thieves. But if Dawson was the gang leader, why did he have to sneak around helping himself to his own haul? That was clear enough: there was someone above him. Could it be the Broomhall they had mentioned?

Dan had not heard of him and Hardyman had not mentioned him, but someone who could strike fear into the heart of a nasty piece like Dawson must be some sort of criminal bigwig. Had Kean been interested in Broomhall?

The next step had to be to find out who this mysterious Broomhall was.

# Chapter Eight

In the morning Dan crossed London Bridge into Southwark again, and continued down Borough High Street. If anything, it was busier than a weekday as apprentices and workers took advantage of their leisure hours to drink, gamble, and torture small animals in the name of sport. Dan made his way through the Sunday crowds and turned right into Union Street, a small spur down to Red Cross Street, at the corner of which stood Union Hall Magistrates' Office.

He had already been to Bow Street to check through the files of known or suspected felons and found no mention of anyone called Broomhall. That in itself might not mean anything; it could be an unknown alias. He waylaid Lavender on his way up to Sir William's room with an armful of papers and asked him if he had ever heard Kean mention Broomhall. The harassed clerk answered that no, he had not, and he was surprised that Dan should think that Kean or any of the officers ever confided important information to him.

If the man was not known in Bow Street, it might be that someone in Southwark had heard of him. Union Hall lobby was crowded with Saturday night's arrests waiting to have their details recorded. They were a drink-sodden collection of men and women, many bearing outward signs of their debauchery in red eyes, trembling limbs, and cuts and bruises sustained from fights or falls. They stepped sullenly aside to let Dan through to the desk.

The constable looked up from his ledger, ready to bawl instructions at another hapless criminal, and recognised Dan.

"Good day, Officer –"

Dan interrupted before the constable shouted his name across the room. "I'm looking for Reeves. Do you know where I might find him?"

"You're in luck. He's just come in. Go through."

Dan went into the clerks' room where a couple of patrolmen, their night duties over, sat waiting to summon the energy to go home. Through heavy-lidded eyes they were watching the performance of a short, wiry man with a broad mouth and sharp eyes beneath thick eyebrows and a shock of black hair. He sat on a chair in front of them, flapping an imaginary fan and fluttering his eyelashes.

" 'Oh, sir, I never heard of no Jack O'Shea,' " he lisped in a high voice. "And all the time I could see his foot poking out from beneath her petticoats and Bill behind me was nearly bursting with trying not to laugh. So I said, 'Well, me dear, if you see him, you'll tell him that Officer Reeves is looking for him.' And she said, 'Oh, I'm not likely to see him.' 'No,' said I, 'but you're feeling him right enough!' And with that, I lifted her skirt and there was the big booby on his hands and knees, almost suffocating between her thighs, and she falls back in a swoon crying, 'La, la! Murder! Save me! Save me!' Aye," Reeves said philosophically as the laughing patrolmen stood up to take their leave, "that pair are of one mind all right. Shame it's such a dim one."

Dan clapped his hands. "Bravo! You should be on the stage."

Reeves twisted round in his chair and grinned up at him. "Dan Foster! Don't often see you Bow Street boys down in the backwoods."

Dan held out his hand. "How are you, Reeves?"

"Well enough. So what's the reason for this royal visitation?"

"I'm looking for information. Just between you and me."

"What is it you want to know?"

"Have you heard of a man called Broomhall?"

"What's your interest?"

"His name came up in a case I'm working on."

"What's he done?"

"Nothing so far as I know. I'd just like to know who he is."

"I do know of a Broomhall, as a matter of fact. Edward Broomhall, one of your parliamentary reformers, though I've never known him do more than jaw about it. Runs Division Fourteen of the London Corresponding Society here in Southwark. Calls himself President. They hold their meetings in the Boatswain and Call."

"Boatswain and Call?"

"Have you heard of it?"

"No. Where does Broomhall live?"

"Has a watchmaking business on Borough High Street."

"What's he look like?"

"God's gift. That's what he thinks, anyway. Do you want me to keep an eye on him?"

"No." Dan put on his hat. "Thanks, Reeves."

They shook hands and Dan went back to Borough High Street. He had passed the watchmaker's on his way to Union Hall without noticing it. It was a modest place flanked by a chop house and a cheese shop, the windows shuttered for Sunday closing.

While Dan stood on the opposite side of the road taking this in, he thought over the information Reeves had given him. With it, Kean's note made some sense: *14 B&C 1/9*: Division Fourteen of the London Corresponding Society, Boatswain and Call, 1 September – the day Kean died. Had he gone to an LCS meeting? If so, why? And how was Broomhall, the President of that meeting, connected to Dawson and his gang?

He thought about going into Broomhall's shop and questioning him. The problem was, he had too little to go on. If Broomhall did know anything about Kean's death and Dan asked the wrong questions, he would only succeed in putting him on his guard.

He needed more information. He had to persuade Sir

William Addington that there was a case to be investigated, and that he was the man to do it. And with two men in Newgate charged with Kean's murder, that might not be easy.

On Monday morning Dan stood in front of Sir William's desk waiting for him to finish reading Kean's note. He had managed to catch the chief magistrate as he was about to go downstairs to hear the morning's cases. The old man's initial impatience had vanished as Dan outlined his findings, such as they were. By the time he had finished, Sir William had forgotten that he was running late for court.

"So you are suggesting that Kean's death could somehow be connected to this man Broomhall of the London Corresponding Society?"

"Yes, sir. There's the link to Dawson –"

Sir William held up his hand. "There's no need to go through it all again, Foster. I do understand. But why should we re-open the case when we already have two men in Newgate charged with the murder?"

"Men who don't know anything about how or when or where the murder was committed. Nor do we have any evidence that they have the wherewithal to cut up a corpse."

"And all you have is Kean's note. It could mean anything. It doesn't prove he was at an LCS meeting in Southwark."

"Not in itself, no. But I think we should take a look."

"Absolutely out of the question. Any investigation into the London Corresponding Society falls into Sir Richard Ford's remit."

"If it was connected with their political activities, yes. But this is a criminal matter. A murder. That's not something Sir Richard's Home Office spies would want to handle, is it?"

"No, too far beneath them. Solving crimes is for lesser mortals like us, who don't have their own chambers in the Home Office, or number the Home Secretary amongst their personal friends."

Dan said nothing to this, though it was common knowledge

that the Duke of Portland, who was Home Secretary, and magistrate Sir Richard Ford were close friends. Sir William could work himself into a jealous fury without his help.

"Surely, sir, we have enough to at least make a few enquiries? The note suggests that Kean was at Division Fourteen in Southwark shortly before he died; his corpse was anatomised; Dawson runs a body snatching business in Southwark; Dawson is connected to Broomhall, the President of Division Fourteen. It seems like a lot of coincidences."

"But what was Kean doing getting himself mixed up with the LCS?" the magistrate demanded. "By God, if Sir Richard Ford has been employing my men without my agreement I'll have something to say about it. It's bad enough that I have to hand over my officers whenever he decides the safety of the realm requires them. I'll not have him poaching them behind my back."

"But why would he use Kean? He had no experience in such matters. He was a good, dogged investigator, though. Maybe he was looking at Dawson and his body snatchers, and found out Broomhall is mixed up with them. But whatever he was on to, it got him killed."

"Dammit, Foster. I committed Reynolds and Wallace myself. Are you saying I was wrong?"

Dan knew better than to answer yes. "Of course not, sir, not on the basis of the evidence you had at the time. Now we have new evidence – evidence I know you won't ignore."

Sir William did not seem heartened by Dan's faith in him. He put the note on the desk and smoothed it flat. "This isn't enough to go on, Foster."

"It isn't much, sir, but I don't believe there's an officer here who wouldn't agree with me that we should follow it up."

"Have you said anything to anyone else about this?" the chief magistrate asked sharply.

"Not yet, sir. I thought it best not to until we knew something definite. It would only cause more upset."

Dan stared innocently in front of him, leaving Sir William

to work out the implications of that for himself. If word should get out that the chief magistrate had been less than thorough in the pursuit of a colleague's murderer...Sir William frowned.

"What is it exactly you propose?"

"I should follow Kean's lead. Get myself into Division Fourteen and find out what it was that drew him there."

"If he was there."

"Yes, sir."

"Sir Richard will have to be consulted. I'll go through the Home Secretary first. If I can secure his approval, there's nothing Sir Richard can do about it."

Dan remained silent. It did not do for a principal officer to involve himself too directly in his superiors' rivalries.

"The Home Secretary won't be pleased, Foster. He wanted a quick conviction to send a message to the criminal fraternity."

"And if the real murderer gets away with it, what message will that send?"

Sir William handed the note back to Dan. "Say nothing to anyone else about this, and take no further action until I've given you authorisation. Make sure you stay close to the office tomorrow to be ready when I send for you."

It was ten o'clock the following morning when Sir William returned to Bow Street and sent for Dan, who was in the clerks' room writing up some reports. When Dan went into his office, the chief magistrate was calming his nerves with a brandy.

"Foster, if you ever come up with an idea like that again, keep it to yourself."

"The Home Secretary won't let me look into it?"

"I did not say so. He was so appalled when I raised the doubts about Reynolds and Wallace, I would have let the matter drop there and then. Having committed myself to it, I had no choice but to press on. His Grace insisted on sending for Sir Richard, who played hell and the devil when he found out about Kean. Turns out he has a man in Division Fourteen, and Kean's clod hopping, as he put it, could have jeopardised this man's cover."

Sir William paused to take another sip of his drink, giving Dan the opportunity to say, "Then his agent would know if Kean had been there! All we have to do –"

"– is ask if he ever saw him. Yes, Foster, the Home Secretary and two magistrates did manage between them to work that out for themselves. When Sir Richard calmed down, that is precisely what we did. After waiting half the night while Sir Richard's team tracked down a spy so valuable no one could remember his name or where he lived, we at last learned that Kean had been going by the name of Scott and had been attending Division Fourteen meetings for some weeks."

"Then I was right!"

"I wouldn't make that a cause for celebration just yet. The Home Secretary was most put out, but he did eventually acknowledge that there is no point in hanging the wrong men. Sir Richard has agreed, perforce, to your investigation. Of course, he refused to give me any details of his agent and he has stipulated that you are to make no attempt to discover or have any contact with him. Says he won't have you interfering with his vital work for the nation."

"I wouldn't dream of it, sir."

"He also said, with no little satisfaction, I would add, that since the passing of the Treason and Sedition Acts, the radicals are cautious about admitting strangers to their meetings. You won't be able to stroll in off the street."

The two Gagging Acts, as Dan had heard them called, had been passed a couple of years earlier. They limited the size of political meetings to fewer than fifty attendees, and curbed what could be said at such meetings by extending the definition of treason.

"I told him that wouldn't be a problem," Sir William continued. "Though I don't know how you're going to do it."

"By going straight to the top," Dan said. "I'll strike up an acquaintance with President Broomhall."

Sir William let himself be reassured by Dan's confidence. "Then you're to make an immediate start. I want this kept between us until we know whether or not it's taking us anywhere. The trial of Reynolds and Wallace will be discretely delayed in the meantime. You'll report directly to me, but not here. Sir Richard has, for a miracle, put some of his resources at our disposal. There's a house he uses for meetings with informers, hiding witnesses and so on where we can meet – number five, Butcher Hall Lane. I'll be there after dark next Monday to hear your first report. If anything significant happens before that, you can send me a message from that address. Carry on, Foster."

The cupboard where Dan kept a few overnight things was next to Tom Clifford's desk. Never one to mind an interruption, the clerk known to the officers as Inky Tom lifted his pen from the neatly ruled page of the Watch Book into which he had been copying the descriptions, serial numbers and makers' names of timepieces filched over the weekend. His sandy hair was piebald from his habit of running his ink-stained fingers through it.

"Going somewhere, Mr Foster?"

Dan ignored this. He took his razor case out of his bag and put it in his pocket. A good blade was the one thing he could not do without even when working undercover, but in the places where his work took him it was the sort of detail that might arouse someone's curiosity. So the expensive blade was set in a cheap, cracked handle and nestled inside an old case. He bundled up a couple of clean shirts; he would buy whatever else he needed. He put his tipstaff in the bag and locked the cupboard.

"I'm handing in my weapon," he said, placing his Bow Street pistol on Tom's desk.

"What shall I say if anyone asks for you?"

Dan was already moving to the door and ignored this too.

He left the office and headed to Monmouth Street at Seven Dials, the centre of the ready-made clothes trade. Sellers ranged from street hawkers pushing barrow loads of rotting, flea-filled garments to shops with goods displayed in sparkling bow windows where smart assistants measured and fitted their customers as if they were the nobility. Avoiding both extremes, Dan fitted himself for the part of an out-of-work servant to people in the middling rank of life. He bought, new, some breeches and black stockings, and to these he added a second-hand coat of reasonable quality in dark grey wool. The shop assistant found him a smart green-striped waistcoat and a small-brimmed black hat to top it off.

That done, Dan purchased some more expensive items, the sort of things servants with a desire to ape their masters might adopt: a smart muslin neck cloth; shoes with plated buckles; a couple of linen shirts. He said he needed a greatcoat, hat and scarf for travelling, and chose everything in black.

He took the clothes to the gym at Cecil Street and waited in the little parlour while Noah finished a training session with a young man fresh out of Eton. The boy was resplendent in white breeches with a satin sash, silk stockings, and hand-made pumps. Someone should have told him that his fancy togs would not last long in the gymnasium.

Noah came in and poured himself a coffee. "What's in the parcel?"

"Servant's garb. I'm going after Kean's killer. I need an unmarked gun."

Occasionally Noah turned his gym into a shooting gallery for clients who required coaching, and kept a few weapons and ammunition in a locked chest. He placed his cup on the table. He knew better than to ask Dan any questions about his assignment; if Dan could tell him where he was going, he would.

Instead, he said, "Have you been home?"

"No. I don't have time. Will you tell them?"

"It's only round the corner from the office."

"I'm not going back to the office."

Noah let Dan's excuse lie between them for a moment before reciting the familiar arrangements. "You don't know how long you'll be; Caroline knows where your will is kept; if there's anything urgent we can get word to you via Bow Street." He hesitated. "Any messages?"

Not for Caroline, and whatever Dan longed to say to Eleanor must remain unsaid. He stood up.

"Can you take my clothes home for me?"

"Of course." Noah sorted through the clutter of odd gloves, old sporting papers, unpaired hand-weights and smeary bottles of embrocation on the table until he found a bunch of keys. "You get changed and I'll go and get you that pistol."

# Chapter Nine

By late afternoon Dan was walking along Gainsford Street in Southwark. Ships' masts spiked the sky above the tenements and warehouses that lined the lanes down to the wharves. Much of the river's mud had made its way onto the road, turning stretches of it into a quagmire churned by heavily burdened donkey carts and horse-drawn wagons. Most of the premises were devoted to sea-going trades: chandlers, rope makers, shipping agents and the like. There were butchers and bakers, and cheap eating houses where the windows ran with condensation so that the diners in their short sailor's jackets seemed to be sitting at the bottom of a tank.

Ahead lay the filthy slums of Jacob's Island with its vermin-ridden houses, brothels, taverns, cockpits and gambling dens squatting over a sewage-filled creek. Dan did not intend to look for lodgings there and turned back. Close to the quays there was no shortage of rooms to rent. He settled on a back parlour in a small house in Thomas Street, furnished with a bed, table, chair and wash stand. It was not the dirtiest room he had ever seen, and the landlady was not the most slatternly. She was sharp, though, demanding a week's rent in advance while her son, a hulking great youth, stood by to make it clear that any breach of the rules and he would be the one to deal with it. But there were not many rules. She could not tell sailors they had to be in by ten, or that they could not bring women back. So long as they paid and did not break anything, the landlady did not take much notice of her lodgers.

Dan gave her a week's rent plus the extra for sheets, towels and candles, and she left him to settle in. It did not take long to unpack his few belongings. There was a closet, but when he opened the door it let out such a gust of musty, mousy air he decided he would rather fold his clothes over the chair. This done, he went out.

The fruit and vegetable market on Borough High Street was still open, and the inns and restaurants were doing a brisk early-evening trade. Dan walked past Broomhall's shop, taking care not to be seen by anyone on the inside. A selection of new clocks and watches was set out in the small bow window on one side of the door, a display of second-hand goods in a similar window on the other. The new pieces were at the cheap end of the market, but there were one or two of silver and gold which would appeal to sailors fresh off a ship with their pockets full of wages. When their money ran out they had only to cross the shop to the counter where goods could be pawned or sold back at a reduced price.

Dan bought a couple of sausages with a few roast potatoes at one of the food stalls. Munching on these, he settled down on the opposite side of the busy road. After a while the traders started to pack up. A young fair-headed man bearing a lamp appeared in Broomhall's window and took out the trays of merchandise. A few minutes after the display had been reduced to empty shelves and the goods locked away somewhere in the interior, the front door opened and the young man stepped out into the street to close the shutters over the windows. He was a slight figure in a dark blue coat, brown breeches and an eye-bruisingly garish waistcoat of red and yellow stripes. When his work was done, he went back inside for a few moments, then re-emerged, turned left, and set off at a moping pace along the High Street.

Now, Dan thought, with any luck Broomhall will be coming out to get his own dinner. Dan would follow him, strike up a conversation, bring it round, as men often did in taverns and coffee houses, to politics...

The lamplight moved about the ground floor for a short time before disappearing. A minute later it reappeared in an upstairs window. An hour later it was still there.

The stalls were empty, the boxes and baskets of produce gone, and most of the stallholders with them, when Dan noticed a ragged boy grubbing around the gutters. He was barefoot and bare headed, with a ring-wormed face, sores around his lips and red eyes crusted yellow at the corners. Dan recognised the boy's look of concentration. He had worn the same expression himself when he hunted for market scraps: fruit that was only half rotten; lumps of meat the dogs had not found first; trodden-on pieces of bread with a few cleanish bits still left on them. Not that the dirt stopped you eating it. The boy was not collecting it all for himself. The filthy sack he carried bulged, but still he slunk along the street, keeping well out of the way of the few remaining traders' cuffs and kicks.

Another quarter of an hour went by and Broomhall did not budge. There was nothing to be learned by staring at a window. Dan would come back tomorrow and go into the shop, pretend he wanted to buy one of those pinchbeck watches.

The boy had scavenged all along the street, and was heading back towards London Bridge. The sight of him gave Dan an idea. He pulled up his coat collar and started off after the urchin. He occasionally lost sight of him amidst the throng of men and women going about their business or pleasure, but a little ducking and dodging brought him back into view again.

Just before London Bridge, the boy turned left into a dark lane lined on either side with unlit, narrow-fronted buildings, their walls and windows encrusted with grime. At the top of the lane the boy turned right into an alleyway. Dilapidated warehouses loomed overhead, blocking out what little light the moon might have given.

The alleyway opened out into a quayside lying almost beneath the bridge. Water lapped around a set of slimy stairs where a row of watermen's boats, stored for the night, gently knocked against one another. The boy headed for a pile of crates, coiled ropes and spars on the quayside and, without a backward glance, ducked down and disappeared. Dan was just in time to catch a glimpse of his heels as he wriggled into a tunnel through the lumber. If he had been the boy's age he would not have hesitated to dive in after him, knowing what he would find: a maze of tunnels opening out into a tiny unsafe cavern where a group of children huddled like mice in a nest.

Such groups formed and reformed all the time. They were loose associations at first, but then someone would emerge who was bigger and stronger than the rest and before long they would all be working for him. It was usually a him, though Dan had once run in a gang led by a girl. After a few weeks there would be a leadership challenge, or they would be driven from their den, or the night watchman would discover them, and the group would disperse. You would be on your own again, until you fell in with someone else.

Dan had fallen in with Weaver. Not that there was any accident to it. Weaver sent scouts out into the streets to round up stray children. He promised food and shelter, but you had to work for it: picking pockets, burgling houses, selling yourself. Useless to try and keep any of your earnings. It didn't matter where you hid. Weaver's boys always found you and beat the rhino out of you. And after you grew up, if you did grow up and weren't smart enough to get away, your only value to him was for sale to the hangman when he turned you in for the reward. It was said that many a boy and girl had added to the old devil's earnings in that way.

In his work as a Bow Street Runner Dan had often wondered if he would run across Weaver. He had dreamed of the moment the trap opened and the villain took the drop, imagining his hanging as a slow, agonising business. But their paths had never crossed again and he could only assume that Weaver had died. Slowly and painfully, he hoped.

Dan stopped at the entrance to the den, weighing up his options. He could wait a while in case the boy came out again, or he could come back early in the morning as the quayside began to fill with porters, dockers and draymen and catch him as the children dispersed for the day.

Dan heard scuffling and darted out of sight. A girl appeared on her hands and knees at the tunnel entrance. She looked cautiously about, hauled herself out and straightened her ragged skirt. She padded to the end of the alley, but instead of leaving it, she stood on the corner, on the fringe of the foot traffic passing back and forth over London Bridge. The lights on the bridge flickered across her face. It was impossible to guess her age; hers was the face of a creature old in vice and experience.

Before Dan could approach her to ask about the boy, she came back into the dark alleyway with a man. He was powerful and broad-shouldered, dirty and unshaven. A whaler from the look – or the smell – of him. His heavy black jacket stank of blood, smoke and oil. He negotiated in broken English. They agreed on sixpence. She led him further into the darkness and leaned against a wall. His body blocked her from Dan's view.

He was still unfastening his loose sailor's trousers when Dan hauled him off her. He spun round, cursing in a language Dan did not recognise, all rolling r's and z's.

"Give the girl her sixpence and get going."

The girl lowered her skirts and scrambled out from behind him. Torn between the desire to flee, the suggestion that her sixpence might still be forthcoming, and the possibility that there might be more money to be made from the stranger, she stopped a little way off.

Understanding spread over the sailor's broad, boorish face. Whatever it might be in his own language, the buttock and file trick was common throughout the world: a girl lures a man to some dark spot and with the help of a male accomplice robs him. Since Dan did not speak the man's language, he could not put him right. He could, however, guess with a reasonable chance of certainty the meaning of the words that gabbled out in a blast of gin and garlic. *"I haven't had what I paid for – you and your punk won't get one over on me – I'm going to beat you to a pulp."* No doubt punctuated by obscenities which rang impressively in his harsh tongue.

"Give the girl her money," Dan repeated.

"Fuck off."

He knew some English then. He turned and spat at the girl, who skipped nimbly out of the way, and started to shoulder his way past Dan.

Dan grabbed his lapels and slammed him back against the wall. He pinned him there with his right arm across his Adam's apple, cracked his head against the brickwork. While the whaler came to terms with that, Dan reached for the knife at his belt and threw it across the alley.

"Give the girl sixpence." Another slam of the head. "Now." Slam.

"Da! Da!" the man blubbered. He fumbled in his pocket, produced the coins and flung them on the floor. Dan shoved him away. He staggered off, his curses echoing between the buildings.

The girl snatched up the money and turned to run. Dan grabbed her arm. "No, you don't."

The girl struggled and swore but he did not loosen his grip. She gave up and tried wheedling.

"If you let me go, I'll go and find the next pigeon. Split it fifty-fifty, eh?" When he did not respond to this offer, she grabbed at his crotch and said, "Is this what you want?"

He shook her off and pulled her back to the quayside. She tried weeping but was not very good at it and soon gave up in favour of swearing at him. As they drew near to the lair she fell silent and avoided looking towards it in the hope that Dan did not know it was there.

"I want the boy. The one that just went in with the sack. Go and get him."

There was no point in feigning innocence. Innocence was something she had never had much familiarity with in any case. Understanding dawned on her wizened face. The wrong kind of understanding.

Dan did not attempt to explain. "Just send him out to me."

She wriggled inside. Several minutes passed and Dan was

beginning to think they had got away through another tunnel when a red and white face appeared from the shadows. The boy hesitated at the sight of the dark figure towering in front of him. Dan reached down, pulled him out and set him on his feet.

The boy rubbed his hand across his nose. "Ann says you wanted me. I want sixpence."

"What's your name?"

The boy gawped. It was not a question he was used to answering. "Nick," he said, though he did not seem certain of it. "Nick," he repeated with growing confidence.

"Well, Nick, if you do as I say you'll get a great deal more than sixpence. Are you listening?"

# Chapter Ten

The next morning Dan sat at the window of the White Hart's coffee room, from where he had a good view of Broomhall's shop. The High Street was already busy; it was never entirely deserted. The sailors, drunks and prostitutes who roamed the district from dusk to dawn had vanished, and the traders had arrived to set up their stalls. Their robust voices mingled with the cries of street sellers; the whines of beggars and ballad singers; the drone of a hurdy-gurdy; the din of horse-drawn traffic.

Occasionally Dan turned the pages of his newspaper. Someone was advertising a new design of coffin, secure enough to keep out body snatchers. Good luck with that, he thought. Broomhall's assistant arrived, knocked and was admitted. Dan watched him lay out the trays of clocks and watches. An hour passed, during which several passers-by stopped to browse the merchandise. Three or four went inside, spent a few moments there, and came out again.

At last a tall man dressed in black breeches and a dark green coat stepped out of the shop and clapped a hat over his short, carelessly-arranged hair. In his late thirties, he was dark-complexioned, with large brown eyes beneath thick eyebrows, a long nose, a shapely mouth over a cleft chin. Officer Reeves's summation of his character had been well-observed: Broomhall knew that he was at the height of his vigour and good looks. Neighbours cried good morning to him; men admired the fit of his clothes and his confident stride; women took second glances.

Dan folded his paper and left it on the table beside his

empty coffee cup. He sauntered after Broomhall, scanning the street as he went, spotting Nick's small figure slip out of the White Hart's coach yard and fall in behind the watchmaker.

As they drew near to the George, their way was blocked by the recent arrival of a stagecoach. Passengers milled about looking lost, their luggage piled in the road around them. It was the spot Dan would have chosen when he was Nick's age. All was bustle and confusion: a good place for a small pickpocket.

Just then Broomhall set up the cry: "Stop thief!", but Nick had already eeled his way through the crowd and was pelting along the High Street. Broomhall started after him. Dan pushed his way through the passengers, leapt over a pile of boxes, and chased after them. A couple of men who had been standing outside one of the taverns joined the pursuit. Dan did not bother trying to overtake them: he knew where Nick was going.

When Dan got to St Saviour's Church he paused on the threshold of the graveyard. There was no sign of the boy. Cursing, he stepped onto the path between the graves. He had gone only a few paces when he felt a twitch at his pocket and, turning, he saw the mottle-faced boy grinning up at him.

Nick handed over Broomhall's pocket book. It contained Broomhall's Corresponding Society membership ticket with the motto "Unite, persevere and be free" printed on it, a much-thumbed copy of the Society's rules, a couple of old restaurant bills, and a handful of bank notes.

"Good work, Nick. And here's what I promised."

The boy pocketed the coins. "Got any more jobs like this?"

"Might be, another time. If I want you, I'll find you. Now you'd better get going."

Nick nodded, turned on his heel and ran. He was soon lost to sight as he weaved between the headstones before dropping down into the road towards the wharves.

Dan hurried back to the High Street. He came up to Broomhall in time to hear him thanking the two men who had tried to help him.

"It was a good effort," Broomhall said. "The vagabond was just too quick for us."

The men mumbled their goodbyes and strolled away.

"I think this is yours," Dan said.

Broomhall glanced in astonishment at the proffered pocket book. "How the deuce did you get that?"

"By catching the thief."

"But he got away again?"

"No. I let him go."

"You let him go? Why?"

"Because I don't hold with fat magistrates hanging starving children."

The remark piqued Broomhall's interest, as it was intended to do. "Fat magistrates, eh? Look, I was on my way to Surrey Street to transact some business. It won't take long. Why don't you accompany me and then I will buy you dinner by way of thanks?"

"That's a good offer, and one I accept," Dan said.

They set off in the direction of Blackfriars Bridge, setting their backs to the decrepit gables of the Marshalsea and the smoking chimneys of the King's Bench prisons where men and women languished for want of sufficient to pay their debts and prison fees. Perhaps, Dan thought, that was why they were always so sharp and busy around here. It was a grim warning for the businessmen, publicans and landladies, the manufacturers and piece workers whose premises huddled around the gaols: *fail and you too may end up in here.*

Broomhall offered his hand. "I'm Edward Broomhall, clock and watchmaker. My shop is on Borough High Street."

"Daniel Bright, gentleman's servant, between situations at present," Dan said, adding bitterly, "having been dismissed to spare a gentleman's embarrassment."

"How so?" asked Broomhall. "Unless you prefer not to talk about it."

"I don't mind. I'm not the one who did anything wrong. Some money went missing from the master's drawer. When his wife found out the thief was their son, she accused me of taking it to save him from his father's anger. The father knew it was the boy, of course, but to spare trouble for himself he went along with it. Said if I went of my own will he'd give me a good reference. It was that or prison. It's a rich man's law, rot 'em."

Broomhall agreed that, scandalously, this was so. The conversation moved on to general matters. Dan asked Broomhall how long he had lived in Southwark and how long he had run the shop. The other answered that he had been born in Southwark and inherited the business from his father. Dan suggested that he must have seen a great many changes, and Broomhall answered that he had. He pointed to many of the buildings around them, which stood on the green fields and ponds he had played on as a child. They turned into Surrey Street and walked down to St George's Circus with the obelisk in the centre where Surrey Street joined the New, Lambeth and London Roads. Just before they reached the Circus, Broomhall stopped outside a silversmith's.

"My business is here, but I shall only be a few minutes. Why don't you go and take a table for us at Johnson's and I will join you shortly?"

Johnson's Coffee House and Tavern was by the Surrey Theatre and next door to a home for street women. At this time of day none of its inmates were to be seen. They were probably being preached at inside the Magdalen's prison-like walls. There was always a high price in humility to be paid for charity, as Dan recalled from his own days on the streets. He and the other children had scattered like rats from a fire when they saw beadles from the foundling hospitals on the prowl.

The place was already filling up but Dan managed to secure a booth. He ordered a coffee while he waited, which was not long.

"Business all done?" he asked as Broomhall settled into the high-backed wooden seat opposite.

"Yes…Simpson makes parts for my watches in his workshop. That's why I had so much money on me. Today was settlement day. If you hadn't intervened, things would have been very awkward."

The waiter came over, flicked his cloth across the table to remove imaginary crumbs and said, "Good day, Mr Broomhall. Well, I hope?"

"Hungry, you hope!" Broomhall laughed. "What's on today, Frank?"

Frank tilted back his head, closed his eyes and chanted, "Asparagus soup, turbot, choice of beef roasted, beef boiled, beef stewed, ham, or mutton chops, with potatoes and carrots, choice of apple pie or Windsor pudding."

"Roast beef for me."

"Same here," said Dan.

"And a bottle of your excellent hock."

"I'll stick to coffee," Dan said.

The waiter hurried off, bawling the order to the kitchen and barman as he went. A boy brought the wine a few moments later.

"Abstention and syrup of brimstone?" Broomhall asked, pouring himself a glass. "Following doctor's orders?"

"No, I just don't like wine."

Broomhall sipped. "I'm sure this would change your mind if you tried it. But I don't insist." He cast a sly glance at Dan. "So, Mr Bright, since you got a good look at the whelp who robbed me, what do you say to coming to Union Street with me when we have eaten to report the crime?"

The Magistrates' Office was the last place Dan wanted to visit. Nor would reporting the boy match the character he wanted to establish with Broomhall. It was not something Dan Foster, who often exercised his discretion in the matter of arrests, would do either.

"I wish I could be of assistance, but I am afraid that one street cub looks much like another to me. I doubt I would recognise him again if I saw him. Besides, I should think he is well away from here by now."

"But don't you think it our civic duty, for the sake of our

neighbours, that the robbery should be reported so that the police can keep our streets clear of this thieving tribe?" Broomhall needled, testing him out.

"No, I do not, and if it comes to reporting a crime, which is the greater crime: that our streets are overrun by starving children, or that our rulers would rather hang them than feed them?"

"I see this is a subject on which you feel passionately, Mr Bright."

"Forgive me. I spoke hastily."

"Not at all. I agree with you. And the plight of these children is no accident. It's not Providence, or fate, or fortune, that brings them so low. It is the way the rich have arranged the world to suit themselves. The children are of no use to them, so the children must starve."

He waited for Frank to put their bowls of soup in front of them before he resumed. "The laws as they stand are designed to protect men of property; it is a cruel nonsense to turn them on the destitute. Sadly, it is a state of affairs which cannot change while it is those self-same men of property who make the laws in parliament. If only men like us had a say in choosing the law-makers. Then we might see some changes."

"Changes? How do you think they would come about?"

"By parliamentary reform, Mr Bright. By annual parliaments and a vote for every man."

"Every man?"

"Why not? Do we not all live in and labour for our country?"

"That's true."

"Reform one abuse, and the others will disappear," Broomhall continued, when their empty soup bowls had been replaced by platters of fish. "The laws will be simplified, judges unbiased, juries independent, taxes reduced, the necessaries of life within the reach of the poor, prisons less crowded, and old age provided for." He smiled. "And no more fat magistrates."

Dan laughed. "You paint an attractive picture. I'm guessing

that you are now going to tell me how all this might come about?"

"Only because I think you are capable of understanding." Broomhall lowered his voice. "You have heard of the London Corresponding Society? You have heard, for example, that we are revolutionaries whose aim is to overthrow our country's constitution? It's a damned lie, sir! What we seek is the restoration of the British constitution as it was originally framed before the Norman invasion, to give us back our liberties and do away with corruption in parliament. Reform, Mr Bright, is our programme."

"And how do you plan to achieve it?"

"By teaching the people to have a due sense of their rights and their duties. That is the only way. But you could see for yourself what manner of men we are. Why don't you come along to one of our meetings?"

"I'm not sure. I don't know much about such things."

"You know enough to recognise wrongs that need righting, and that is all it is."

Dan had the chance to appear to think this over while the waiter brought the main course. "When is the next meeting?"

"Tonight at eight."

"There's no harm in finding out about it, I suppose. Where?"

"At the Boatswain and Call in Maze Pond, the back of Guy's Hospital. I'll call for you and introduce you...what is your address?"

"I've got rooms in Thomas Street."

"Where all the houses are falling down and infested with bugs! No, no, Mr Bright, we can do better than that. I have a friend in Tooley Street who has a room that has just become vacant. Why don't we go and look at it after dinner?"

"Thank you, I'd like that."

For the rest of the meal they swapped remarks about the excellence of the food. After the apple pie they drank a coffee and Broomhall settled the bill. Another party pounced on their table as soon as they stood up to leave.

"Is your friend an LCS man too?" Dan asked as they strolled along Tooley Street.

"No, Chambers is much too careful these days. But I think you'll find him interesting."

They stopped at a shop window full of badly-drawn cartoons printed on cheap paper. Dan could see that it was not quality that mattered in this market, but the quantity of bums and bubbies the customer got for his money. Central place in the display was a book on a wooden stand open at one of the illustrations. Dan, twisting his neck the better to see what was going on in the scene, wondered if it was possible for a man and woman to get into the position shown or, for that matter, out of it. He looked at his companion in surprise. Broomhall laughed, took his arm and drew him up the steps.

They had been seen from inside the shop and the door opened as they reached it. They were greeted by a fine-looking woman in her middle years with a clear, wholesome complexion, bright hazel eyes from which flashed a hint of green, and auburn hair beneath a white cap. Her dress was neat to the point of modesty and there was a pleasing Welsh tinge to her voice which, for all that Dan was unfamiliar with the nuances of the accent, struck him as that of a woman born to better things.

"Mr Broomhall," she said. "I see you were showing your friend *The Adventures of a Comely Country Wench.*" She turned to Dan and added with an air of pride, "It's one of our most popular publications."

"And with good reason, I don't doubt," Broomhall said. "How do you do, Mrs Chambers? We've come about the room."

"You'd better come in then."

In the shop a thin, puny-shouldered man with grey hair straggling about his pale face was unpacking a box of books. He peered at Dan over a pair of green-tinted glasses. Dan took him at first for Mrs Chambers's father.

"Mr Chambers, this gentleman is going to look at the room," she said.

"Yes, yes, my dear," he murmured absently. "Oh, is that Mr Broomhall? What a pleasure to see you!"

Broomhall held out his hand. "How do you do, my dear fellow?"

Dan and Mrs Chambers left the two chatting. She led him through the door at the back of the shop into a parlour crammed with books, some in boxes, others stacked in tottering piles. Three girls sat at the long plain table which took up the remaining space. The elder two, who were about sixteen and fourteen, had brushes and paints in front of them and would have looked like any young misses at their watercolours had they not been diligently colouring in lewd prints. Their little sister, with bent head and protruding tongue, copied addresses from an order book on to slim parcels of discretely wrapped books. She did not look up from her work, but the other two regarded Dan with demure curiosity.

Mrs Chambers paused at the table to gather the scattered papers she had been working on before she went out to the shop. Dan caught sight of the title page: *Amora, or the Countess of Love*. That explained her pride in the book in the window: she was an authoress. He had walked into the middle of a busy family manufactory.

The room was upstairs at the back. It looked out over a yard in which stood a large shed with a padlocked door.

"We used to have a printing press in there," Mrs Chambers said. "But now we send the work out. It is cheaper than keeping a pair of apprentices. This was the room they slept in."

It was certainly superior to the Thomas Street establishment. The sheets and blankets were clean and fresh, and there was a gaily-coloured rug on the floor. There was a wash stand with a clean bowl and unchipped jug, and a table, chair and chest, all smelling of beeswax.

They agreed terms. Mrs Chambers would provide breakfast, coals, towels and bedding, water and candles, and suppers by arrangement.

"The shop closes at ten, but here is a key if you are later."

She took Dan downstairs, left him in the shop with the other two men, and returned to her writing.

"Mr Broomhall has just been telling me about the service you did him this morning," Chambers said. "Let me shake you by the hand, sir, for your quickness – but more than that, for your kindness. The parish ignores these children when they starve, but is hasty enough to punish them when they steal."

"I was just telling Chambers that you are coming to your first London Corresponding Society meeting tonight," Broomhall said. "And asking him if he could provide you with some reading material that might be useful."

"I have just the thing. Come with me."

He led Dan and Broomhall back to the parlour.

"My love," he said, "would you keep an eye on the shop while I talk to Broomhall and – and –"

"Bright," Dan said.

Mrs Chambers, used to the constant interruption necessary on attending a business, rose from her seat. The three men went out through the kitchen and crossed the yard, and Chambers opened the padlock on the shed door with a key from his pocket. The building was empty save for an old desk piled with books and magazines, with a tray of letter presses nearby. Chambers rummaged through the literature.

"Something for someone attending his first LCS meeting, you say?"

"That's right." Broomhall erupted into a coughing fit. "Must be the dust in here. I'll leave you to it and go and get a glass of water."

Chambers, busy with his books, did not notice him go. "I have just the thing," he said, thrusting a pamphlet at Dan. "Here is the *Address to the French National Convention*. And the *Address to the Nation at Large*…William Frend's *Peace and Union*…some copies of the London Corresponding Society's *Moral and Political Magazine*." He lowered his voice. "Don't let Mrs Chambers see them. She doesn't like them in the house, you know…I'll just lock up. You go through."

Dan thrust the offending publications under his jacket and went back across the yard. The back door stood open and neither Broomhall nor Mrs Chambers, who were standing in the kitchen, heard him approach. They were too busy kissing. Kissing and arguing.

The woman tilted back her head. "But why did you have to bring him here?"

"Because I want to be sure he is who he says he is. You can keep an eye on him for me. Tell me if he has any visitors, receives any letters. You will do that little thing for me, won't you?"

Before she could refuse, he kissed her again.

Dan heard the shed door close and Mr Chambers fumbling with the padlock. He tiptoed back into the yard and then returned to the house, treading heavily and scraping his shoes on the doorstep. The couple leapt apart.

"That's better," Broomhall said, patting his chest as if recovering from a coughing fit. "Thank you for the water, Mrs Chambers."

Her husband came in and invited Dan and Broomhall to take a glass of wine. Broomhall said he had his own shop to look after, and Dan said he would go and fetch his things from Thomas Street. The eldest girl had been sent to wait in the shop. On his way out, Broomhall winked at her. She scowled at him and turned away.

"That's a strange family business," Dan said when they were outside. "It doesn't seem to fit Chambers and his family somehow."

"He didn't always sell salacious literature. His was once one of the best radical bookshops this side of the river. He had a spell in prison for selling copies of Tom Paine's book, *The Rights of Man*. He was never charged with anything and they let him out after a few months. But it ruined his business. He had to sell his printing press and, as you've seen, diversify his trade. I doubt he would have taken that way if he had not been driven to it by dire necessity and a wife who has a sounder head for business than he does. I hear from those who are knowledgeable about such things that Mrs Chambers has discovered a talent for a certain type of literature."

Dan, thinking of the *Comely Country Wench* and the *Countess of Love*, nodded. "And yet their daughters behave as if they are misses in a mansion."

"Yes, those girls are like white roses growing in a midden heap."

Broomhall gestured at their surroundings to illustrate his point. Around the quays foul-mouthed lumpers shifted bales and crates. A filthy beggar sat in the road with his back against a wall, his bare ulcerated legs stretched in front of him. A drunken woman peeped out of an alley and slurred, "Buy us a drink, me darlings!"

# Chapter Eleven

The pool that had given Maze Pond its name was long gone, aptly replaced by a bewildering network of narrow streets and courts behind Guy's Hospital. Broomhall explained that, like most divisions of the London Corresponding Society, Division Fourteen had often had to change its meeting place as landlords threatened with prosecution turned them away.

"But the landlord at the Boatswain and Call is on our side," he said. "And the constables don't come into the Maze Pond if they can help it."

Dan could see why. The occupiers of the crowded, rotten tenements spilled out into the streets. Hard-faced women, savage children and brutish men sat on doorsteps or hung about on corners. They all seemed to be in a perpetual state of readiness to offer violence to anyone who so much as looked at them. Broomhall was unaffected by their hostility. He strode amongst them as if they were his friends, and for the most part there was a lifting of the mood as he passed. But no amount of friendly smiles could change the stale atmosphere, heavy with the stench of cess pits, open drains, rotting food, gin, and unwashed bodies.

Broomhall led Dan past the inn's front door and turned into a narrow alley where no light penetrated and the flagstones were damp and slippery. A few steps brought them to a side entrance, where Broomhall rapped a distinctive rhythm on the door. It was opened by a man in dust-covered smock and trousers.

"Citizen, this is Citizen Bright," Broomhall said. "He is my guest for the evening."

The door-keeper nodded an acknowledgement and stood

aside to admit them. They climbed a steep flight of wooden stairs towards the buzz of voices coming from the room above. Clouds of smoke billowed across the narrow landing from the open door. A man with a cash box and a bundle of tickets sat behind a table at the entrance. While Broomhall gave him the two pennies for Dan's entrance fee, Dan moved into the room. Instantly the chatter ceased and he was confronted by a crowd of wary faces.

"Citizen Bright is with me," Broomhall announced.

There was a rustle of relief and the talking and smoking started up again. Broomhall took Dan over to a burly, broad-shouldered man who stood with his back to the door, talking with another man. His neat, dark clothes were not those of a labourer. They were almost clerkly, though he did not look like someone who spent his days bound to a desk.

"Citizen Bright," said Broomhall, "may I introduce Citizen Metcalf. He has been a member of this division since it started. He will be able to explain the proceedings to you and answer any questions you have." He nodded at the long table at the top of the room. "My place is over there."

Metcalf regarded Dan stonily from beneath thick black eyebrows. His jaw was shaded by the day's growth, his dark hair cut short. His face was as blank as that of a pugilist in the middle of a bout, his expression carefully arranged so as not to give any hint of where he meant to strike next. Dan was equally careful not to betray the tautening of his own nerves as he shook Metcalf's hard hand. He sensed that this was a dangerous man.

Metcalf had not been chosen to steer the newcomer because of his charm, for it was a quality he lacked. Unsmilingly, he introduced his crony, Simmons, who was tall and bony with a long, lantern-jawed face and knobbly knuckles which he cracked throughout the meeting.

Metcalf gestured at the front row of seats. "Won't you sit here beside me, Citizen Bright?" His voice, deep and emotionless, grated on the ears.

Dan sat down with Metcalf on his right. Simmons slithered into the seat on his left. Dan did not like the arrangement, but had to resign himself to the fact that, with these two at his elbows, this was no occasion to start asking even the most subtle questions about Kean.

Broomhall took his place at the top table. Beside him sat the Division Secretary: a thin, nervous-looking man who had a squint which became more pronounced when he was called upon to speak. The third person at the table was the speaker for the evening. He was one of the Division's tything men, Metcalf explained. They were individuals who each had ten members assigned to them with whom they kept in regular contact. It was a quick, efficient system for passing on news from the committee, such as last-minute venue changes, and also, Dan guessed, warnings of impending raids and arrests.

By the time Broomhall called the meeting to order there were close to sixty men in the room. That made the meeting illegal, the lawful limit being fifty, but as Broomhall said, Maze Pond was largely ignored by the constables. Many of the men were smoking pipes and some had brought glasses of ale up with them from the bar. All removed their hats and placed them under their seats.

"Welcome, citizens," Broomhall began. "First in the order of business: are there any new members to be admitted tonight?"

Dan turned with everyone else to watch two men stand up. For one of them the manoeuvre was something of a struggle. He gripped the back of the chair in front of him and stood awkwardly, one hip higher than the other. Dan glanced down and saw that one of his boots was built up to accommodate a club foot. His clothes were patched and ragged, his eyes large and intense in his skeletal, pockmarked face.

"Citizen Upton, who is it you wish to introduce to the Society tonight?" Broomhall asked the lame man.

"Citizen Broomhall, I present Citizen Warren, a tea merchant of Tooley Street and known to many of us herein assembled."

Warren bowed and one or two members nodded in recognition.

"And you vouch for Citizen Warren? He is well known to you?"

"I hereby swear that I am able to vouch for the here-assembled party Citizen Warren who has a domicile in Tooley Street in this Borough of Southwark and who seeks –"

"Yes, yes," Broomhall interrupted. "There's no need to swear an oath. Does anyone second the application?"

Someone mumbled something from the back row which was taken as a second and Broomhall continued, "Citizen Warren, has Citizen Upton explained our requirements to you?"

"He has," the tea merchant replied.

Dan wondered if Warren valued the commodity he traded in too much to drink it. He was a fat, red-faced man with a bulbous, crimson nose which suggested he spent more time at his wine glass than his teacup.

"Then I shall put the qualifying questions. Question one: are you convinced that the parliamentary representation of this country is at present inadequate?"

"Inadequate and imperfect," corrected Upton.

"Thank you, Citizen Upton," Broomhall said drily.

"I am," answered Warren.

"Question two: are you persuaded –" Broomhall saw Upton open his mouth and hastily said, "*Thoroughly* persuaded that the welfare of these kingdoms requires that every person of adult years in possession of his reason and not incapacitated by crimes should have a vote for a member of parliament?"

"I am."

"Question three: will you endeavour by all justifiable means to promote such reformation in parliament?"

"I will."

"Then your application for membership is accepted. The secretary will collect your quarter's dues and give you a copy of the rules and the addresses of the Society after the meeting."

Warren and Upton sat down looking pleased with themselves. Broomhall and the Division Secretary conferred briefly over their papers. Most of the penny candles in the room were concentrated on and around the front table for the benefit of the delegates, leaving the corners and rear of the apartment in shadow. Looking around during the short pause, Dan noticed a man huddled against the wall at the end of the row behind him, scribbling in a notebook held close to his eyes.

Metcalf, following Dan's gaze, said, "That's Spy Wheeler. Every division has its own Jerry Sneak, some more than one."

So much, Dan thought, for Sir Richard Ford's spy and his vital work for the nation. "You know he's a spy but you admit him?"

"No point trying not to. They'll only send another and he'll be just as easy to spot." He paused and fixed Dan in his grim gaze. "They always are."

Broomhall announced, "I shall now give my report from the meeting of the executive committee on Thursday last."

This part of the proceedings took some time as several members rose to ask questions as the various items came up. By the time it was over, the room was hot and close, but no one opened the door for fear, Dan assumed, of eavesdroppers lurking on the stairs. The same caution prevented opening the windows, and it was not surprising to see one or two heads lolling during the tything man's talk. Nor was the heat the only explanation for the slumber that stole over the gathering. Wheeler stayed awake to note down the particulars of the speech, which Dan considered quite an achievement on the spy's part.

The meeting ended with a song which had Spy Wheeler's pencil racing across the page: "*But cease ye fleecing senators / Your country to undo / Or know we British Sans Culottes / Hereafter may fleece you.*" Dan, who did not take it too seriously, enjoyed the sing-song.

In the hubbub as the room emptied, Broomhall caught up with him.

"What did you think of the meeting?" he asked.

"A lot of talking. Can't say I understood half of it."

Broomhall laughed. "That wasn't one of our best speakers – no one ever understands a word he says. I hope you will give us another chance and come to the next meeting."

"I think I will."

"Good…I won't walk back with you. I have one or two things to clear up here first. Goodnight, Mr Bright."

They shook hands and Dan moved towards the door. He hung back in the shadows on the landing while the men in front of him clacked down the stairs and vanished into the dark alley below. When they had all gone, he crept back and, keeping out of sight, looked into the room. Broomhall and Metcalf were in a private confab by the table, Simmons standing sentinel close by. The only way in was the door Dan had just passed through, so there was no chance of sneaking back to listen.

He put on his hat, moved quietly down the stairs and took up position at the end of the alley. Twenty minutes later the three men came down. When they parted with Simmons, Dan let him go and stayed with Broomhall and Metcalf. They led him to Broomhall's shop on Borough High Street. Broomhall went inside and Dan heard him slide the bolts across his door. It did not look as if he was going out again that night, so Dan shadowed Metcalf on the off-chance he was up to something of interest.

It seemed that radicals kept more regular hours than the villains Dan usually had to deal with. He watched Metcalf let himself into a lodging house on Joyners Street, noted the address and made his way back to Tooley Street and his own bed.

# Chapter Twelve

On Monday evening Dan went back over the river and headed for his appointment with Sir William Addington. Not that he had much to report. Since the London Corresponding Society meeting in Maze Pond he had kept a close watch on Broomhall. Borough High Street was well provided with inns and eating houses, which had given him a good excuse to dawdle in the vicinity of Broomhall's shop during the daytime, and after dark there were plenty of shadows in doorways, passages or alleys to hide in.

He had seen precisely nothing. Broomhall never went to the warehouse on Horsleydown and Dawson never came to the shop, though Metcalf was there every day at different times. Sometimes he stayed an hour or more, sometimes only a few minutes. Dan had so far failed to discover how Broomhall and Dawson were connected. If there was a link, it was possible that Broomhall used a go-between to maintain it. Perhaps Metcalf was running back and forth with messages. Or possibly they sent Simmons. Or someone else.

Broomhall himself gave no sign of being involved in anything unlawful other than running political meetings that exceeded their legal quota. Perhaps, Dan thought, he should approach the question from another angle. There might be more benefit in watching the warehouse to see if any of Broomhall's friends went there, linking him to Dawson that way.

Occasionally ducking into an alley or passageway or stopping to look in a shop window to check that no one was following him – not that he had reason to think anyone was, but it always paid to be careful – Dan walked along Cheapside and turned into Butcher Hall Lane just after entering Newgate Street. Behind the iron gates of Christ's Hospital the boys in their blue petticoats and yellow stockings filed out of the great hall on their way to their beds. From the opposite side of the road the clatter of dishes and hubbub of conversation floated out of Crish's Beef Shop on waves of savoury smells. Bright light poured through the steaming windows; Dan crossed the road to avoid it.

He crossed back to look for number five, which turned out to be the house next to Crish's. An unlit carriage without any identifying insignia waited outside, the driver and footman standing guard beside it.

A man in black breeches, boots and jacket, with the lower half of his face covered by a black silk scarf, opened the door of the house. With his hand on the pistol in his pocket, he scrutinised Dan before allowing him inside. Dan followed him into the unlit hall, beyond which he saw a dim light through the half-open door of a cold, disused kitchen. He caught the faint sound of a foot shifting: there was another man on watch at the rear of the house. Dan passed the silent bulk of a third guard on the landing.

In the first floor room at the front of the house, Sir William Addington stood near the tiny hearth where a feeble fire burned. Another man sat on a rickety chair behind a rough and none too clean wooden table on which were a decanter and a couple of glasses. Dan, who had not expected to find Sir William in company, and certainly not such detested company, halted in surprise. It seemed that when Sir Richard Ford gave his approval to his colleague's investigation, he had not meant to give him a free hand.

"Come in, come in, don't stand there gaping," Sir William said irritably. "And shut the door behind you. Sir Richard Ford wants to hear your report."

"There isn't much to report yet, sir. I've made contact with Broomhall, attended one meeting of Division Fourteen, and told Broomhall I'll go to the next one. Broomhall comes over as friendly and open, but he's cautious. He's got my landlady, who also happens to be his lover, spying on me. That might be just because of his LCS activities; they are careful about who they let in." Dan thought it best not to mention that he had won Broomhall over by his criticism of fat magistrates.

"Tell me about the Divisional meeting," Sir Richard said.

"It wasn't very interesting. They swore in a new member. Talked about their committee. Nothing very startling."

"I'll be the judge of that. All you have to do is tell me exactly what happened. Can you do that?"

"I can, but –"

"Can you do that, Officer?"

Dan glanced at Sir William, who nodded.

"Yes, sir."

The smell of roast beef saturated the walls, forcing itself on Dan's attention whenever there was a pause in the proceedings. The pauses were frequent as Sir Richard mulled over each piece of information before signalling that Dan could continue. Sir William preferred intelligence to be delivered rapidly and without straying from the point, but Ford wanted every detail: how many had been at the London Corresponding Society meeting; the substance of the speeches; who said what.

"But you have your own spies to tell you all this," Dan ended. "On which point, you should be aware that they know Wheeler is working for you."

"The man is an incompetent blunderer," Sir Richard answered. "However, he will be a useful decoy now you are in place."

"I'm not there to spy for the Home Office."

"You're there to gather information," Ford retorted.

"About Kean's murder."

"That's enough, Foster," Sir William said. "No one's forgotten Officer Kean. But indeed, Sir Richard, it was my understanding that you did not want my officer trespassing on your jurisdiction."

"The situation has changed now that we can no longer

95

trust Wheeler's intelligence. At best, they will not talk about anything important in front of him; at worst, they will use him to feed us false information. Luckily, Foster is already well placed to take over from him."

"But I was sent to find Kean's murderer," Dan said.

"I assume that it has not escaped even your notice that peace negotiations have broken down and we are still at war with France. The French are once more looking across the Channel, and their Dutch allies have amassed a fleet at the Texel. The threat of invasion is becoming very real again. The corresponding clubs, united societies and friends of liberty are all Frenchie lovers to a man. We can't afford to leave these traitors unchecked in our midst at such a time."

"But you can't take me off my case."

"Can't I? And I suppose I can't put you back in the foot patrol either."

"That you can't," Sir William said. "He's under my command."

"And I have my authority directly from the Home Secretary."

"You have made sure we are all aware of it," Sir William answered.

He and Ford stared angrily at one another. After a moment, Ford said coldly, "I think you misapprehend me. There is no need to take Foster off the case. Far from it. I want him to stay where he is. But he is to seize on any opportunity to get close to Broomhall and his allies, and he will report on everything that passes while he is there. Unless you think that is beyond his ability."

"It's not a question of ability," Dan said. "I haven't so far been able to connect Broomhall to Dawson and the body snatching, and I'm thinking a change of tactics would be worth trying – watching the warehouse instead of Broomhall's shop. I can't watch Broomhall and Dawson at the same time."

"The resurrectionists are not important," Sir Richard said. "From now on your focus will be on the London Corresponding Society."

"But –"

Sir William interrupted Dan. "I and my officers will, of course, do all we can to assist the Home Office. Your instructions will be carried out."

"Good."

Sir Richard Ford rose and without another word strode out of the room. He flung the door wide, the draught all but extinguishing the sickly fire. A few moments later the front door opened and closed and the guards bundled the magistrate into the coach waiting to whisk him back to Whitehall.

"So now I'm one of Sir Richard Ford's spies?" Dan demanded.

"You're whatever I tell you to be," Sir William answered. "So just be glad I don't decide to put you back in the foot patrol myself. And Foster?"

"Yes, sir?"

"Let's have less argument in future."

Towards the end of Tuesday afternoon, Dan bought some savoury pies at a butcher's stall on Borough High Street. Then he stopped a street trader pushing a barrow of old clothes. The man was black, thin and stooping, old before his time. Probably a servant turned out when he lost the youthful good looks that had made him a fashionable accessory for a lady's carriage.

"Have you anything to fit a boy, so big?" Dan asked, holding his hand at chest height.

The barrowman sorted through the heap of ancient, patched garments. Dan chose some breeches and a shirt and jacket which were none too clean and had been well-worn. Anything better would turn the wearer into a target for robbers. He hesitated over a pair of shoes and decided against them, not being able to judge the size.

Having completed his purchases, he headed through the busy streets towards London Bridge. A constant stream of goods poured in and out of the warehouses. Crates and barrels swung from pulleys above Dan's head, nearly rumbled over his toes in over-burdened carts, or trundled across his path on wheelbarrows. The crashing and banging echoed from wall to wall, mingled with the workmen's foul-mouthed banter and the horses' ringing hooves and plaintive neighing.

On the quay by the children's hideout, Dan dug out an upturned crate and sat down to wait for them to return from a day of scavenging, begging and thieving. The smell of stale urine drifted from the nearby alleyway, mingled with the yeasty gusts borne on the wind from the massive vats of Thrale's brewery. After a while he did not notice it. He watched the boats sliding up and down the river, the smaller skiffs and wherries dodging back and forth from the ocean-going vessels anchored in the middle of the stream. The wharf men going about their work cast curious glances at him, but no one disturbed him.

Last evening Sir Richard Ford had decreed that he should shift the focus of his investigation to Broomhall's political activities and away from Kean's murder. Striding back to Tooley Street after their meeting, Dan had invented many uncomplimentary names for the magistrate who had thus reduced him to the level of a common informer like Wheeler. Going undercover to catch a murderer or thief was one thing, but he had never agreed to be a government spy. If he was to ensnare his fellow men, let it at least be because they had committed a crime.

Sir William hadn't been a lot of use, as usual. One mention of the Home Secretary and he had caved in to Sir Richard's demands. Not with any good grace either, and he had taken his anger out on Dan. And now Dan was to spend more fruitless hours outside Broomhall's shop although he thought there might be more to be gained by watching Dawson's warehouse. It was not until he had crossed London Bridge, looked down at the dark quay and imagined the children sleeping in their den that it had struck him there was a way to do both.

Dusk fell and the quayside quietened down. Doors banged shut, keys turned in locks, tired men and horses plodded back to bed and stall, boats were secured for the night. A rat ran over Dan's shoe; he flicked it away. It righted itself and scuttled off, sniffing at the ground as it went, on the lookout for edible spills: grain intended for the flour mills; leather for the tanneries; bones for the glue makers.

A ragged, barefoot girl emerged from the alleyway, a hunk of dirty bread clutched in her fingers. The lights had not been lit on London Bridge and she did not see him in the gloaming as she crept into the den. A few moments later another girl arrived. After a little while Dan spied the skinny, filthy figure he was waiting for. He stood up. Behind him one of the lamps on the Bridge flared into life.

"Nick!"

The boy stopped in his tracks, slewed round on tiptoe, ready for flight.

"Remember me?"

The boy stepped forward cautiously. "Mr Bright."

"I got you these."

Nick glanced at the bundle of clothes over Dan's arm, sniffed at the meaty smell rising from the bag of pies. Dan held one out. Nick snatched it and tore a bite out of it.

"I've got another job for you, if you want it."

"What?" mumbled Nick, pastry cascading out of his mouth.

"There's a warehouse next to the cooper's yard on Horsleydown. I want you to keep an eye on it. There's a ruined house by it, you should be able to sleep safely there. I'll show you when you've finished eating."

Nick looked at the bag; he had not finished yet. Dan handed him another pie. The boy's hunger was not satisfied until his belly was stretched round and taut beneath his thin rags. Not a healthy way to eat, but when good, clean food rarely passed your lips, the only way. He shoved his last pie into his shirt.

"It's for Ann."

Dan gave him the bag. "Enough there for all of you. But business first. Come on."

It was Nick who led the way, though. The boy had a keen instinct for not being seen, and he knew the dark byways of the district. Amidst the ruins of the tumbledown house, Dan explained what was wanted. Nick was to keep watch at night, when the gang would be active, and report anything he saw.

"They're resurrection men, Nick. Do you know what that means?"

The boy shuddered. "Course. Is that your line too?"

"I'm in lots of lines. Let's just say they're in my way. Will you do it?"

"Can I bring Ann here?"

"You can bring who you like. Just make sure none of you are seen."

"'Tain't very likely."

"I know. Meet me on the wharf same time tomorrow. Here." Dan dumped the clothes over the boy's arm. "I'll leave you to it."

When he reached the empty doorway, Dan paused and looked back. Nick stood where he had left him, his spoils clutched to his chest, his mottled face a mixture of wonder and yearning. What vistas the interest of a well-dressed and generous man opened up to someone in his situation! Glimpses of another life where there was enough to eat, to wear, somewhere safe to sleep. Then the boy's habitual mask of pinched cunning descended. He turned, hunched his shoulders and pattered away into the rubble.

Dan tried to shake the image out of his mind. He could not afford to raise the boy's expectations. It would make Nick careless, forget to look out for himself on the street. You couldn't afford to dream or hope, not when you had to survive.

# Chapter Thirteen

Dan left Nick and walked towards his lodgings. He had not gone very far along Tooley Street when he saw Chambers's eldest daughter, Evelyn, in front of him. He almost did not recognise her: she was nothing like the miserable girl who drooped over her work in the back room at the shop. Taking advantage of her freedom, she browsed in brightly-lit shop windows; lingered at smoking braziers spitting roast chestnuts; laughed at the blandishments of the stallholders who wanted her to buy their wares.

He watched her go into a stationer's and, curious about the alteration in her, stopped to peer in through the window. She stood at the counter where a young man showed her a box of watercolour tablets. With hardly a glance at them, she sealed the purchase with an impatient nod. The man reached beneath the counter and brought out a sheet of wrapping paper. With a teasing flourish, he produced two letters he had hidden in its folds and slid them along the counter. Evelyn laughed and snatched them up.

This bodes ill, Dan thought. A clandestine love affair, and with what manner of man? The sort who could not or would not openly declare his love, who separated a girl from her parents, who taught her deception. Like white roses on a midden heap, Broomhall had called the Chambers girls. Evelyn was probably no better able to handle the situation than the most sheltered girl in the highest social circles.

While the assistant wrapped her purchase, his eyes straying constantly to her face, she opened the first letter and scanned it quickly. Her shoulders sagged; she folded it and put it in her pocket. The young man frowned in earnest sympathy. Generous in his love for her, Dan thought, for love it clearly was, yet he was willing to play postman for her and her lover.

Less eagerly, expecting only further disappointment, she opened the second letter. She read it once, twice, a third time, then threw her arms around the young man's neck – he had to lean over the counter to facilitate the manoeuvre. Carefully, she put it in her pocket and turned to leave. The young man called her back and handed her the parcel. She laughed at her forgetfulness, and danced out of the shop.

Dan raised his hat. "Good news, Miss Chambers?"

She gasped. "News? I don't know what you're talking about. Why are you following me?"

"I wasn't. I saw you go into the shop."

"I've been buying watercolours. If you don't mind, I must get home. Mother is waiting for them."

She tried to push past him but he blocked her path. "How do you know you can trust him?"

"Trust who?"

"Your lover."

"I haven't got a lover."

He smiled. "Come, Miss Chambers, I've just seen you jump for joy over a love letter."

"A love letter? Do you really think I'm that stupid?"

"If it's not a lover, what then?"

"It's none of your business."

"It might be your father's business."

He had hit a soft spot. "It's to help Father," she protested.

"A man he does not know secretly carrying on with his daughter will help him?"

"There is no man, I tell you!"

"So if your father finds out about those letters, there's nothing for him to worry about?"

"I've been offered a situation as a governess and I'm going to accept and I'm going to save all my money and when I have enough I'll find a home for us far away from *her*. Satisfied now?" She brushed away an angry tear. "Let me go. They'll be wondering where I am."

"They'll have more to wonder about when you run off to your new employers. When are you going to tell them?"

"I can't tell them. They won't let me go if I do."

"So it's to be a note on the mantelpiece and a midnight flit?"

"What choice do I have?"

"I don't know unless you tell me. But look, Miss Chambers, we can't talk here. There's a pastry shop over the road. Why don't we go in there for some tea?"

"Why should I?"

"Because I want to help you."

"Does that mean you won't say anything to Father?"

"If you can convince me you know what you're doing, I won't say anything."

He held out his arm. She gave in, put her hand on his sleeve and let him lead her across the busy street. It was not one of London's finest establishments, but it was cheerfully lit by candles and wall sconces. The tea was not bad and it came with a plate of little cakes. Evelyn cheered up at the novelty of being out with a male companion, even if he was only the lodger, and was soon nibbling at the sweets.

"So," he said, "tell me why you want to go and work for strangers when there's a place for you in the family business."

"Family business! We had a family business once. Everyone came to our bookshop. Mr Godwin, Mr Thelwall, Mrs Wollstonecraft. She had to find work as a governess too, you know. And when I've got some experience and saved enough money, I'm going to follow her example and open a school for girls. I'm going to employ someone to teach them Latin and Greek, and they'll do mathematics and history, and German and French, and no sewing or shell work or paper flowers. And I'll make sure they all read *A Vindication of the Rights of Women*."

"I hope you get your school one day...Broomhall said your

103

father lost the business when he went to prison."

"Yes, but he could have started again. It was her. She said he had to make more money. The print shop was her idea, and the books and pictures. And now instead of the greatest minds in the world, we have to bow and scrape to the grubbiest."

"No doubt your mother was thinking about your financial security."

"Security! What security is there for us? What decent man will consider marrying us while we live in that place? And now I know what's in the minds of the other sort when they look at me. It's like poison. And it's all her fault. She can't even stand by Father now she's brought him to this."

"What do you mean?"

"Haven't you seen them? Her and Broomhall? She thinks I don't know, that I'm as blind to her faults as Father."

"He doesn't know?"

"No, and I dread him finding out. And as if Broomhall's not bad enough, there's his horrible friends. Metcalf, who just stares, and Simmons whose breath smells like a cesspit, and that ugly beast Scott. I'm sure he's a highwayman. He's so mean looking."

"How so?"

"His eyes are always red from drink. And he has a scar on his face, here." She pointed to her left eye.

That was definitely Kean. Dan wondered how he had managed to get so friendly with Broomhall.

"Broomhall brought him to the shop?"

"Only once. But he came back on his own two or three times after that."

"When did you last see him?"

"I don't know. A little over two weeks, I think. But you do see now why I have to get away?"

"It's not an ideal situation, I grant you that. But things could be worse. And that's not just a meaningless expression. How did you get the job?"

"I put an advertisement in the *London Chronicle*."

"That's resourceful, but you need to be very careful about accepting situations from people you know nothing about."

"But Mrs Harris has told me everything."

She passed the letter over to Dan.

He looked at the address. "Liverpool. Quite a distance."

"She said they'd send money for the coach and someone will meet me at the other end."

Dan read the letter. "Her husband is a merchant and she has three children all under ten. You will have your own apartments, dine with the family, be in sole charge of the nursery. Sounds like a dream job. And a high salary, for a first post...Before you write back to accept, will you let me make a few enquiries first? Check that the Harrises are who they say they are? And if it all works out, I'll book your place on the coach myself."

"But how can you find out about them?"

"I know a man who can help me." He was thinking of Captain Ellis. He would send him the letter with a note asking him to make some postal enquiries about the Liverpool family. "Is it a deal?"

"Very well."

"Good. And now you've eaten all the cakes, we'd better be getting back."

Evelyn reddened. "Oh dear, didn't you have any?"

"Not much of a sweet tooth," Dan said, as they stepped outside.

# Chapter Fourteen

On his way to his second London Corresponding Society meeting the next evening, Dan went down to the wharf to look for Nick. He leaned against a warehouse wall, a conspicuous figure on the deserted quayside. He knew that Nick was already there, looking out for him from some hiding place. It was what Dan would have done if he had been in the boy's position and about to meet a man he knew little about, in case he turned up with a constable or beadle in tow. Or worse: a receiver or pimp like Weaver.

After a few moments the boy's quick figure appeared from the shadows. He wore the breeches and jacket Dan had given him. They made him look almost civilised.

"So did you see anything last night?" Dan asked.

"Four men brung in some bodies. All wrapped up in sacks, they was."

"How many bodies?"

"One apiece. Except the tall carroty-head. He just ordered the others around."

"Did they leave the bodies there?"

"Didn't see 'em come out again."

"How long were the men in the warehouse?"

"Not long. Half an hour. I heard St John's clock."

"Did you get a good look at any of them?"

"Not very. They was wrapped up. One of 'em was very short."

That would be Capper who had helped Dawson steal the teeth. "Did you see the man whose pocket you picked?"

"Nah. I'd a known him. He's a reg'lar cove."

"How close did you go?"

"Climbed onto the wall."

"No one saw you?"

Nick snorted.

Dan handed him some coins. "Good work. See you same time tomorrow."

Nick jauntily touched his forelock and pattered off, his bare feet slapping along the dark alley. Should have got him some shoes, Dan thought.

At the Boatswain and Call, Dan paid his entrance fee and found a seat in the crowded room. Broomhall sat at the top table with the Division Secretary. Dan spotted Spy Wheeler, but the meeting began without Metcalf and Simmons. It followed the same pattern as last week except that there were no new members.

Before moving on to the important business of the day, Broomhall asked the Secretary to read out a letter they had lately received. The spindly man unfolded the paper and read it in a harsh voice as rapidly as would any man impatient to have done with a task that offended his dignity.

*From The Female Patriots at No 3 New Lane Gainsford Street Horsleydown to their brothers and friends in liberty, greetings.*

*Since forming our group six months ago we have been at pains to educate ourselves as to the state and condition of our nation and the means of remedying the great evils which arise from the abuse of the Rights of Election and Representation and the Force and Fraud which withholds the right of all men and women*

(here there was an outburst of groans and guffaws)

*to share in the government of the country and we do solemnly declare our belief that the aims of the London Corresponding Society, being the securing of a fair, equal and impartial representation of the people in*

*Parliament, being the only redress for such a calamitous state of affairs, we do request of our brothers that we be granted membership of the Society. Signed –*

Here the Secretary broke off, unable to make himself heard above the protests.

"What is this, a joke?"

"An she was my wife, I'd soon teach her what her rights are!"

"Have we come here to listen to this taradiddle?"

"Move to the business in hand, Chairman!"

"I haven't had my supper yet. Why are we wasting time on this?"

"Citizens, citizens!" Broomhall shouted. "Order, please! Have the goodness to allow our Secretary to finish reading."

"I have done," his colleague said. He put the paper on the table in front of him and regarded it with distaste.

"It is my duty as President," Broomhall said, "to lay before you all correspondence sent to the branch. I have done so. Am I to take it that the answer you wish me to convey to the female patriots is no?"

The audience loudly and passionately signalled that was their wish. The Secretary made a note for the minutes and Broomhall moved on to report the business from last Thursday's committee meeting. The main topic had been the discussion of a proposed open-air meeting to protest about the Government's heavy-handed response to the meeting held at the end of July in a field at St Pancras.

Dan remembered how the ministry had reacted. Sir Richard Ford had declared the meeting illegal, but the London Corresponding Society had gone ahead anyway. Like every other police officer, Dan had been on duty that day, along with two thousand constables and two thousand soldiers, with another six thousand soldiers ready to be called up at a moment's notice. From where he had been standing, close to the veterinary college, he had seen no disorder. He had nabbed half a dozen pickpockets, but once stolen goods had been restored to their owners, had had to let them go. Bow Street was too crowded with arrested radicals to accommodate thieves as well.

Now the LCS plan was to gather again to protest against the illegality of the arrests of their speakers and the breaking up of that meeting. Dan could not decide if it was the persistence of courage or delusion. Whichever it was, they insisted on their right to hold a peaceable demonstration. The question before the Divisions was whether or not they should also send another address to the King to replace the one left unanswered on 31 July.

Upton stood up. He held on to the back of the chair in front of him. His voice was weak and he trembled as he spoke, but his message was uncompromising.

"What good have petitions ever done us? They've always been ignored in the past. Parliament is never going to reform itself and all the asking in the world won't make it."

The cries of "Hear! Hear!" and "Sit down!" were about equal in volume.

Broomhall called for silence. "Let us conduct the debate according to the rules of the Society," he said. "As for Citizen Upton's remark, it is beside the point. We are not going to petition the King, but present him with a remonstrance. We will ask him to restore universal suffrage as it existed in King Alfred's time."

"Petition, remonstrance, what difference does that make?" returned Upton.

This provoked a renewed tussle between applause and jeers. Broomhall called the meeting to order, but it ignored him and disintegrated into little groups shouting at one another. The hubbub was at its height when the door opened. Metcalf stood in the doorway, with Simmons behind him. The President sprang to his feet, drew his watch out of his pocket and made a show of consulting it.

"Citizens, we have run out of time and will have to continue this discussion next week. Thank you all for coming!"

Taken aback by the abrupt ending, the audience turned their anger on their President but Broomhall had already snapped the watch shut and left his seat. There was nothing else to do but shuffle away, some to replenish their glasses in the downstairs bar and others to go home. Dan darted out of the room and waited in the dark alley. When the rest of the company had dispersed, Broomhall, Metcalf and Simmons emerged. Broomhall pulled the door to and wordlessly the party headed for the street. Dan pulled up his collar and hurried after them.

They headed east, avoiding the main roads, and before long were following a winding course roughly parallel with Tooley Street and the river bank. In the dark, Dan did not recognise anything until the bulk of a church rose up before him opposite a roofless house, a cooper's yard, a pair of gates fastened with chains. They were on Horsleydown outside Dawson's corpse repository.

Broomhall unlocked the wicket and they stepped into the warehouse yard.

Dan took the route he had identified on his last visit: over the wall. He dropped down, crouched in the shadows for a few moments to see if there were any sentinels. No one appeared so he ran across the yard. He pressed his ear to the warehouse door but could not hear anything through the thick boards. Gripping the latch, he cautiously opened the door and slipped inside.

A line of light lay under the door to the room with the butcher's block in it. He crept closer, tried to make out individual voices in the murmur of conversation within. The door stood slightly ajar and he could see Broomhall standing by the butcher's block, Simmons behind him. The resurrectionist Dawson lounged at the side of the block. There was no sign of Metcalf.

Behind Dan the warehouse door banged, the echo reverberating around the building. He jumped out of sight behind the crates. Two sets of footsteps drew near. There was no mistaking

Metcalf's bulk. Dan had not seen the man beside him before, but his silhouette with its short jacket, wide trousers and round, narrow-brimmed hat – so different from Metcalf's coat, boots and breeches – was enough to tell him that he was a sailor. The gang must be shipping corpses to other parts of the country, possibly to Scotland and Ireland too.

"The United Patriots welcome you, citizen," Broomhall said to the traveller. "You must be in need of refreshment after your journey. Simmons, will you do the honours?"

Who, Dan wondered, were the United Patriots and how did they fit in with the London Corresponding Society? Presumably they were a breakaway group, one that was clandestine where the LCS was cautious. They hadn't gathered in this blood-stained place for a cosy debate either.

Simmons's lanky figure passed out of sight, heading towards the side table. He reappeared and handed the sailor a glass of spirits.

"You are right about that, citizen mate," the sailor said, snatching the glass and taking a large, grateful gulp. "Been freezing me bollocks off on that damned coach roof all the way from Dover."

"You have a letter for us from Calais?" Broomhall asked.

With a knowing wink, the sailor reached inside his jacket and brought out a packet sealed with red wax. He complacently sipped his rum while Broomhall examined the seal before opening it and taking out the sheet of paper folded inside.

"Pass me that candle," Broomhall said, handing the empty packet to Simmons.

Metcalf handed a light to Broomhall, who held it up to the paper. When he had finished reading he folded the note and put it in his pocket, his expression unchanged.

"What does he say?" asked Simmons.

His words were lost in a whirl of movement and an explosion of sound. Someone screamed, "Fuck!" The men scattered through a cloud of smoke and powder. All except the sailor, who stood staring at Broomhall in astonishment, his hat gone, a red circle in the middle of his forehead. His glass fell from his fingers and smashed on the floor. He sank to his knees and slumped over on to his side. Broomhall stepped towards him, a second pistol in his left hand, took careful aim and fired again.

It was lucky for Dan that the men in the room were all so taken up by their own amazement they did not hear his exclamation and recoil of surprise. In the shocked silence he remained huddled where he had instinctively flung himself, hands on the floor, his body taut, ready to sprint.

Broomhall turned and flashed a smile at his companions. "Sorry to alarm you, patriots, but I'm advised that the man's become something of a liability since he took to smuggling French goods across on the packet. The captain already suspects him and is on the verge of ordering a search. We can't risk our letters falling into the hands of the authorities."

Broomhall handed his spent pistols to Metcalf, who moved towards the side table. Dan heard the heavy clatter of the guns as he put them down. When he came back into view it was to hand the rum bottle round.

Simmons was the first to take a swig. It put new heart into him. He passed it on to Dawson and glanced pitilessly at the dead packet boatman. "What news then?"

"Excellent news," Broomhall said. "The French say they will soon send an agent to make contact with us."

"What we need is guns," Simmons said. "Will they supply some?"

"That I don't know yet. Obviously, I will raise the matter when I get the chance. In the meantime, we must continue our own exertions. This news should put heart into the patriots! I'll announce it at the Chequers tomorrow…I think we're done for tonight. Dawson, get rid of that." He indicated the body on the floor.

"On me own?"

"Simmons, stay and give Dawson a hand. Lock up when you've done."

Broomhall and Metcalf left Dawson and Simmons to their task.

"Thinks he's the bloody Emperor of China!" Dawson muttered.

"Shut it," Simmons said. "Let's get on with it and get out of here."

Dawson drew a bunch of keys from his coat pocket, selected one and unlocked the storeroom. Simmons retrieved the sailor's hat, then the two men lugged the corpse inside. After much puffing and panting and thumping of dead-weight, they re-emerged. Dawson locked the storeroom door, while Simmons seized a lantern from a hook and went out to the rear of the warehouse. He returned a few moments later carrying a bucket of water. He sloshed it over the blood, which trickled down the sloping floor into the open drain.

After a last look around to make sure all was tidy, they left the room. Dawson fastened the wooden bar across the door. Dan listened for the sound of the front door closing and their footsteps fading across the yard.

As before, he got out by the window and over the wall. He had just landed when a small figure loomed out of the darkness and hissed, "Mr Bright!"

"Nick?"

"I saw you go in after 'em. Then I heard a shot. Did you shoot someone?"

"No, but I saw someone who did. You have to be very careful around these men, Nick. Don't ever let them see you."

"I won't."

"Can you tell me where the Chequers is?"

"Pickle Herring Lane. Shall I show you?"

"No, I'll find it tomorrow. Here's some money. Get yourself some breakfast in the morning."

Nick took the coin and disappeared into the shadows. Dan hurried off to his lodgings in the opposite direction. He had got Broomhall and Dawson together at last, and that was cause for satisfaction. It was marred by having to admit that

Sir Richard Ford had been right. There was more going on here than body snatching. That was just a sideline, and a lucrative one – a useful source of funding for the United Patriots' treacherous activities.

At the Boatswain and Call, Dan had heard the London Corresponding Society defending the legality of their protests and insisting on their right to demonstrate peacefully. At Dawson's warehouse the United Patriots had discussed their need for guns and shown by the murder of the packet man that violent deeds backed their violent talk. Broomhall had despatched the sailor without giving it a second thought, and the others had been willing accessories.

Plenty of interest for Sir Richard Ford there, though Dan's information on the United Patriots was still vague. The spy master liked detail, so best give him some or else risk being accused of incompetence. A trip to the Chequers was in order.

He wondered how much of this Kean had discovered. Whatever he knew, it had been enough to get him killed. The likelihood was that he had been murdered in the same way as the sailor and by the same hand. And now Dan was following the same path as Kean. It was not a comforting thought.

# Chapter Fifteen

Pickle Herring Lane was a pitted road of crumbling ware-houses, cranes and pulleys, all provided to service the vessels moored in the Thames. Dan recognised the tavern from the faded square of chequers painted on the outside wall. He pushed open the door and stepped down into a stinking gloom lit by cheap, smoking candles.

Gangs of stevedores and warehousemen stood swilling in groups, while around the damp walls those lucky enough to have found a seat made themselves as comfortable as they could on stools made of old barrels clustered around sticky trestle tables. The smell of tobacco and spirits, filthy bodies and unwashed clothes, river mud and horse manure, brick dust and tanned hides hung heavy beneath the stained rafters. Dice clicked, men swore and swaggered, poxed women wheedled, drunks sang. Ugly fighting dogs with massive shoulders and gleaming fangs barked and growled, whined into silence when kicked. There were white faces, yellow faces, black faces; sailors, beggars, thieves; women old and raddled, women young and raddled.

Swathed in his dark coat, his scarf pulled up to his face and his hat low, Dan took a seat in a corner with his legs outstretched, his arms folded across his chest, a bottle and a glass of daffy on the table in front of him. He scanned the room. Broomhall and company were not in sight.

A scrawny woman in a skimpy, ragged dress cut low to reveal her bony shoulders lurched close to his table, eyeing him up. He pushed his glass towards her and she sat down, gleefully seizing the gin. She gulped and offered it back to him.

"You have it," he said.

She gave a smile that did not reach her clouded eyes. The few teeth that still clung to her blackened gums looked as if they would give up and let go at any moment. She was young in years, though her life was nearly over, eaten away by drink, pox, malnutrition.

Dan located a thickset, bowlegged man playing cards with three other men. At his feet lay a scarred bulldog and a cudgel. From time to time he looked over at the woman.

She emptied the glass and stared greedily at the bottle. Dan refilled the tumbler. She drank again, making sucking noises.

He leaned forward. "Is there somewhere we can go?"

"There are rooms upstairs." She licked her lips and winked at him in a ghastly effort at flirtation.

"Who else goes up there?"

"No one. Just us girls."

"Bet they ain't cheap. Is there anywhere else we can go?"

"Out the back."

"What's out there?"

"A skittles alley."

"There'll be lots of people about then," he grumbled. "I ain't doin' it like a dog in the street."

"You're partiklar, ain't you? There's a reg'lar club in there tonight; none of 'em'll be out for hours. We'll be as private as you like in the yard." She giggled, the breath catching in her throat. "Bet you have a yard hidden away in that coat of yourn."

"Maybe I do, and maybe you should do something about it."

"Two shillings."

"What is this, Covent Garden? One shilling."

"One and six pence."

"For that, I expect more than a five-minute fumble. And I warn you, no tricks from you and your pimp."

"M – my pimp?"

"The man with the dog face over there. Oh, that is his dog. Anyways. No tricks, else I'll slit your throat."

"Charming bugger, ain't you?"

"You'd better believe it."

He grabbed the bottle of gin and followed her through the packed room. Her bully was too busy with his cards to do more than flick a glance at them. She lifted the latch of a door at the side of the bar and led Dan out into an enclosed cobbled area dimly lit by the murky glow from the tavern windows. The boundary on the right was formed by the windowless wall of a neighbouring warehouse. The river flowed beyond the end wall, which was about six feet high, with crates of empty bottles stacked against it. On the left was a long, narrow skittles shed with a sagging roof. Patches of light shone through the internal shutters which, due to the state of the roof, did not hang properly over the warped, grimy windows.

The woman led Dan over to a coal bin against the warehouse, close to a rubbish heap seething with plump rats. She wriggled into a sitting position on it, hitched up her skirt, pulled him towards her and wrapped her legs around his thighs.

"Let's have a drink first," he said, putting the bottle to his lips and taking care that none of the gin went down his throat. He held it out to her and she took it and drank.

"Go on," he said. "It's cold out here. Keep the warm in."

She drank some more and put down the bottle.

"I need a piss," he said.

He moved towards the far corner, leaned one hand against the wall and pretended to undo his breeches with the other. Looking back he could just see her sitting there like a child told to wait quietly. Her patience only lasted seconds before she reached for the bottle and raised it to her mouth.

She passed out a moment later, still clutching the near-empty bottle. Dan gently prised it out of her hand. He searched her skirt until he found a threadbare pocket and put two shillings inside. With any luck, she might get to keep it for herself. He laid her down on her side to make sure that if she vomited, her stomach contents would not lodge in her throat to choke her. She looked like just another corpse in a gutter then, a heap of human rubbish to be swept up by the night carts or tossed into the river.

He went over to the skittles alley and worked his way along the side of the building, looking for a gap in the shutters. He found none until he came to the last window. It had no shutter, most of the panes were missing, and the few that remained were cracked or loose. He peered inside the room, allowing his eyes to adjust to the jumble of dark shapes which gradually turned into boxes, discarded furniture, broken skittles and game boards.

It was not difficult to get inside and drop down onto the rotten floorboards. He crept to the door and slowly lifted the latch, using his scarf to stifle the noise of rusty metal which had not been disturbed in ages. The door opened on to a corridor running across the rear of the skittles alley. There was a door in front of him which, like the windows, did not fit its frame.

He knelt down and looked through a gap. A score of men sat on two rows of chairs in front of a table, their angry, indignant faces pointing towards Dan, their voices raised in discontent. He recognised many of them from the Boatswain and Call, amongst them lame Upton, his tea-merchant friend Warren, and Broomhall's doleful shop assistant. Simmons stood guard at the door at the far end of the room.

Broomhall, his back to Dan, sat behind the table with Metcalf on his right and struggled to calm them down. He gave up and sank back in his chair, rolling his eyes at Metcalf.

Metcalf stood up, brought his fist down on the table and roared, "That's enough! The next man who speaks out of turn will have me to answer to."

The noise subsided.

"Patriots!" Broomhall cried. "I understand your feelings. I know that many of you think we have waited long enough. I well know that you are all men of courage, ready for action, but waiting until the time is right is as much a part of our service as action. Maybe it's the hardest part for men like us, impatient for our country's good. Our friends in France have promised us aid, but if we move before that aid is secured all will be lost. In the meantime, we must focus on preparing ourselves for the great day, quietly, diligently, without drawing attention to ourselves. In particular, we must carry on going to London Corresponding Society meetings as normal and do nothing to alert them to our existence." He flashed the smile that Dan was beginning to realise always presaged danger for someone. "Upton."

"Here!" Upton stood up and glanced nervously at Simmons, who had moved closer to his seat, thoughtfully cracking his knuckles. Upton grew more agitated as Broomhall let seconds pass. He trembled, bit his lips, broke out into a sweat.

"Your remarks at the LCS meeting last night bordered on betrayal," Broomhall said at last.

"I never said anything that might arouse suspicion," Upton protested.

"You questioned LCS policy. Is that the action of a whole-hearted Corresponding Society member?"

"It was a debate. I only said what many others are thinking."

"Your role, Upton, and the role of every United Patriot, is to hold his place until he is called upon. That means that for now we must appear to go along with many things we disagree with, things we know to be futile and cowardly. But I promise you that the opportunity for dealing with the London Corresponding Society and other false friends of reform will come in good time and we'll harvest their heads along with those of Pitt, Portland and all the other peers and placemen. Ours is a great cause, gentlemen –"

Broomhall's speech had almost reached a stirring crescendo when a dog started to bark in the yard, and a man yelled, "Where's the bugger got to?"

At once the quiet, diligent and patient patriots threw aside their chairs and jostled for the door. Cries of "It's a raid!", "The militia!", "Death or glory!" filled the air. Over all boomed Metcalf's "Order! Order!"

Broomhall rose, drew out his pistol and commanded, "Simmons, go and see what's happening."

The thin man nodded and slipped outside. Broomhall and Metcalf forced their way through the throng and met him at the door when he returned with the girl's pimp in tow.

"What's going on?" Broomhall demanded. "Is it the Runners?"

"Runners, 'ere?" the whoremaster sneered. "Not fuckin' likely. I'm looking for the cully what came out here with my girl."

"Who came out here?"

"Never seen him before. I came out to see what was taking him so long, found the bitch dead drunk and not a penny the richer and the scab gone."

"How many times have you been told that no one's to come out here while we're having our meeting?"

The pimp shrugged. "Got to make a living."

"You're sure he's gone?"

"If he ain't and I get my hands on him, he'll wish himself in hell with Satan and his imps by the time I'm done with him."

Broomhall jerked his head at Simmons. "Take some men and go and make sure there's no one in the yard. The rest of you search the building."

Simmons grabbed a lantern and lit it from one of the candles, then led his group outside, the pimp following. Metcalf and his men spread out through the skittles alley, shining lights into dark corners as they went.

Dan dodged back into the lumber room and dived behind a pile of broken chairs. Seconds later the door swung open and two figures appeared on the threshold. The first held up his candle and shone it around the room.

"Clear," he said.

"That's not clear," the other retorted.

He went inside and pounced behind piles of furniture, pushed boxes out of his way, even got down on his hands and knees and looked along the floor for hidden feet. He reached the tangled pile of chairs behind which Dan crouched in the dirt. The man put his candle down on a wooden box and took hold of one of the chairs. He was so close Dan could have grabbed his hand.

He looked back over his shoulder. "Here, come and give me a hand with this lot."

Dan sprang to his feet, toppling the chairs on top of the two men. They crashed to the floor where they lay entwined in a mesh of sticks and slats, choking and cursing as a dust cloud exploded around them. Dan grabbed hold of the windowsill, hauled himself out head first and rolled down into the yard.

Simmons's party had already gone back inside. He had seconds to get to the end wall and over it before they worked out what had happened and came after him. One stride – shouting from inside the skittles alley. Two – thumping and banging as the men in the lumber room freed themselves. Three – he was flexing his fingers, ready to grab the parapet. Four – he was nearly there, about to spring onto the crates and haul himself up.

A pale shape shot across the yard, emitting a yowl of bloodthirsty delight. Its slavering fangs gleamed in the dark. Its neck and shoulders bulged with hard muscle. It was the pimp's dog – and there was no way Dan could outrun it.

# Chapter Sixteen

A woman screeched, "Filthy shag-bag!" From the corner of his eye Dan saw the girl he'd brought outside swaying in the middle of the courtyard. She flung the empty gin bottle in his direction. It hit the dog with a loud clunk, bounced off and broke. The dog yelped and swerved aside. Dan jumped onto one of the crates. It tilted under his weight, but his foot was only on it for a second before he swung himself up and over the wall. Behind him the crate tipped over, spreading bottles across the cobble stones.

He did not know if the girl had been aiming at him, the dog or just the world in general, and he was not going to stop and find out. He heard footsteps running towards the wall, then curses and confusion as the men got tangled up with the rolling bottles. There was a slap and a scream, and the pimp's voice rose above the rest.

"What the fuck have you done to my dog? He's got a fight on Saturday. He'll be no good now."

"Who was that?" Broomhall demanded.

"A cheating cull," the girl slurred. "Had his way and didn't pay me."

Dan had landed on a narrow strip of wharf near Pickle Herring stairs, only a few dark alleys away from Tooley Street. He took the coat off, bundled it up and threw it into the river. When he turned into the main road he stopped running, became just another man out for the evening.

He knew that he should report his discoveries to Sir William Addington as soon as possible. He could go to Butcher Hall Lane now and send a message to the magistrate. But if he did that it would mean he would be missing from his bed in the morning, and Mrs Chambers was bound to report his absence to Broomhall. There was no reason Dan could see why Broomhall should link him to the disturbance at the Chequers, but it might just seem like too much of a coincidence to the suspicious and sanguinary revolutionary. And whatever it was that the United Patriots were plotting, it was not going to happen in the next few hours. Dan decided the safest course was to go back to his room.

He let himself quietly into the shop. The family had gone to bed, and provided no one woke, he could always claim he had been in an hour before this. He drew the bolts on the front door and tiptoed upstairs. He undressed in the dark and got into bed. After the stresses of the evening he did not expect to sleep, and was surprised when the next thing he knew was Mrs Chambers knocking on the door with his shaving water.

He grabbed a quick coffee from a stall near London Bridge, then made his way to Butcher Hall Lane. He was admitted by one of the men he had encountered on his first visit and asked him to send for Sir William Addington. The man immediately sent a messenger to Bow Street.

"The United Patriots?" Sir Richard Ford said. "I've never heard of them."

"I think they've kept their existence a secret even from the London Corresponding Society," Dan answered.

The glance Sir Richard gave Sir William plainly conveyed his opinion that he thought his man a fool. Dan had described his recent discoveries to Sir William: the London Corresponding Society meeting and the murder of the packet man the evening before last; his own narrow escape at the Chequers on the previous night. The magistrate had promptly sent to the Home Office for Sir Richard. While they waited for the spy master, Sir William asked Dan, "Where do you think Kean fits into all this?"

"We know he went to LCS meetings. Now Miss Chambers

tells me he was thick with Broomhall. Whether that means he also gained access to the United Patriots I can't say, but I suspect that he did and it's what got him murdered, probably by Broomhall. He's one of the coldest killers I've ever seen. An executioner."

It was a matter Sir Richard did not pursue when Dan repeated his report to him. Instead he picked away at the details Dan had gleaned about the United Patriots.

"You seriously think that the United Patriots are separate from the London Corresponding Society?" he asked.

"Not only separate, but enemies. Broomhall intends to get rid of the LCS if his plan succeeds."

"I shouldn't read too much into that," Sir Richard said. "There is never any loyalty in revolution. One faction lops off another faction's head, then along comes another faction to lop off theirs. You yourself have reported that the United Patriots are all members of the LCS."

"It's their main recruiting ground," Dan answered, "but beyond that they're just using it as a cover."

"Yet we know that Broomhall regularly attends LCS committee meetings. Really, Foster, your intelligence is most – unintelligent."

"My officer risked his life to get this information," Sir William protested. "As it's of no use to you, I'm pulling him out now and issuing a warrant for Broomhall's arrest for the murder of this sailor and the suspected murder of Officer Kean."

"No, wait. I spoke hastily. I did not mean that the information is of no use to me. It is just that it is incomplete. What exactly are the United Patriots planning?"

"Isn't that obvious?" Sir William retorted. "Insurrection."

"Yes, that of course. But what's really of moment here is their connection with the French. That's what we need to target if we're to ensure an end to the danger once and for all."

"What about Broomhall and Kean?" Dan asked.

Sir Richard fluttered his fingers dismissively. "You don't

have enough evidence to convict Broomhall for Kean's murder. Without his body you don't even know if he was killed in the same way as the sailor."

"But I know both their bodies were disposed of by Dawson and his resurrection men."

"But can you prove it? Even if you could, it's hardly enough to secure a conviction against Broomhall for Kean's death. Of course, you can bring him to the gallows for the murder of the packet boatman. But your colleague's murder won't get to court."

Dan turned to the Bow Street magistrate. "Sir William?"

Sir William shook his head. "I am afraid Sir Richard is right."

"Hanging is hanging. I can live with that."

"But His Majesty's Government cannot," Sir Richard said. "We must sift this matter to the bottom. We need to know what the United Patriots are plotting. More importantly, we must intercept that French agent. To those ends, you must get yourself accepted into their confederacy."

"Why can't we just arrest them?" Dan asked. "Raid the Chequers and round them all up?"

"Because that would simply be cutting off a Hydra's head. The French know that the only way they can beat us is not from fighting us from without, but from within. There will always be other complainers and outcasts ready to accept their help. We must break the French spy network to strike at the heart of the beast."

Dan did not know what a Hydra was, but he got Sir Richard's meaning. He also knew that he could not refuse and keep his job. Sir William must have had the same thought about his own position, for when he spoke again he was all for conciliation.

"I think, Foster, that we should see this as an opportunity to satisfy all our needs," he said. "Finding the truth about Kean's death and bringing down these contemptible wretches are one and the same thing. I have every confidence that you can achieve both aims."

"That's gratifying, sir," Dan said.

"And I'm sure," Sir William continued, either not noticing or choosing to ignore Dan's sarcasm, "that His Majesty's Government will show its appreciation in its usual munificent way."

Sir Richard laughed. "Point taken, Sir William. I am aware that a great deal is being asked of your officer. I will see that he gets a reward. And now you have secured an incentive for him at no cost to yourself, what is to be his next step?"

"Do you have any suggestions, Foster?" Sir William asked.

Dan thought for a moment. "If I could impress Broomhall I was of his way of thinking and might be useful to him, I might worm my way into the United Patriots."

"You have an idea?" Sir Richard asked eagerly.

"Unless you can think of a better one," Dan said. "But I'll need your help."

# Chapter Seventeen

Leaving the two magistrates to return to the safety of their offices, Dan left the house and started walking to the river. He changed his mind and turned towards Covent Garden instead. A man heading back to danger deserved at least a couple of hours' respite. Besides, he had not had anything to eat yet.

There was no one home. Dan stoked the fire in the stove, put the kettle on to boil, threw eggs and bacon into a frying pan. There was fresh bread in the pantry, and butter and milk. On the sideboard was an issue of the *Sporting Magazine* he had not seen; Eleanor had put it aside for him as usual. He heaped food on his plate, poured himself coffee, and settled down to read.

The front door opened and footsteps sounded in the hall. Eleanor came in, flustered and tired from shopping and carrying her basket from the market, but at sight of him a smile transformed her face. "Dan!"

He started to get up, but she said, "No, no, finish your meal. What is it, a late breakfast? Can I get you anything else?"

"I think I'm done, thanks. Afraid I finished all the bacon. Where is everyone?"

"Caroline and Mother have gone shopping." She put down her basket and set some water to warm for washing the dishes. "So are you home now?"

"No. Have to go off again in a bit."

"They're sending you on another case already?"

"No. Same case."

The opportunity to be alone together seldom came and they had got into a habit of thinking it was their own willpower that kept them apart. But though she seemed busy with the dishes and he with his reading, they were acutely sensitive to each other's presence. Watching Eleanor's neat, thorough way of working, he was reminded of Evelyn Chambers. The girl too could appear calm at her work, though within she seethed with longing to be free of everything that prevented her happiness.

He refilled his coffee cup. "I met a girl who wants to run away."

She turned to face him, her curiosity awakened. "Elope, do you mean?"

"No. This girl has other plans. She wants to be independent."

"How will she do that?"

"She intends to set up a school. Says the girls will learn Latin and Greek and that they won't do sewing and shell work. What is shell work?"

"You stick little shells on things. Boxes, mirrors, that sort of thing. It's supposed to make them look pretty. A waste of a woman's time, if ever there was one."

"So you'd not miss the shell work if you went to Miss Chambers's school?"

She laughed. "Not at all. But sewing is useful. And she might find few parents willing to send their daughters if they are to learn no practical skills at all."

"Is that so? I'll tell her."

"Who is she, this girl?"

"The daughter of a radical. Her father used to run a bookshop, but he was arrested for selling seditious books. He was ruined, and now he sells bawdy pictures for a living. The girl helps in the family business. She hates it."

"I don't blame her. But how do you come to know her?"

"She gave me some useful information about Kean."

"Are you any closer to finding his killer?"

Dan hesitated. He did not usually talk about his work at home. He thought of Kean sharing his cases with his wife, seeking her opinion, her sympathy. Why shouldn't he enjoy Eleanor's sympathy now?

"I do have a suspect, and a number of accomplices. A man who fancies himself as the next Robespierre and is plotting a revolution with the help of the French. If it was up to me I'd make the arrests now before anyone else gets hurt. But the ministry don't value lives that way. Except their own, I suppose. Sir Richard Ford would rather I stayed in Southwark spying on them."

She pulled out a chair and sat down next to him. "Was Kean murdered because he found out about their plans?"

"I think so, yes. Or got too close for comfort. I do know they're a nasty bunch. They're funding their activities with body snatching."

Impulsively, she put her hand on his arm and gazed up at him anxiously. "It sounds dangerous. You will be careful, won't you, Dan?"

It was what he had wanted, to make her show her concern for him, but he felt guilty now she had. He put his hand over hers. "I shouldn't have said so much. There's nothing to worry about, I promise you. Only don't say anything to the others."

"I won't. But I wish you were safe home."

"So do I. I miss you, Eleanor."

"And I you."

He moved his hand beneath her chin, gently tilted up her face. She was so beautiful, her eyes wide and brimming with love for him, her lips trembling, her face flushed. He bent his head and kissed her. His arms went around her and they clung to one another.

"God, Eleanor, what are we going to do?"

"What can we do?"

"There must be something. Caroline's no happier than I am. What's the point of dragging on like this?"

The front door opened and closed. Dan and Eleanor moved apart. Caroline came in, beribboned packages rustling in her arms. Her eyes narrowed, flicked from her sister to her husband. He was turning the pages of his newspaper; she had risen from her chair and picked up his cup to take it over to the sink.

"Dan!" Caroline exclaimed. "What are you doing here?"

"I live here," Dan said. It was meant to sound light, but came out harshly.

"I wouldn't know it," she retorted. "You're never here."

"Move along in, lovey," said Mrs Harper from the hall. Caroline stepped out of the doorway and the old lady trudged in and dumped her shopping on the table. "Oh, these blessed bunions! Put the kettle on for a pot of tea, there's a love, Nell. And here's Dan!"

Dan stood up. "I was just going."

"Going?" Caroline cried. "The minute I come in, you're going?"

"I only dropped in to see how you were all doing. I'm still in the middle of something."

"Oh, I can see you're in the middle of something."

Dan picked up his hat and moved towards the door. Enraged by his lack of response, Caroline drew back her arm and flung one of her parcels at him. It missed and smashed into the dishes in the sink. The second one skidded across the table.

"Caro, Caro!" Mrs Harper cried. "What a state to work yourself into. You know Dan has his work. Let's pick these things up and have our tea."

"I'll give him his work!" Caroline swooped over the table and swept off the newspaper and the packages her mother had just deposited. One of them split, scattering comfits. Mrs Harper fluttered behind her, uttering soothing noises. Caroline flung her mother off, sending the old lady spinning.

Dan threw his hat aside and caught hold of Caroline's wrists. "Caroline! For God's sake, calm down."

"Let – go – of – me!" Caroline shrieked. For a moment she and Dan stood locked together, swaying. She puckered her mouth and spat into his face. He shoved her into a chair and held her down while she struggled to free herself.

Dan glanced over his shoulder at Mrs Harper. "Has she been drinking?"

"She had a glass of liqueur with her ice-cream," Mrs Harper said. "There's no harm in one little glass."

"One while you were looking," he muttered. "Caroline! Listen to me. You are going to quieten down."

"Or what? You'll hit me?"

"Don't tempt me."

"Dan!" Eleanor gasped.

Caroline laughed. "Oh, didn't you know about that, Nellie? Do you want to see my bruises? Look!" She wriggled and thrust her shoulder forward.

"I've never hit you in my life," Dan said. "And don't you say I have."

She smirked up at him. "Not for lack of wanting to."

He gazed down at her for a moment, then put his hands under her arms and hauled her to her feet. She let herself fall limp in his grip, her head lolling back, and gave no resistance when he half-dragged her upstairs, her mother following. Dan got her into the bedroom. The bed was made, but strewn with handkerchiefs and dresses, and on the floor was a jumble of shoes. He cleared a space and sat her on the bed.

He crouched in front of her, trapping her hands in his. But she had stopped raving and fallen into an exhausted slump, her dress awry, her hair dishevelled. Her fair complexion was blotched and swollen; her eyes red and puffy; her nose and mouth glinted with tears. The girl he had married had been merry and quick-tempered, her moods as puzzlingly changeable then as now. It was a puzzle he had solved long ago.

He pushed back a strand of her damp hair, smelt the sickly liqueur on her breath. "What happened to you, Caroline?"

Hope sprang into her eyes. She clutched his arm. "Oh, Danny, Danny, why don't you love me?"

He looked helplessly at Mrs Harper, who was gathering up the discarded dresses. There was no aid for him there; the old lady saw everything, and refused to know anything. Because he could not think of anything else to do, he sat down next to his wife and put his arm around her. Her head sank on to his shoulder and she sobbed into his jacket.

"Hush," he said, "hush!" and gazed through the window at the jumble of tiled roofs and smoking chimneys.

When Dan went downstairs, Eleanor had tided away the broken dishes, gathered up the parcels and mopped the spills. She sat by the fire, her hands loose in her lap, her face pale. She looked up at him when he came in, quickly looked away again.

He stood awkwardly in front of her. "She's lying down."

"I'll take her some tea in a bit."

Lying palely in a darkened room, Caroline would take the tea from her sister with a feeble "Thank you". Her rages always ended like that: in invalidism and denial.

"You know she will have forgotten all about this by tomorrow."

Eleanor glanced sharply at him – did he really think that? He avoided the challenge in her eyes. In truth, he wasn't sure. Embarrassment and mortification locked Caroline's lips, and sometimes drink fuddled her memory, but there was no way of distinguishing between her silence and forgetting.

"What we were talking about before. It was wrong, Dan."

"I know."

She nodded as if something had been agreed between them. He waited but she did not say any more.

"I'd better be going."

She did not reply.

# Chapter Eighteen

"Liberty is in danger of being annihilated by private influence and corruption unexampled in the annals of the world. Nothing can avail against them but zeal, discipline, activity. It particularly behoves us not to sleep upon our posts."

Stirring words. Dan glanced around the room. Pity that only the spy Wheeler was still awake to hear them. The upper chamber at the Boatswain and Call was hot and swirling with pipe smoke. The speaker droned on in a nasal twang like that affected by some Methodist preachers.

Dan blocked out the talk on *Reform in Parliament* and tried to detect if anything was happening outside the room. It might have been his imagination, but wasn't that the tramp of feet? And a snatch of song? And wasn't it drawing closer?

Still the speaker snuffled on. Broomhall was in his place at the top table, dreamily sketching on a scrap of paper. In the row in front of Dan, Metcalf sat with folded arms, giving an occasional jerk to nudge Simmons awake. Upton's thin face was unhealthily flushed, his lids falling heavily over his glittering eyes. Someone at the back was snoring.

Suddenly a window shattered, showering glass on the startled men sitting beneath it. The draught of cooler air brought with it the smell of smoke from guttering torches. Flickering lights chased streaks of shadow along the alley. A voice yelled, "For King and Country!" The space between the buildings rang with the pounding of feet, the roar of voices.

The outer door splintered beneath the thuds of rams and cudgels. Broomhall sat up, his eyes wide with surprise. Metcalf and Simmons were out of their chairs, as were many others.

Some, still half asleep and slow on the uptake, stood goggling at one another. Others grasped the situation more quickly and turned to face the danger. Dan grabbed a chair and smashed it on the floor, handed the pieces around as makeshift weapons. Metcalf and others followed his example.

When Sir Richard Ford came up with a King and Country mob he certainly did not do it by half measures. The gang pounded up the stairs, kicked open the door and poured into the room. It was led by a butcher wearing a bloody apron and armed with a stun hammer, and composed largely of Smithfield's apprentices: rough lads raised to cruelty in the slaughter house.

For seconds the two sides panted and glared at one another. Then Broomhall yelled, "For Liberty!", the butcher, "Death to traitors!", and the two factions crashed into one another.

Dan despatched the first man to come at him with a crunching blow to the chin. The second went the same way. The space around Dan cleared as the attackers veered shy of his fists and he was able to look about him. Broomhall was not doing badly; no one had drawn blood from him yet. Metcalf shuffled like a bear, his great paws knocking men to left and right. Simmons moved nimbly in and out of the fray wielding a chair leg, inflicting bloody wounds with precision. Upton, hampered by his club foot and too frail to join the fight, stood behind the table, pitching whatever came to hand at the enemy: bottles, glasses, papers, ink. Wheeler had taken a smack across the ear and slumped back into his chair by the wall, from where he watched the melee with an outraged expression: this was not what he had signed up for when he agreed to spy for the Government.

The butcher was in his element, cracking skulls here, arms there. He was not fussy about his targets. Armed or unarmed, on feet or knees, bleeding or not, any man within range felt the weight of his hammer.

Another man lurched at Dan and knocked him off balance. Dan righted himself, ducked and drove a punch into his midriff. He squeaked, "Ooof!" and doubled over.

The butcher had turned on Upton, was hacking at the table with the little man trapped behind it, his back to the wall. Splinters flew to the left and right, while an ever more frantic Upton struggled to break free. The table finally collapsed, the butcher kicked the wreckage aside, and grabbed Upton by the throat. He shook him from side to side, his dangling feet drumming against the wall, his teeth rattling.

Dan stepped up and tapped the butcher on the shoulder. He dropped the crippled man to the ground and swung round. Dan let him have it full in the face. The brute stood stupidly gazing down at Dan, then gave a great roar and went for him with the hammer. Dan dodged, defended himself with his left hand and brought in a stinger to the man's ear. The man shook his head, his face scarlet with rage, swung back his arm and lunged again. Dan deflected the blow, grabbed the butcher's arm and slammed it back against the wall.

The hammer fell to the ground, but the butcher still had his enormous fists and powerful arms. Dan knew that it was not force that would win him this fight. Speed and accuracy were needed here: a blow on that ear again, the kidneys, the temples...in fast, out quickly, trusting the accumulation of well-aimed attacks on the man's vulnerable spots to wear him down. His opponent's lumbering punches missed home or landed on his dancing target with a fraction of the power behind them, though that was still enough to raise bruises. The rage in the man's eyes gave way to confusion, then they glazed over as the blows began to have their effect. He sagged, groaned, and after a last couple of cracks to the nose, lost consciousness and slid down the wall.

Seeing their leader go down took the heart out of the apprentices. First one, then another beat a retreat. When the butcher opened his eyes it was to find himself alone amongst his enemies. With a cry of dismay, he struggled to his feet, lurched across the room and stumbled down the stairs.

Broomhall led the victors in three cheers. The jubilant men

sank exhausted onto the chairs that remained intact, looked for their hats, mopped their blood, felt for broken bones. Shards of glass, wrecked furniture, scraps of torn clothing and scattered papers littered the room. Wheeler had gone.

The landlord arrived with a couple of barmen and demanded, "Who's going to pay for this?"

"Let Metcalf know the cost of repairs," Broomhall answered, "and he'll see the bills are settled. In the meantime, bring up some brandy and glasses. Oh, and a bottle of small beer. And if you've any cloths to spare for bandages, they'd be welcome." Before the landlord could say anything, he added, "I'll pay for those too."

Dan, meanwhile, helped Upton on to his feet and half carried him to a seat. He was white-faced, his eyes closed, and struggling for breath. Dan loosened his collar.

"Where does it hurt?"

Upton's eyelids fluttered open and he gave a weak grin. "Where doesn't it?"

The brandy arrived, along with a jug of hot water and some cloths. Dan grabbed a glass and put it to Upton's lips. Broomhall and a couple of his men handed round the other glasses.

"I got this for you," he said, handing Dan the weak ale. He turned, raised his own drink and cried, "To Liberty!"

When the toast was drunk, Broomhall nodded down at Upton. "How is he?"

"Might need help getting home," Dan said, putting down his beer after taking a sip for the toast. "Is anyone else hurt?"

"Not seriously. You put up an impressive fight."

"I've no time for bullies."

"These are no ordinary bullies. The Government actively encourages them and they know that they can attack us with impunity. They call themselves loyalists, but what are they loyal to? A corrupt government, a rotten system. We have no choice but to fight back."

Dan looked around at the wrecked room, the bloodied

radicals. Most of them had nothing to do with the United Patriots, knew as little of its existence as the mob that had attacked them, and would have been horrified to discover it in their midst. The London Corresponding Society did not stand for bloodshed, yet such violent incidents against them were nothing new. So Dan was not entirely acting when he said, "There's no arguing with that. I've seen enough. When merely to talk about the need for reform becomes a crime, the time for talking is over."

Broomhall smiled. "Having seen you in action just now, I'm glad you're on our side. You've fought for our freedoms on a small field tonight, Bright. Do you not see yourself participating in the battle – in the war?"

"I would, and gladly. But how?"

"Some of us have formed a group for the defence of the nation's rights and liberties. We have been forced to the view that the time has come for us to seize the initiative. To take action against our oppressors. There's danger in it, but there's hope too: the hope of a better future. Would you like to be part of that future?"

"For the chance for men to live a decent life? You can count me in."

"You must understand that once in, there's no backing out. We are all sworn to the cause and to secrecy."

"I'm willing to pledge myself."

Broomhall slapped Dan on the shoulder. "Excellent! Metcalf," he called.

Metcalf stepped over. He looked at Dan with no friendly eye and said, "Yes?"

"Mr Bright has proved himself a soldier in our cause," Broomhall said. "I have invited him to join us."

"Lots of men can fight with their fists," Metcalf said.

"But lots of men do not stand with us."

"How do you know he will?"

"He is prepared to take the oath."

"To say words?"

"And to do deeds," Dan said. "Or do you think you're the only man with the courage to act?"

"I think I'm an honest man," Metcalf retorted.

"That's enough," Broomhall said. "You forget yourself, Metcalf. I have said Citizen Bright is in, and so he is. You can go and help with the tidying up."

Metcalf, who obviously considered the work beneath him, locked glares with Broomhall. Eventually he lowered his eyes, muttered, "Very well," and, with a last venomous glance at Dan, turned away.

"A bad-tempered cove," Broomhall said. "But he has his uses...I will call for you at ten tomorrow evening, Bright."

# Chapter Nineteen

From the shop below, Dan heard the door open and Broomhall's jaunty greeting, which was answered sharply by Mrs Chambers. Dan shrugged on his jacket, snuffed the candle and went downstairs, taking care not to make a noise. The girls had gone to bed and the parlour was empty. He could hear Mr Chambers in the kitchen, bolting the back door. Mrs Chambers and Broomhall were alone. Dan crept to the door from the parlour to the shop and quietly opened it an inch or so.

Mrs Chambers stood at the counter, an open ledger in front of her. She was prevented from giving it any attention by Broomhall. He stood behind her, his arms around her waist, nuzzling her neck.

"I have to finish the day's takings."

"But you promise you'll come on Saturday evening?"

"Yes, I'll be there."

"What will you tell him?"

"The same as I told him last time, that I'm visiting a friend. He never remembers."

Broomhall laughed. "It's a wonder he recalls his own name."

"That's enough. Whatever he's lost, he's sacrificed it in the cause of liberty. Your cause."

"Yes, of course, my cause," Broomhall said placatingly. "I didn't know you still cared about him."

"I don't hate him. His was once the keenest mind in the movement. Thelwall, Godwin, Tooke – dolts compared to what he was. His ruin and imprisonment broke him, and we've got his King and Country to thank for that."

"I do like your passion."

There was a brief interval during which he expressed his admiration with kisses.

She wrenched herself free. "I've got passions, and one of them's a passion for the revenge you've promised me and all the people who have suffered under this corrupt ministry."

He watched her as she wrote an entry in the book. "How's Bright getting on?"

"He's polite to Mr Chambers, kind to the girls. And he's the first person I've seen Evelyn behave halfway civilly to for a long time."

"Do you want me to warn him off?"

"I don't think Evelyn's in love with him. She's too cold for that."

He laughed. "Not like mother, like daughter, then."

"Don't think you can say what you like to me."

He held up his hands. "I don't, I assure you!" He took out his watch. "Where is he? Can you go and call him?"

Dan noisily turned the door handle and walked in. She snapped shut the book, locked the front door behind the men, pulled down the blinds and carried the lamp to the back room.


At the Chequers there was a man on duty outside the courtyard door to turn back anyone who had no business with the United Patriots. After the disturbance to the last meeting, they were taking no risks. Metcalf and Simmons stood guard inside the skittles alley. They waved Broomhall and Dan through, Metcalf as usual eyeing Dan in no welcoming spirit.

Before long there were about thirty men seated in front of Broomhall. The meeting started with Broomhall introducing Dan to the United Patriots. He was then made to swear an oath affirming that he *undertook as a member of the Society of United Patriots to do his duty and defend the rights and liberties of the people, and free his country from tyranny, even at the cost of his life, and by force of arms if necessary, in obedience to the discipline and commands of the duly appointed officers of the*

*United Patriots. And that he pledged himself to the cause and to his fellow Patriots, and he undertook to hold no communications concerning any business, actions, plans, and membership of the Society with anyone outside the Society.*

"And now to business," Broomhall said. "At our last gathering here, some amongst you –" He paused and swept the room with his gaze until Upton and one or two others shifted uncomfortably. Having achieved this result, he resumed, "– expressed the wish that we should take untimely action likely to jeopardise our cause. Though I could not sympathise with your lack of discipline, I did sympathise with your zeal. Tonight, patriots, I can tell you that we have great news from our friends in Paris. They have despatched their agent and he will be with us within the next few days. All that remains to be done is to finalise arrangements with him."

There was an outbreak of cheering, hand shaking and congratulations. Broomhall raised his hand to silence the hubbub.

"To that end, I need to know how far in a state of readiness we are. I will hear your reports. O'Brian."

Broomhall's shop assistant stood up and announced in a voice that seemed to come from some deep, cold place where hope and enthusiasm had no existence, "We have five kegs of gunpowder."

"Not enough," Broomhall said. "We will be setting off simultaneous explosions at key sites around the city. Lay in three times as much, at once."

"Does that include all the British bastilles?" called out Upton.

"No, we'll concentrate on opening Newgate," Broomhall answered.

"And the Old Bailey?" the little man persisted.

"The exact details are yet to be determined, but if we do target the law courts I'll make sure you're on that detail. For now, can we get on? Simmons."

Simmons stood up, reached into his pocket and pulled out a bone handle. He pressed a hidden spring and a long, pointed blade shot out. "Our friends in Sheffield have promised to supply five thousand of these kooto secrets. See, the blade won't sink back when it's used. And you can't open or close it until you know where the secret switch is."

He demonstrated the mechanism and passed the weapon around. For some moments there were clickings open and shut, murderous stabs at the air and murmurs of appreciation as the knife the French called the *Couteau Secret* made its way along the rows.

"When will they deliver?" asked Broomhall.

"In a sennight."

"Good. Once we've lit the flames and people have taken to the streets, we must make sure we have plenty of weapons to hand round...How is the armed training progressing, Simmons?"

"We've been drilling over Citizen Warren's tea shop in Tooley Street this last month. Until the pikes arrive, we're using mop handles."

Dan was hard pressed to suppress a guffaw at the image of the United Patriots marching up and down an attic with mops on their shoulders. He transformed it into a cough as Simmons continued, "I've also set up armed bands at Lambeth, Holborn and Tothill Fields, making an extra thirty men."

"Well done, all of you. Now listen carefully. We are at a critical point and there has never been a greater need for secrecy. For that reason, your unit and deployment will not be revealed to you until we are ready to launch our attack."

The men were disposed to start complaining at this lack of trust.

"Patriots," Broomhall said, "I promise I will tell you as soon as I can. There are many strands to draw together before all is ready. Suffice it to say that on the night we strike a blow for our nation's freedom, you must be ready to go where you are sent and do as you are ordered. It will be vital that every man carries out the part allotted to him with all diligence and determination."

The meeting ended with the distribution of brandy and a toast to liberty.

Simmons came up to Dan. "I'm putting you in the Southwark unit. Our next training session is tomorrow. Come to Warren's at ten."

"To train with mop handles?"

"Until we have the real thing," Simmons snapped.

"I didn't say I wouldn't be there. Only I wonder how useful it's going to be."

"I wouldn't start throwing your weight around so soon if I were you. It's what Broomhall's ordered."

Simmons moved away. Metcalf intercepted him. Simmons glanced back at Dan as he answered the other's question. He's reporting back on our conversation, Dan thought.

As soon as he could get away, Dan hurried towards the lights of London Bridge. Ridiculous the Patriots might be, but that did not mean they were not dangerous. He knew how easy it was for violence and anarchy to spread. He had been a boy when the Gordon Riots broke out, and like most people in the crowds, he had had no idea what issues lay behind the disturbances. People cried "No Popery!" as they attacked chapels; "No prisons!" as they stormed Newgate and released the murderers, rapists and thieves; "No tolls!" as they fired the toll houses on Blackfriars Bridge. There were a hundred causes, and no causes.

For Dan and the rest of Weaver's boys and girls the cause had been bellies full of food and drink, pockets full of loot. They had carried watches and silver plate, silk and lace, gold and jewels back to the old receiver's filthy rooms, where he examined them with his eye glass. The stick he used for doling out beatings lay on the table beside him, motionless for once while he recorded their takings in his book. When he had finished he ordered the children out again with a few kicks and slaps to send them on their way.

Dan had spent nights fighting his way into houses from

Southwark to Holborn, clawing through his fellow-looters to grab what he could. For the first time he could remember, his bare feet knew the feel of carpet beneath them – and recorded the fact in many a filthy print. His hands left streaks of dirt on shawls, bedspreads and curtains, dimmed the polish on the bureaux and drawers he broke open.

On the fourth night of the riots, mobs had attacked number four Bow Street, the home of Magistrate Sir John Fielding and the base for his Runners. They had made a bonfire with the furniture and burned files of intelligence reports gleaned from a network of informers, including the descriptions of wanted felons and conviction records. Dan had not been amongst the crowds in Covent Garden that night. Given how his life had turned out, it was just as well.

And that was what Broomhall and his United Patriots were planning to unleash on London. Dan had all the information Sir Richard Ford needed – and more than enough to see the men responsible for Kean's death hang. Swiftly, he made his way to Butcher Hall Lane and rapped on the door.

"I need to speak to Sir William Addington and Sir Richard Ford now," he said as soon as he was inside.

"I think it's time to bring the existence of the United Patriots to an end," Sir William said when Dan had finished his report. "Don't you, Sir Richard?"

The other magistrate, who sat at the table with his chin resting on one hand, did not immediately reply. At last he lifted his head and said, "No."

"No? What more d'ye want, man? They're amassing arms, setting up their own militia, planning to wreak havoc on the city. We've enough to hang them all twice over."

"Five kegs of gunpowder isn't much to start a revolution on," Sir Richard objected. "And according to Foster's information, they won't be making a move until they have secured French assistance."

Dan sighed. He could see where this was going.

"But in the meantime they are expanding their arsenal and growing more dangerous by the day," Sir William said. "We can't afford to leave them unchecked."

"But that is what we must do, until we have drawn in the enemy agent."

"And what happens if they decide not to wait for him? We should at least issue a warning to potential targets, put the militia on stand-by, double the King's guard."

"And alert them to the fact that we are on to them? No. We must let the game play out a little while longer."

"So you propose doing nothing?"

"For the time being, yes."

So Dan went back to Southwark.

Just after ten the next evening, Dan knocked on Warren's door. It was opened by Upton, who pointed to the darkness at the back of the shop. "Up the stairs."

Dan made his way past the bins of tea and climbed the dark stairs to the landing. The doors were all closed, the rooms silent and dark. Another set of steps, more like a ladder, took him to the square of light shining from an open trapdoor. He poked his head through this and found himself in a long attic beneath the roof space looking at a tangle of Patriots' legs. They were bunched together at the far end, chatting. Dan hauled himself up and joined them.

After a few minutes Simmons lowered the trapdoor and called the men to attention. The poles were handed out. Simmons was the only man with a gun, which he wore ostentatiously in his belt as he ordered the men around. He warmed them up with some stretching and jumping exercises, then formed them into pairs. Dan's partner was a young, double-chinned man called Isaac whose stomach bulged over the top of his breeches and who was in need of a wash. For an hour or so they paraded up and down the attic, trying not to hit their heads on the sloping roof, then Simmons let them have a break.

They queued up for cups of weak beer from a tapped

barrel in the corner. Simmons sent one of the younger men to take some to Upton, who was still on guard at the door. Dan sat on the floor next to Isaac and a short, barrel-chested Scotsman called MacGregor.

Isaac took a huge slice of fruit cake out of his pocket and bit into it with yellow teeth. Still chewing, he joined in the toast to the coming revolution before they got down to the serious business of talking.

Dan looked around the attic. "I thought there'd be more of us."

"There will be more," Isaac said through a mouthful of cake. "There's groups all around the country just waiting for us to get things started."

"The French prisoners in the hulks are going to break out any day now and join us," said MacGregor.

"And there's half a dozen men o' war ready to mutiny, sail up the Thames and turn their guns on Parliament," added Isaac.

"Sounds good," Dan said. "I hope we're going to be issued with more than wooden sticks when the time comes."

"The French are going to send us some guns," Isaac said.

"I'll fight with my bare hands if necessary!" MacGregor declared. "And death to anyone who stands in my way."

"If everyone here's of the same mind, we can't lose," Dan said.

He had been wondering if Kean had got as far as drilling with the United Patriots, and if so what he had made of their training regime. Not much, he guessed. Maybe he could draw out his companions on the subject.

"We'd be better off with an instructor who knew what he was doing," he remarked. "Aren't there any such in the United Patriots?"

Isaac looked fearfully over his shoulder. "Mind you don't let Simmons hear you say that. He's touchy on the subject."

"He ought to be," Dan said. "I've seen better soldiers in a toy box."

"Hush!" MacGregor said, though he was grinning. "There

was a soldier put in charge for a while. Man called Scott. Mean devil, but knew what he was talking about. Put Simmons's nose out of joint something wicked." He chuckled at the memory.

A professional soldier would have been a useful addition to the United Patriots, where military expertise was in short supply. That must have been how Kean, as Scott, got in with Broomhall.

"We could do with him now," Dan said. "Where is he?"

MacGregor and Isaac looked at one another.

"Up and left," MacGregor said. "Or so they say."

"What's that mean?"

"It means that one day he was strutting round at Citizen Broomhall's side, and the next he had gone," MacGregor answered. He drained his cup. "Looks like Citizen Simmons is ready for us. Better get on."

Isaac clambered to his feet. Simmons had set up a table at the top of the room. They gathered around while Simmons demonstrated loading and unloading his gun, carefully omitting the gunpowder stage.

"Did you all get that?" he asked.

Although they nodded, many seemed uncertain. Simmons sighed. "Here," he said, singling out Dan. "Let's see how much you've taken in."

Dan took the pistol from him and moved the hammer to half cock. He picked up the powder flask and made a show of pouring powder down the barrel, following it with the ball wrapped in paper. He clicked the frizzen down, moved the trigger to full cock and swung round, pointing the pistol into the attic.

"And bang," he said.

"So you know your way around a gun," Simmons said. "Maybe you'll be some use after all...All right. That's enough for tonight."

# Chapter Twenty

The following evening Dan joined the Chambers family for dinner. Afterwards Mr Chambers went back to the shop, and when the girls had helped her clear the table, Mrs Chambers got ready to go out.

"I'm off to visit Mrs Hope now," she said, pulling on a pair of gloves. "I'll be back before the shop shuts. Evelyn, there's some ham for your father's supper. Make sure he eats it."

"As if you care whether or not he gets his supper," Evelyn muttered without looking up from the repair work she was doing to one of her little sister's paper dolls. Lydia knelt on a chair next to her, anxiously watching her deft fingers glue the figure's feet back on to the stick used to move it about.

Mrs Chambers ignored her daughter's sullen mumble. "And mind you put all those things away when you've finished with them. I don't want to come back to a mess." She pointed at the cardboard theatre the girls had arranged on the table.

"Yes, Mother," the two younger girls chorused meekly.

As soon as their mother had gone, the middle girl, Sarah, cried, "Will you stay and watch our play, Mr Bright?"

"I'm sure Mr Bright's got better things to do, Sarah," Evelyn said.

"No, I'd like to see the play," Dan said. "What's it about?"

"A lady who wants to marry a highwayman but her wicked uncle won't let her and anyway he isn't really a highwayman and he stops the uncle stealing all her jewels and then he marries her."

"Now you've told him all the story," said Lydia.

"No I haven't."

"Yes, you have."

"I haven't. Evie, tell her."

Evelyn laughingly rolled her eyes at Dan. "Now you see what you've let yourself in for. Lydia, here's your highwayman. What are you going to call him?"

"Dead Leg Jack."

"He hasn't got a dead leg," Sarah objected.

"It's just a pretend name. His real name is Lord Frederick Fotheringay."

"That's enough," Evelyn said. "Stop bickering and let's get started."

The girls pulled the jerky curtain across, reopened it with a flourish and, kneeling on chairs on either side of the theatre, poked their characters on to the stage. Then they stopped to argue about what should happen next. After Evelyn had arbitrated on this dispute, the scene went reasonably well, although Lady Arbella's habit of falling flat on her face every few minutes was a trifle distracting. (Sarah: "It should be Ar-A-bella." Lydia: "No, it's Arbella.")

Evelyn was a different girl with her mother out of the way. She threw herself into her little sisters' game, and revealed a talent for storytelling which rivalled her mother's in ingenuity and certainly surpassed it in wholesomeness. Mr Chambers popped in from the shop once or twice to see what all the noise was about. Looking at his daughters, he lost his vague, troubled look, his eyes softening into fond pride.

When the play was done and Dan had duly applauded and cried "Bravo", he left the girls packing their toys away and wandered out to the shop.

"Quiet tonight?" he asked.

Chambers, who was sitting behind the counter, looked up from his reading. "Yes, it's usually busier on a Saturday."

He closed his magazine. Dan glanced at the cover of the London Corresponding Society's *Moral and Political Magazine*.

"What Mrs Chambers's eye doesn't see," Chambers said.

Dan, who knew that Mrs Chambers had gone to visit Broomhall, thought the indulgence of his own pleasure the least the old gentleman deserved.

"It's the last issue," Chambers continued. "They couldn't afford to publish it any more. Pity."

"It is," said Dan, who had found the journal hard going and had not noticed its passing. "You still have a lot of friends in the London Corresponding Society, don't you?"

"Not really. I attended meetings in Bond Street, you see."

"But you know some of the men in Division Fourteen."

"I know Mr Broomhall and I've met one or two of his friends. And you, of course."

"I find it hard to remember everyone's name. What's Mr Broomhall's friend called? The big, dark-haired fellow."

"I expect you mean Mr Metcalf."

"And is it Scott? The man with the scar?"

"Mr Scott? I thought he'd left the district."

"Did you know him?"

"He called here once or twice. Not a very sociable man. He bought some of Mrs Chambers's books."

So Kean had had a taste for bawdy literature. Dan was just digesting the information when the door opened.

"Well, well, talk of the devil!" Chambers cried. "We were just talking about you."

Metcalf gave Dan a suspicious look. "Were you?"

"I was going to tell him how well you stood up for our liberties when we were attacked by the King and Country mob," Dan said.

"Tut, tut, a dreadful business," Chambers said. "There seems to be no end to this ministry's wickedness."

"There doesn't," Dan agreed. Metcalf shifted impatiently. "Sorry, Metcalf. You've obviously come to buy something. I'll get out of the way."

Metcalf looked daggers at Dan. "I'm not here to buy. Mr Broomhall wants to see you. That is," he glanced at Chambers, "he requests the pleasure of your company at a little supper he's organised."

"Delighted to accept," Dan said. "If you'll excuse me, Mr Chambers."

"Yes, yes, goodnight, Mr Bright."

"So where are we going?" Dan asked Metcalf once they were in the street.

"You'll see."

Dan saw a few moments later. They were on Horsleydown outside Dawson's corpse repository. Metcalf led Dan inside.

"What is this place?" Dan asked.

"You'll see."

"Are you just going to say 'you'll see' all night?"

Metcalf curled his lip in a half grin, half sneer. "You'll see."

They walked past the crates and into the room with the butcher's block. Dawson and Simmons were waiting for them with the little pug-faced man, Capper. Metcalf offered Dan a brandy, which he refused. No one said anything.

The door swung open and Broomhall appeared, glowing with good humour after his hour with Mrs Chambers.

"I'll have one of those," he said, striding up to take his place behind the butcher's block. He gulped some brandy. "And now to business."

"Ain't no one else coming?" asked Capper.

"No, it's just us this evening," Broomhall answered pleasantly. "Or, more specifically, just you, Capper."

Capper began to look uncomfortable. He glanced at Dawson and Simmons but their faces gave nothing away. Simmons stared back at him, cracking his knuckles.

Capper wiped a hand across his mouth. "Is it a special job?"

"In a manner of speaking," Broomhall said. "I hear you've come into an inheritance lately."

"I ain't had no 'eritance. What gave you that idea?"

"Forgive me. From the way you've been throwing your money around over the past fortnight, I thought you must have been remembered in someone's will, perhaps for some act of kindness or generosity."

Capper gave a sickly grin. "Not me, chief."

"Then you won it at cards?"

Capper, whose breath had begun to wheeze through his flattened nose, said, "That's it. Cards."

"Are you sure?"

"Yes. It was cards."

"Not teeth?"

"T...teeth?"

"Teeth you stole from the storeroom here, and that were meant to be sold for the benefit of the cause. You do realise that when you took them you weren't stealing from me, or from your fellows, but from the people, for whose liberation those funds were intended?"

Capper, who seemed baffled by this argument, shook his head, then nodded. "I never took no teeth. Who says I did?"

"The lady you beat up two nights ago."

"Lady? A common, lying, trumpery whore!"

"Yes, I was giving her the benefit of the doubt. Still, even a whore seeks vengeance when she's wronged."

Capper looked to Dawson for help, but the red-headed man ignored his silent appeal.

"Whatever she's told you is a lie. I never took no teeth."

"Come, come, Capper. The temptation was there, I understand that. The problem is that we can no longer trust you. You have betrayed the people. And that, my friend, is treason." Broomhall reached into his pocket, took out a pistol and placed it on the block. "The penalty for treason is death."

Capper's mouth fell open and a string of incoherent noises came from it.

Dan tried to nudge his mind into action but he could not think clearly. This was not like watching a murder from behind a stack of crates. Broomhall was making him a party to it, testing his nerve. Dan could no more save Capper than he could have saved the sailor, not without risking his own life. He had to stand by and let it happen.

No. He could not accept that. There must be something he could do, something he could say. But no clear course of action came to him.

He realised that Broomhall was speaking again, flashing his big smile. "But I'm not going to kill you, Capper."

Capper sagged with relief, licked his white lips.

Broomhall pushed the gun along the table. "Bright is going to do it."

# Chapter Twenty-One

Dan willed himself to return Broomhall's stare, keep the flicker of dismay out of his own eyes. He was aware of Metcalf's face beyond Broomhall's shoulder, the lips in a mocking curve gleaming red against his dark chin. Dawson sucked in his cheeks, giving his face a haggard, skeletal look. Simmons was watching Capper.

"You are sworn to defend the people from the enemies of their rights and liberties," Broomhall said softly.

Dan reached out for the gun. "Only one way to deal with enemies."

He cocked the pistol, turned it slowly on Capper. The man stared back at him, transfixed with terror. There was no tremor in Dan's arm, no pity in his face. He took careful aim at the man's heart. He would drop his arm at the last second, send the ball through the man's thigh. He hoped that his agony would be enough to satisfy Broomhall's need for revenge.

Capper found his voice, managed to croak, "Dawson! It was –" before he hit the floor.

Dan had not fired. The shot was Dawson's. Dan, Broomhall, Simmons and Metcalf stared at the resurrectionist in shocked silence. Dawson let out a long sigh of relief. As well he might, Dan thought. If Capper had lived a few seconds longer, he would have revealed Dawson's part in the theft.

Dawson shrugged and raised his eyebrows. "The man was one of mine. Least I could do was kill him."

There was a long, tense silence. Broomhall's expression was unfathomable. His features kept slipping in the candlelight, looking now angry, now surprised, now amused. Metcalf was like a cat about to spring, ready to dole out whatever punishment Broomhall commanded, be it beating or death.

Broomhall clapped his hands together, the sound bouncing from the stone walls. "Well, that's that. Get the carcass out of the way and let's get on."

He beckoned to Dan, Metcalf and Simmons to follow him out of the room. Behind them, Dawson grabbed Capper's legs and dragged him across the stones. He did not complain or ask for help. He knew he had had enough luck for one day.

Outside in the yard, Broomhall said, "It didn't go exactly as I'd planned, but you were up to the job, Bright, and that's the important thing. I shall need men like you about me over the next few days."

On Tuesday morning Dan, letter in hand, looked into the parlour where the girls were at work around the table while their parents were in the shop.

"Miss Chambers, I wonder if you would be so kind as to sew a button on to my jacket for me?"

Evelyn's head jerked up, an indignant refusal forming on her lips. Dan tapped the letter with his forefinger. Understanding dawned. She put down her pencil and said, "Of course, Mr Bright."

She followed him out of the room into the passageway by the kitchen.

"I've had a reply from my friend about the Harrises in Liverpool," he said. "It's good news. They're a respectable merchant family, though it seems that Mrs Harris is an invalid with something of an ill temper. That probably accounts for the salary they're offering: they're hoping to get someone to stay. Here. You can read it."

Captain Ellis had been careful not to address his letter to Dan, or to sign his own name. Dan had taken delivery of it last evening at Butcher Hall Lane, when he went to report progress to Sir William Addington and Sir Richard Ford. Sir Richard had been pleased to hear that he had won Broomhall's trust, though Dan had not kept back any details of the Capper murder. It had been Sir William who told him when they were alone that he was authorised to take any steps necessary to protect himself. There would be no questions asked. As if that would make it any easier to kill a man on the orders of a cold-blooded murderer.

Evelyn read the brief report with increasing excitement.

"Mr Bright, thank you so much. I shall write back today to accept the post."

"You'll be on your own, a long way from home. Are you sure that's what you want?"

"So much for your promises. You said you'd book my coach."

"And I will. I just want you to understand what it means."

"It means getting away from here."

"Then let me know when you want me to book the place."

"Thank you!" Before he could stop her, she rose on tiptoe and kissed him on the cheek.

The parlour door opened and a gasp of surprise came from the doorway. Evelyn whirled round to face her sister, Sarah.

"What are you doing there?" she snapped.

The girl's eyes widened. "Nothing. I was sent to find Mr Bright. Mr Broomhall's here for him."

"Then you've found him, so go and get on with your work. And not a word about this to anyone, do you hear? Or I'll pull your ears off."

Sarah's mouth fell open and she fled back into the parlour.

"I wasn't expecting him," Dan said in answer to Evelyn's unspoken question.

She returned the letter to him and they went back to the parlour where her little sisters were whispering and giggling. They fell silent at her frown. Dan continued to the shop. Mrs Chambers stood at one of the bookshelves, making a show of tidying the books, her back turned to Broomhall and her husband.

"Oh, Mr Bright," Chambers said. "I hadn't realised you were going away today."

Broomhall smiled. "Don't say you forgot to tell your landlord about our little jaunt to Canterbury, Bright?"

"I think I must have," Dan answered. Which was hardly surprising, as this was the first he had heard of it.

"Well, no harm done. Go and get your things, there's a good fellow. Our coach leaves within the hour."

Dan hurried up to his room and threw a few overnight things into his bag. He wondered if he dared risk scribbling a note to Sir William and asking Evelyn to get it to Butcher Hall Lane. He decided it was too dangerous an errand to burden the girl with, resourceful though she was. There was no knowing what Broomhall would do if he found out.

"We aren't going to Canterbury, are we?" Dan asked once they were in the street.

"No, but explanations can wait. Our post-chaise will be ready."

Metcalf was waiting for them in the busy yard of the White Horse.

"What's he doing here?" he asked when he saw Dan.

"I've asked Simmons to stay and keep an eye on things here. Bright is coming in his place."

"I can manage without him."

"I do not doubt your efficiency, Metcalf, but an extra pair of hands is always welcome, is it not? Now, let's get going."

Dan stood aside to let Broomhall climb into the coach. When he was settled, Metcalf shouldered Dan out of the way and got in next to him. Dan shrugged, stuffed his bag under the seat and took his place opposite them. Metcalf folded his arms and stared stonily at Dan as the post boy mounted and the stable boy let go of the horses' heads.

"Will you be wanting anything else?" the landlord asked, putting the last of the dishes on the table.

"Only to be left alone," Broomhall answered.

The landlord pursed his lips and shuffled out of the room.

Broomhall shivered. "Why the hell does anyone choose to live in the middle of a marsh? Isn't that fire going yet, Metcalf?"

Metcalf, busy building up the blaze, did not answer. Dan stood at the window looking out at the darkness. When they had arrived there had been enough light to see across the flat, swampy ground to the flat, grey sea. Now the leaping red flames of the fire and the flickering yellow flames of the candles were reflected on the black glass and cast a faint glow on the ground beneath the window. Dan pulled the musty-smelling curtains together and turned back into the room.

They were in the George in Queenborough, a mile or two out of Sheerness. The parlour, off a stone-flagged passageway leading to the tap room and kitchen, had the air of not having been used for some time. The wooden walls and furniture felt damp and clammy. Moisture trickled down the small, deep-set windows. Yet the copy of *The Times* left by the previous occupant on the round table in the window bay was only two days old.

There was a perpetual gloom in the room which neither the firelight nor candles did anything to disperse. The dark heavy furniture, the age-blackened walls, and the smoke-stained ceiling seemed to suck the energy from the flames.

"Sit down and eat," Broomhall said.

Dan did so. Metcalf ignored the chair next to him and moved as far away as the table allowed. Dan took no notice. He was hungry. Maybe it was the sea air. He piled food on his plate and Metcalf followed his example. Broomhall only picked at his meal, though he kept his glass full.

They had not long finished eating when there was a knock on the door. Metcalf beckoned to Dan to take up position on one side of it. When Dan was in place, he opened it. Three men stood in the passageway, the smell of marsh hanging about them.

"Old things have passed away," hissed one of the newcomers. He wore a shabby, salt-stained coat, unbuttoned to reveal a pair of pistols in his belt.

"Stand fast therefore in liberty," Metcalf answered, opening the door wide.

The man looked about the room, one hand on the butt of his pistol.

"All well," he said over his shoulder.

"Very good, Captain."

The faintly-accented voice was closely followed into the parlour by the speaker. A tall man with an athletic figure, he was muffled up in a cloak weighted with seawater and mud. He took it off and removed his wide-brimmed hat and scarf to reveal plain but elegant clothes: high boots, dark breeches, dark blue jacket, and linen that looked as fresh as if he had just finished dressing. He was in his forties, his hair tinged with grey, clean shaven, with a long scar down the right side of his face and a cold glint in his blue eyes.

Broomhall rose. "Welcome, monsieur!"

The two shook hands while the captain took off his coat and hat. His dark hair was tied back with an old ribbon. He was thin and ferret-faced, deeply tanned, the skin around his pale eyes crinkled, his mouth a narrow, humourless line. The man bringing up the rear was a common sailor, huge and well-built with massive arms ending in fists like hammers. His head was shaved and half of one ear had been sliced off in some old fight. There was a skull and crossbones tattooed beneath it, a dripping dagger under the gold ring in his good ear.

"Perhaps you could send for some clean plates and fresh food?" the Frenchman asked.

At mention of food the seaman's mouth split into a happy grimace. Dan would not have been surprised to see that his teeth had been filed. They had not, but that did not make him look any less menacing.

"Of course," Broomhall answered. "Bright. More wine as well."

Dan hurried out to find the landlord. He ordered more food, another bottle of wine, soda water for himself. When he got back the men had settled themselves around the table and

Broomhall was making introductions.

"This is Citizen Metcalf, and here is Citizen Bright, both good, trustworthy fellows."

"Captain Lewis," said the captain. "And this is Seaman Glutton. At least that's what we call him. Glutton for punishment, see? Giving it, that is."

Glutton smirked. "Ain't never taken none."

Broomhall said, "And Monsieur – ?"

"You can call me Citoyen," the Frenchman answered.

There was a short pause while the landlord brought in pies and roasts and took away the dirty plates and glasses. Broomhall poured wine. The Citoyen helped himself to some slices of pie. When he had done, his companions dived in less daintily.

"Well," said the Citoyen, "you have a proposition for me?"

"It's simple enough," Broomhall answered. "We overthrow Pitt's corrupt ministry and with your help install a government fit to rule over free-born British men."

"I shall need more detail than that."

"On the appointed day, we will set off explosions around London. This will provoke the London mob into action, leading to widespread confusion and disorder which my agents will be careful to encourage. We'll add to the effect by storming Newgate and releasing the prisoners. This will lead to attacks on other prisons, which are always favourite targets when the ire of the people is aroused. The resulting lawlessness will divert a substantial portion of the armed forces."

"London has survived riots before, has it not?"

"Yes. But that's just the beginning. The crux of the plan will take place outside the city. The Secretary of State for War, Dundas, has a house in Wimbledon. The King and Pitt often join him there for a weekend of guzzling and card playing. Though, of course, the King travels with a guard, Warren House is vulnerable to attack. With one stroke, a company of bold, determined patriots will rid England of the German hog-butcher and his key ministers. And that will bring the Government down."

# Chapter Twenty-Two

A man who had lived through the French Revolution was unlikely to be moved by Broomhall's bloodthirsty plans, and the Citoyen accepted the announcement without any display of emotion. Captain Lewis swore and laughed; Glutton gnawed at a chicken bone; Metcalf sat with arms folded, a satisfied look on his face.

"And you have support around the country?" the Frenchman asked.

Broomhall's eyes flickered. "Yes. We are in contact with many other units throughout Britain."

The Citoyen gave no sign that he saw through this braggadocio. "Weapons?"

"We have amassed significant arms depots in London and elsewhere. However, if France could provide us with guns, a few more would not be unwelcome."

"How many men do you calculate you can muster?"

"The British people are ready to cast off the yoke. Once the first step has been taken, the nation will follow our lead."

"Do you have any military on your side?"

"There are many disaffected soldiers in His Majesty's Army who will join us. As for the Navy, you know of course about the recent mutinies at Spithead and the Nore. Although the Government made some concessions to the sailors such as improving victuals and paying overdue wages, there are many who feel they did not go far enough. There have been further outbreaks across the fleet."

The Citoyen drew out a snuff box and took a pinch of the dark brown powder. The box was solid gold, Dan noticed, engraved with what looked like a coat of arms. The Frenchman, noticing his curiosity, smiled as he slipped it back into his pocket.

"The spoils of revolution." To Broomhall, he said, "It does seem that you have thought of everything. However, you must understand that my government cannot commit itself too lightly. The answer, therefore, is this: you do your part, and as soon as we have intelligence that the coup is underway, we will come to your assistance."

"But we're taking a big risk," Broomhall said. "We need a better assurance than that."

"We will be waiting for your signal. What more can I promise? You cannot expect us to launch our fleet until events are favourable. You provide the favourable events and we will come."

"How do we know you'll be ready?"

"The fleet is as ready now as it will ever be. Of course, if you can settle the date on which you plan to start your coup, I can take the information back to France with me."

Broomhall took a large gulp of wine. Now the moment had come to set things in motion, he hesitated. He swigged another large mouthful of courage then gabbled, "Ten days from today. Will that give you time?"

"With a fair wind, yes," the Frenchman answered.

"Then, Citoyen, *Vive la Révolution!*" Broomhall cried, raising his glass.

The others joined in the toast.

Metcalf jabbed a finger at Dan's glass. "Can't be right to call that a toast."

"What's that?" Captain Lewis asked. "Not water?"

Broomhall slapped Metcalf's arm. "Bright doesn't like wine, Metcalf. It's not a crime."

He drained his glass and sent Dan for another bottle. When Dan brought it back, the captain had got his pipe going, Glutton was dozing with his hands on his bulging belly, Metcalf was stoking the fire and the Citoyen, his face betraying nothing of his thoughts, was sitting with his arms folded on the table, listening to Broomhall's maundering.

Broomhall, waving his glass for emphasis, sloshed wine over the table. "And then, Citoyen, with your backing, we restore order and set up a new government. Of course, there'll be some dead wood to clear away. You had similar in France."

"Aristos' heads on spikes, do you mean?" cackled Captain Lewis. "Throw in a few revenue men while you're at it."

"Aristocrats, the corresponding societies, chattering intellectuals. And as you are present at this historic meeting, you will all have your part to play in the new order. Captain Lewis, I'm putting you in charge of the Navy. Glutton."

The big man snorted and started awake.

"Collector of taxes. Don't worry, I'll find someone to do the counting for you."

They all laughed at this, Glutton louder than anyone.

"Citoyen, you will be our Ambassador for France. And Bright, I think you are capable of high office. My deputy, perhaps."

"Ready to stand at your side," Dan said smartly.

"What about me?" Metcalf demanded.

"Metcalf, Metcalf, Metcalf. What am I to do with you? A steady man, a plodding man, an unimaginative man. What say you to spy master?"

"Spy master?"

Broomhall was too drunk to notice that Metcalf had taken offence. They drained the last bottle in a storm of self-congratulatory toasts.

The Citoyen stood up. "I wish you luck with your plans, Citizen Broomhall."

The two men shook hands. The Citoyen, Glutton and Captain Lewis gathered up their things ready for the walk back across the dark marshes to the inlet where they had hidden their boat.

Broomhall made his unsteady way towards the door.

"Light Citizen Broomhall's way to his chamber, Bright," Metcalf ordered.

Dan, surprised that Metcalf did not prefer to do it himself, took a candle from the table. Broomhall, scattering farewell blessings on the Citoyen and his party – "*Vive la Révolution!*" "*Liberté, Egalité, Fraternité!*" – tottered after him. By the time they were halfway up the creaking staircase, he was leaning on Dan and had to be all but carried to his room. He flung himself on the bed and immediately fell asleep.

Although not feeling kindly disposed to the man, Dan thought he had better make it look as if he cared, so he loosened his collar, pulled off his boots and left him snoring, his lips flapping over his open mouth.

Downstairs, the front door was open. The Citoyen stood outside, gazing up at the stars while he waited for his escort. Dan went back into the parlour. Metcalf was deep in conversation with Captain Lewis. He handed something to Lewis which the captain quickly conveyed to his pocket. Before Dan had time to wonder what it was, something struck him on the back of his head and he went down.

When Dan woke up he was lying on the floor in the passageway with his hands tied behind his back. He could only have been out a couple of minutes for the Citoyen still stood in the same spot, though now he had turned to look dispassionately on the scene.

Metcalf dragged Dan to his feet, shoved him against the wall and hissed in his ear, "I know your kind, Bright."

An image of Kean's head in a welter of blood at the bottom of the basket flashed through Dan's mind. Did Metcalf know he was a Bow Street officer? His face was pressed against the plasterwork which made it hard for him to speak.

"And what kind is that?"

"A Johnny Newcome who thinks he can muscle in ahead of those who've done the hard work. I'm Broomhall's right-hand man. You're just a cocky little bugger who'll do as he's told."

It took Dan a moment to grasp the cause of Metcalf's grievance. Were they really arguing over who would be next in line to Broomhall's crazy throne? The thing was so absurd he could not think of an answer. If he had it would have made no difference. Metcalf thrust a malodorous strip of cloth over his mouth.

"I've seen off better men than you," Metcalf said, tying the gag tight. "And I'll see you off too." So saying, he thrust Dan out of the door at the sailors.

Captain Lewis, pistol in hand, grinned at him. "I'd advise you not to try running. A body could rot in these marshes before anyone knew it was there. Now move."

Glutton took the lead. The Frenchman, indifferent to Dan's plight, moved off. Dan twisted his aching head and looked back at Metcalf who stood in the doorway of the George with a satisfied smile on his face. Lewis prodded him with the pistol and Dan turned and concentrated on keeping his balance on the narrow path through the grasses. Behind them the door snicked shut.

A cool breeze sighed across the marsh. The sailors were silent, their eyes, used to scanning long ocean distances, constantly checking the terrain for soldiers on patrol from the Sheerness garrison or marines from the war ships on the lookout for deserters. From time to time Dan lost his footing against a hummock of grass, was pulled up by Lewis or Glutton and shoved forward again. The Citoyen strode on steadily, occasionally stopping to let the others catch up with him.

Dan, his head throbbing, tried to make sense of what had happened. All along he had assumed that Kean died because Broomhall and his men discovered he was a Bow Street officer. Now Metcalf had presented him with a new motive: jealousy. Kean had threatened Metcalf's position in the United Patriots, so he had got rid of him. He had access to the warehouse, and he could have ordered Dawson to dispose of Kean's body.

If Metcalf was Kean's killer, had Broomhall been a party to it, or had Metcalf been acting independently? That he had waited until Broomhall was dead to the world before making his move against Dan suggested that on this occasion at least he was working on his own. If he had taken it upon himself to kill Kean, he must have given Broomhall a convincing explanation for his disappearance. Presumably he would do the same tomorrow, when Broomhall woke to discover Dan had gone: claim Dan had deserted, or produce evidence that he was a traitor to the cause.

Though they kept going, they did not seem to make any progress through the unchanging landscape, but after an hour or so Dan realised they had reached a ridge of sand dunes. Beneath them lay an untidy line of inlets. Across the dark water he saw the shadowy outlines of ships dotted with night lights and the occasional massive, dark form of a three-decker man o' war.

Lewis shoved him down the slope. He ploughed knee-deep through dry sand, falling face down onto a wet strand. The others climbed down after him. Lewis pulled Dan into a sitting position.

"Glutton, go and uncover the boat. Monsewer, you go with him. I'll be along when I've finished this little job."

The Frenchman silently followed the big sailor. He stood at the edge of the waves looking out to sea, fidgeting in his pocket for something. His snuff box, Dan guessed: a pointless detail to be wasting his last thoughts on, but preferable to giving way to his fear and despair. Behind the French agent, Glutton dragged the rowboat out of a tangle of greenery.

Captain Lewis stood over Dan and raised the gun. Dan looked about for something that might help. There was nothing but sand. He could flick some into the captain's eyes, while he struggled with that break his kneecap with a well-aimed kick, get to his feet and run, bound as he was, before Glutton or the Citoyen had time to stop him. Even as he thought it out he was digging his right foot into the sand. The captain cocked the pistol. There was no time left. Dan shut his eyes, felt the tears squeeze out of them, the bile rise to his throat.

Lewis pulled the trigger.

# Chapter Twenty-Three

Dan felt a weight slam into his chest. He fell backwards, dimly aware of a second gunshot somewhere nearby. For what seemed a long, dark time he was unable to move, unable to see, unable to breathe. Suddenly the weight lifted and he was looking up into the Citoyen's face.

The Frenchman dragged Captain Lewis's corpse off Dan and shoved it to one side. He reached behind Dan and unknotted the gag. A knife glinted in his hand and he sawed at the rope around Dan's wrists. The cords fell away. Pain shot through Dan's arms as the blood began to flow again. The Citoyen sank back on his heels and reached into an inside pocket.

Dan's mouth was so dry he found it hard to speak. "What happened?"

For answer the Citoyen brought out a small hip flask, unscrewed the lid and held it out to Dan. "Brandy. Best quality, not the swill we sell to your smugglers."

Dan hesitated, then grasped the flask with shaking hands and took a mouthful. It warmed his blood, stopped his shivering, but made his mouth feel worse. He handed it back.

"Drink," the Citoyen said.

"No. Need water."

The Frenchman swallowed some brandy and put the flask away. "There's some in the boat."

Dan tried to move but the Citoyen pushed him back. "Sit. I'll get it."

While he was gone, Dan looked about him. Captain Lewis lay face down beside him, the back of his head a glistening crater. Glutton's enormous bulk had fallen on its back a few feet from the boat.

The Citoyen came back and thrust a water bottle at Dan. The water was cold, though stale. He swilled out his mouth before gulping down draughts of it. The Citoyen crouched beside him and busied himself cleaning out a pair of the smallest pistols Dan had ever seen. When he put the pistols in an inside pocket, no one would have known they were there.

"Why did you save my life?"

"If I go back to the Directory and say the United Patriots are very well organised, very well equipped and well led, I will put heart into those who want to invade England. If I say they are led by a fool and have no weapons, no support, no likelihood of achieving anything, I put heart into those who say we should not invade England. Now, it is not my desire that we should invade England. It is not at all my desire that we should defeat England. It is my desire that the Directory should fall and the monarchy be restored, and with it my estates at – well, my estates."

Dan found it hard to focus on anything but the pain in his head. "But you work for the Directory."

This being obvious, the Citoyen ignored it. "So, what message do you think I shall take back to France?"

"That the United Patriots are no use to them?"

"That is correct. But do you think that message is the whole truth?"

"You're going to tell me it isn't."

"They don't have a vast stock of weapons. Very well. We could provide them with weapons. They don't have widespread support. But why would they need it? In the last few years governments have learned to tremble when demagogues unleash a mob. It is true the United Patriots are led by a fool, but even a fool's blade can strike home if no one's expecting it. An attack on the King at Wimbledon. It's so insane it just might succeed. Imagine it. A government in disarray, a capital in chaos. Even the most timid Directory members might think twice about passing up such an opportunity. No, it's not such a bad plan after all."

"So you think they could succeed?"

"Not without our help. So, I say to myself, I will make sure there is no help. I will tell the Directory that they are a hopeless cause. But I have some slight anxiety that they may achieve more than they deserve, and then my judgement will be questioned. It is a risk I have to take. But then I see you, and I think, here is a way to make the thing certain. For you, I think, intend to stop them. And since that suits my purposes, I have saved your life."

"Not me. I'm not looking for any trouble. All I want is to get as far away from them as I can."

The Citoyen smiled. "But that is the interesting thing. You are a man who looks for trouble, and a man who is used to finding it. I saw it at the inn. You did not beg, or scream, or cry. You calculated, and you never once stopped calculating all the way here. Right to the end you were looking for a way out. It was only in the very last seconds that you gave in to your natural feelings and considered yourself lost. And I said to myself, 'If I were in his place, that is how I would behave.' For we are the same, you and I. We both have our secret missions. Am I right?"

For a moment Dan thought he heard voices drifting across the water. Then the sounds were gone, and there was nothing but the waves on the sand and the wind through the grasses. The blow to the head was making him imagine things.

"Are you saying you're on our side?"

"No, I am not. If a legitimate government of France was at war with you I would be your enemy."

"You must have done something to help your government get and keep power, else why would they trust you?"

"I have done what I had to do. You would have done the same." The Citoyen stood up. "So you will not answer my question. No matter. If I am wrong about you, then I lose nothing. Can you stand?"

"Yes." Dan got to his feet. "How will you get back to the boat now you've killed those two?"

"I do not intend to go back to Gravesend on Lewis's boat. I have arranged for my own men to pick me up. There is a ship waiting to take me to France."

Again voices sounded eerily from across the waves, but now there was no mistaking the reality of the approaching row boat. It came splashing and creaking out of the chill, rolling shadows. A man in a buttoned-up greatcoat leaned from the prow and peered on to the strip of sand.

"Is all well?" he called softly. "Shots were fired."

"I am well," the Citoyen answered. "Wait there."

Three men jumped into the thigh-high water, pulled the boat onto the strand. Their leader, pistol in hand, waded ashore, his boots crunching on the sand and pebbles. His intelligent gaze took in the scene: the dead sailors, the Citoyen's mysterious companion. He showed no surprise or curiosity, but kept his hand on his pistol in case of lurking danger.

"It is time for me to go," the Citoyen said to Dan.

"Wait...what you said. It's true. My name's Dan Foster. I'm a Bow Street officer and I am here to bring Broomhall and his men down. One or other of them killed a colleague of mine, a man called Kean. Killed him and handed him over to the resurrection men. I'm not going to let them be the death of anyone else, whether it's the King or the most stupid apprentice in a misguided mob."

The Citoyen held out his hand. "I wish you luck, Monsieur Foster."

Dan returned the Frenchman's hand clasp. "And I you."

Dan watched the Citoyen walk down to the boat, click his fingers at the waiting men, and clamber in. The sailors pushed the vessel into the water and jumped in to take their place at the oars. They disappeared into the grey, misty dawn.

Left alone, Dan searched Lewis's pockets until he found a small purse, presumably the money Metcalf had paid for his murder. The price put on his life was ten guineas. The gun

Noah had given him was gone so he took Lewis's, along with a powder flask and cartouche of shot. A trawl through Glutton's pockets did not produce anything useful. Dan turned his face towards Sheerness and set off at a steady run.

The lamps had been lit by the time the post-chaise dropped him at the Bow Street office. Inky Tom was on his way back from the courtroom with a bundle of papers in his arms. From the chamber behind him came the sound of a clanking pail and the slosh of water as the housekeeper dabbed a grimy mop over the day's accumulated dirt.

"Mr Foster," the youth cried, "what happened to you?"

"Is Sir William still here?"

"Yes, but –"

Dan pushed past Tom and ran upstairs. He knocked on Sir William Addington's door and entered without waiting for an invitation. The magistrate, who was gathering his things ready to leave, looked up in surprise. His furious rebuke died on his lips when he recognised a dishevelled and unshaven Dan.

"Foster!" he exclaimed. "What are you doing here?"

"Sir, the United Patriots are planning to assassinate the King."

While he spoke Sir William rang his bell, but Lavender was already on the threshold of the room, staring at Dan in amazement.

"Bring brandy, quickly," Sir William ordered.

"Not for me," Dan said. "But if there's coffee…"

"And send for Sir Richard Ford immediately," Sir William added. "Tell him it is of the utmost urgency."

"Very good, sir." The clerk hurried off.

"Now, Foster, sit down and tell me everything."

It took a long time to tell the story, which had to be told over again when Sir Richard arrived from Whitehall. When Dan had finished, Sir William sat back in his chair and took a long pull from his glass.

"So who do you think killed Officer Kean?" he asked.

"Broomhall was the most obvious suspect. He murdered Kean, or ordered someone else to do it, because he found out he was a principal officer. Only now there's Metcalf, who didn't want anyone to take his place as Broomhall's second in command. He told me he'd seen off other men. Perhaps one of those men was Kean. In which case, the Patriots may not have known he was from Bow Street."

Sir Richard looked at the page of notes he had jotted down while Dan spoke. "You have no clue as to the identity of this Citoyen?"

"None." This was not strictly speaking true. Dan knew that even the little personal information he had gleaned about the Frenchman, coupled with a description, might be enough for the British spies in Paris to identify him.

"You cannot describe him except to say that he is of medium height and build?"

"No. He was careful to sit in the shadows, and afterwards it was dark on the marshes."

"And you believe that he spared your life because he guessed that you were working against the United Patriots, which suits the faction he supports?"

"Yes."

"So you gave him your name and rank, but did not obtain the corresponding identification from him. When I specifically told you it was the agent I wanted to apprehend." Sir Richard paused to let Dan feel the full extent of his displeasure. "Well, I will let my operatives in France have the paltry intelligence you have been able to provide. If they can locate him, he will be a useful man to get on our side. Let us turn now to the United Patriots' planned attack. It will take place ten days from now?"

"That is correct, sir. The conspirators usually meet on Thursday evenings in the Chequers, and I'd say that would be the best opportunity to round them up. But we'll have to be careful putting the men in place. It's not the kind of district where citizens like to lend a hand to the police."

"Thank you, Foster. I think I am capable of organising the operation," Sir Richard said. He rose from his seat. "I will speak to the Home Secretary at once. The arrests will take place a week tomorrow. That will give us plenty of time to prepare. In the meantime, Foster, can you provide a list of names of United Patriot members?"

"Many of them, yes. Some I don't know."

"Very well. Good evening, gentlemen."

"You haven't made a very good impression on Sir Richard," Sir William said when his colleague had gone.

"I shouldn't think he'll be recruiting me to spy for him again," agreed Dan, too tired to attempt to hide his satisfaction. He never wanted to be dragged into Sir Richard Ford's espionage network again.

Sir William cast a sharp glance at him. "You're exhausted. Go home and get some sleep. And I want you to stay in the office until the arrests are made."

"But, sir –"

"You're on desk duties for the next few days, Foster."

"Very good, sir." Dan picked up his hat and stood up.

"And Foster – well done."

"Thank you, sir."


Though Russell Street was closer, Dan did not go home. Instead he walked down to Cecil Street, where he found Noah and Paul, his assistant, closing the gym for the night.

"We're about to have a bit of beef and onions," Paul said, smacking his lips over the stubs of his teeth, which had been broken by a French musket handle at Quebec during the Seven Years' War.

"Good, I'm hungry. First I'm going to the steam baths. Have I got some clean clothes here?"

Noah, busy stuffing used towels into a laundry sack, nodded. "In the cupboard in the parlour. I'll be in in a minute."

Dan went into the parlour and found himself a shirt, breeches, coat and, most welcome of all, a pair of boots. He kicked off his servants' shoes and pushed them away with a grimace of disgust, then sat down on the worn old armchair and started to undo his shirt. Even that felt like a mighty effort. His hand fell into his lap and he let his head fall back, closed his eyes. Just for a minute.

When he woke up he was lying, still dressed except for his hat, bedraggled jacket and muddy stockings, on the narrow bed behind the curtained alcove where he had slept as a boy. Noah and Paul had carried him there and put a blanket over him. They had also washed the matted blood out of his hair.

He pushed the cover aside and sat up. There was no one in the parlour, but he could hear men punching sacks, lifting weights, exercising hard in the gymnasium. Every now and again Noah or Paul shouted instructions: "Arms up! Head back! Watch that stance!" Good, familiar sounds.

Barefoot and in his shirtsleeves, he padded into the parlour. Here a cheery fire burned and there was a pot of coffee next to it. Gratefully he helped himself.

Noah came in, dropped a pair of mufflers on the table. "You've had a good long sleep."

"How long?" asked Dan, rubbing his bristling chin.

"It's four o'clock."

"In the afternoon? Why didn't you wake me?"

"Because you were dead on your feet. And you still look like death."

"Nothing a wash and shave won't put right. And something to eat. I suppose I missed the beef and onions," Dan ended wistfully.

"But not the gammon and eggs. Do you want to bathe or eat first?"

"I'll eat, if you don't mind me sitting at table like this."

"Sit."

Dan did as he was told while Noah bustled about with bread, knives and plates. Paul came in to rearrange everything, then threw some rashers into a pan along with the eggs.

After he had eaten, with Noah and Paul watching his every mouthful and encouraging him to second and even third helpings, Dan told them about his recent adventures.

"And you're on to Kean's killer?" Paul asked eagerly.

"I think so."

"You knew he would be," Noah said. Then, lest the praise seem too high, "And now you'd better go and have that bath, son. You stink."

Dan took his clean clothes and went to the steam baths next door. After he had soaked away the grime of the last few days and woken himself up with a cold shower, he let the baths' resident barber, Mr Faraldo, shave him with his usual grim air of the world about to end.

He bundled up Daniel Bright's clothes to be given to a street pedlar. Though he was glad to be rid of them himself, he knew that they had plenty of life left in them for someone with only pennies to spend. He shrugged on his coat, pulled on his boots, adjusted his scarf and felt himself grow six feet taller. Dan Foster was back.

Now he was presentable, he was keen to get home. He anticipated Eleanor's expression when she saw he had kept his promise to get back safely. He knew that his dream of the two of them together was just that: a dream. All that was real about it was the longing. Yet in spite of it, his steps were still eager.

When he opened the front door there were voices coming from the kitchen, along with the welcome smell of roasting meat and potatoes. Hanging up his hat in the hall, he could have sworn he heard a baby crying too.

There was a baby, lying on Eleanor's lap, with Mrs Harper crowding her daughter and fussing over the infant. Eleanor smiled up at Dan. Seeing her sitting at his hearth with the child was like a stab to the heart, a picture of domestic happiness he would never have. Caroline stared at her sister, her eyes full of envy and discontent. Dan wondered if things would have been better between him and Caroline if they had had a child in the early days of their marriage. The time when they had found pleasure in one another's bodies was long past, and it was unlikely to happen now.

The proud parents looked on. Dan did not know the young, rosy-faced woman, but he recognised the lad sitting beside her. Before he could say as much, the youth stood up.

"Mr Foster, you remember me? Walter Halling. We met in Barcombe."

# Chapter Twenty-Four

Dan put out his hand. "Yes, I remember you. I didn't know that you'd married."

And had a child in double-quick time, too.

"This is Rosie," Walter said.

The girl flashed a look at Dan, then lowered her eyes.

"How did you know where to find me?" Dan asked.

"I went to Bow Street. You were out and they didn't think you were going back today so they told me to come here."

Dan had promised Anna Halling that if she or her son Walter ever needed his help, they only had to ask. He and Anna had been more than friends in Barcombe. She had been angry with him when he left, with good cause. He should have told her he was married.

Walter certainly looked as if trouble had come to him. His face was thin and there were shadows under his eyes. The consequence, no doubt, of a boy still in his apprenticeship taking on a wife and child.

"How's your mother?" Conscious of Eleanor's and Caroline's eyes upon him, Dan was careful to put nothing more than friendly interest into his voice.

"She's dead."

"Dead?" Dan exclaimed, forgetting the need for caution and heedless of Caroline's sudden tensing, her hands clenching in her lap. "When? How?"

"She died in June after she caught a fever physicking a neighbour's child."

Anna had been a healer and herbalist. She would be a great loss to the villagers who could not afford a doctor's fees, or who did not trust modern medicine. He remembered how she had looked after him following his fight with Bristol pugilist Hen Pearce at Kingswood, cared for him with more than balm for his bruises. There had been tenderness for his unhappiness as well. He had thought about her occasionally when he got back to London, even considered going to see her, trying to put things right between them. But work, home, the gymnasium had put her out of his mind. Now it was too late.

"That's terrible," Mrs Harper said. "And not to live to see her grandchild. The poor chick."

The baby, at whom the last remark was aimed, whimpered. Rosie put out her arms and Eleanor handed back the child.

"What's its name?" Dan asked, for want of knowing what else to say.

"Dan!" Caroline laughed, a forced, brittle sound. "He's not an it."

"What's his name, then?"

"Davy," Walter answered.

Named after his grandfather. Dan remembered Anna talking about her husband and his early death in an accident at work. He pulled up a chair and sat down. Eleanor and Mrs Harper served tea. They talked about inconsequential stuff: how expensive everything was in London, the food not fresh, and the crowds enough to make you giddy. Rosie did not say a word. She sat clutching the child, exchanging secretive smiles every now and again with Eleanor and Mrs Harper. Caroline was quiet too.

Dan noticed how evasive Walter was whenever he was asked any questions. How long might they stay in London? That depends. On what? Oh, many things. Was he planning to look for work? Perhaps. So they might go back to Barcombe? He didn't know yet. The lad fidgeted, seemed on the verge of saying something, but after scanning the circle of faces, he would bite his lip and remain silent.

Eventually the conversation ground to a halt. Rosie looked

at Walter. Walter and Eleanor started to speak at the same time. He reddened.

"After you."

"No, what were you going to say?"

"Nothing," he muttered. "We'd better be going, Rosie."

She began to wrap up the baby against the cold, but Walter said, "Wait," and turned to Dan. "Can I speak to you?"

"Of course. We'll go into the next room."

Dan led Walter into the parlour which they hardly ever used. It was too small for comfort, for one thing. For another it overlooked the yard, which for all the flowerbed and pots of herbs tended by Mrs Harper and Eleanor was still a gloomy London court.

Dan gestured to Walter to sit down. The young man shook his head and they remained standing.

"I am so sad to hear about your mother," Dan said. "If there's anything I can do to help you only have to tell me."

"You'll help us?"

A bitter note had crept into Walter's voice, but Dan, knowing how hard it was to ask for a favour, did not take offence. He could not help being disappointed at the boy's lack of trust in him, though. He thought they had become friends in Barcombe. He had taught him some boxing; talked him out of running with the poaching gang led by the blacksmith, Singleton, before he arrested them; set him on a straight path.

"There's no harm in asking for something if you need it," he said. "I can see that things aren't easy for you."

"You can see that, can you?" Walter retorted.

"Your mother knew that when I said I'd help, I meant it. You've come all this way to see me, so isn't it time you told me what's going on? For the sake of your wife and child, if nothing else."

Walter thrust his hands in his pockets and poked at the hearth rug with his toe.

"He's not my child and we aren't married. My mother did catch the fever while she was tending a newborn, just like I told

179

you. That child died and then so did Mother, hours after her own baby was born." He turned to face Dan. "Davy is yours. He's your son."

"Mine?"

"What did you think? That she'd get rid of it for you?"

"I thought no such thing. I didn't know. Why didn't she tell me?"

"Because you'd gone back to your wife. I was going to tell you in the other room. That's what I came here planning to do. I was going to shout it out in front of your people. But when I saw Mrs Foster I couldn't do it. She's so sad. So beautiful. I couldn't do it to her. So." Walter shrugged. "You've got away with it. And I don't want your money, if that's what you think. Davy's my brother and I'll look after him. Oh!"

He gazed towards the door in dismay. Dan turned and saw Caroline, her white-knuckled hand clutching the door handle. Her voice was low, deep, almost a growl.

"I knew it. I knew you'd been unfaithful as soon as you got back from Barcombe. And you so high and mighty. Such a bloody puritan."

"Don't call me that."

"I'll call you what I like. You never let me have a moment's enjoyment without pulling your long fucking face about it. And what are you? Dan Foster the adulterer. Dan Foster the liar. The cheat. The bastard who begets bastards."

"Caroline – please listen to me –"

"Listen to you? I wouldn't give you the snot off my nose. You whoring son of a bitch!" She launched herself at him, beat his chest with her fists, clawed at his face. "You bastard! You bloody bastard!"

He grasped her wrists, held her at arm's length. She kicked and struggled, screamed at him, her spittle spattering his face.

"Get your filthy hands off me, you fucking miserable whoreson, and fuck off back to the gutter!"

Mrs Harper rushed into the room. "What's all this? What's going on? Caro, what are you doing? For pity's sake, calm yourself, lovey. You'll make yourself ill."

Caroline let her mother lead her away. She looked ready to tear herself from Mrs Harper's restraining embrace, spring on her husband and tear him apart.

"What am I doing?" Caroline cried. "Ask him what he's been doing. Ask him whose baby that is." She rounded on her sister. "Or why don't you ask him, Nell?"

Eleanor stood just inside the room. "Dan? Is this true?"

Her disappointment in him was almost harder to bear than Caroline's fury. He rubbed his hand across his face. "Yes."

Caroline laughed. "My husband's not such a fine catch now, is he, Nellie? Leave me alone, Mother. I want a drink." She tore herself out of her mother's arms and turned back to Dan. "Get out of here and don't come back. Ever."

She swept out of the room, shoving Rosie, who stood in the doorway holding the baby, out of her way. Mrs Harper followed her daughter, paused as she passed Dan and said, "You had better go. You can do no good here."

Rosie sidled over to Walter, slipped one arm through his.

"Mr Foster," he said. "I – I'm so sorry. I didn't mean –"

"It's not your fault." He moved towards Eleanor. "Eleanor – let me explain –"

She stepped away from him. "No, Dan. You should do what they say. You should go."

"But, Eleanor, it's not what it looks like."

"Yes it is. Just go." She turned her back on him and walked away.

"Oh, God!" he groaned, dropping his arms and head on the mantelpiece. Rosie and Walter, stricken with guilt, moved softly towards the door.

Dan raised his head. "Where are you staying?"

"We have rooms in Newport Street."

"I'll walk back with you. There are arrangements to be made."

"What arrangements?"

"We can't discuss it here. Come."

He went into the hall for his hat and coat. The kitchen door was closed against him. From inside came Caroline's noisy sobbing, the clink of bottle on glass, Mrs Harper's soothing murmur. Not a sound from Eleanor.

Already in the interlude between day and night the streets had acquired a dangerous atmosphere. Brazen women, alone or in pairs or groups, sauntered towards the Strand or hung about corners and tavern doors, whistling and calling invitations to men as they passed. Apprentices, clerks and shop assistants strolled to their homes or supper clubs, exchanging suggestive banter with the women. Packs of well-dressed young men descended on the restaurants and taverns as a prelude to the evening's frolics in brothels and bagnios. Many of them would be found later with their finery trailing in the gutters or their pockets emptied in alleyways.

Dan, Walter and Rosie walked in silence, each busy with their own unhappy thoughts. Rosie hurried along between Walter and Dan, clutching the child to her chest as if she feared someone would snatch him away. But no one accosted them. This was Dan's beat and he was well known.

The young couple had taken a bedroom and parlour in the lodging house. Rosie put the baby in a basket while she lit the candles and the fire. Then she sat down and took up some sewing: clothes for the child. Walter, throwing his hat onto the bed in one of his old boyish gestures, stood by the fireplace, occasionally stoking the fledging flame into life with the poker. There was evidence that someone slept in the parlour; presumably Walter.

"I told you I don't want your money," he said.

"We'll see about that," Dan answered. "Are you going to take the child back to Barcombe?"

"I can't. Uncle won't have him in the house and I can't afford to give up my apprenticeship. Besides, a Bow Street Runner's bastard won't have an easy time of it in Barcombe, seeing as how you got Singleton and the others transported. Uncle's expecting me to go back without him, and it will be better for Davy if I do. I'll leave him at the Foundling Hospital. As soon as I'm earning for myself, I'll come back for him."

"No."

"What do you mean, no? It's got nothing to do with you."

"No child of mine is going as a foundling. He's my son, Walter, and I'll not have him grow up like that."

"What will you do – hand him over to your wife?"

"When I've found myself some rooms I'll hire a woman to look after him."

The needle faltered in Rosie's hand and tears welled in her eyes. "A hired woman?"

Then Dan understood. "It was your baby Anna was treating."

Rosie nodded. And now she was about to lose another one.

"Would you do it?" Dan asked her.

She looked at Walter. "I would, if I didn't have to live in this great, dirty place."

Walter shook his head. "It's no good, Rosie. I can't take him back to Barcombe."

"Would I be on my own?" she asked Dan.

"I'll hire a servant to look after you. My son will have a home. I'll make sure it's a good one. And you'll be welcome any time you like, Walter."

"Walter?"

"It's up to you, Rosie."

She stood up, stooped over the basket, gathered up the baby. "I'll stay, for a while at least." She carried the child over to Dan. "Do you want to hold him?"

Dan hesitated. He did not know how.

"Like this," she said. "Support his head."

Dan took the hot, wriggling bundle into his arms and looked down at the tightly shut eyes, the mouth working on an imaginary teat, the fingers clasping open and shut. The life of the streets was over and done with for Dan. He would make sure that Davy never knew it.

# Chapter Twenty-Five

For what seemed like the hundredth time, Patrolman Jones tightened his grip on his police rattle and checked his pistols were secure in his belt.

"Stop fidgeting," Dan said. "You're ready."

"Yes, sir."

Dan and Jones stood in the doorway of a dingy office building opposite the Chequers. The patrolman was almost as pale as when Dan had seen him retching into a bucket the night he brought Kean's remains to Bow Street. But his was not the worst case of nerves Dan had ever seen, and he knew how hard the waiting could be.

Dan glanced along the shadowy street. The occasional drop of rain still splashed down, but the heaviest part of the downpour had ended. Captain Ellis sat in the driving seat of a lamp-lit cart, chatting with two workmen who leaned carelessly on the wheel. There were four more men hidden under the tarpaulin at the back. Further down, a card sharper held an audience spellbound by lamplight with the three cup trick. Most of the men following his deft hands were police, as was the player himself – Reeves of the Union Hall office. A group of porters who lounged against a wall, and a crowd of idlers who had gathered around two men on the verge of fisticuffs, were all constables or Runners.

In a street usually thronged with strangers and foreigners, they had managed to stroll, slouch and sneak into position over the last hour or so without attracting attention. Only John Townsend, with the broad-brimmed hat he had refused to relinquish, looked out of place, though he had consented to cover his yellow waistcoat under a dark greatcoat. Luckily the Prince of Wales's self-proclaimed friend and confidant need have no fear of being recognised. Pickle Herring Lane society was as ignorant of John Townsend's appearance as they were of his existence.

There had been no refusing Townsend when he volunteered for the operation. Gleefully, he had supplemented his police-issue cutlass and pistols with a cudgel. The other five principal officers of Bow Street were there, along with many from the magistrates' offices around London. John Lavender, whose experience to date was raiding gambling houses, headed the party stationed behind the tavern to round up any who attempted escape that way.

Dan looked at his watch. The United Patriots had been inside the Chequers for a quarter of an hour. They would be well into their bloody business by now. No doubt thinking themselves close to victory too, since yesterday's news that the Dutch fleet had set sail from the Texel. The Dutch were allied to the French, but their warships had been pinned down by Admiral Duncan's ships and helpless to move against the British. A few days ago Duncan had temporarily lifted his blockade and sailed back to Yarmouth for refitting, and the Dutch had seized their chance to launch their fleet.

The British Navy caught off guard, the Dutch in control of the North Sea, the assassination of the King and his key ministers, Pitt and Dundas: how could the French pass up such an opportunity? The Citoyen's warnings against putting too much faith in the United Patriots might not be enough to hold back the pro-invasion party in the French Directory.

Dan drew his pistols from his belt.

"Give the signal."

Jones raised and twirled the rattle. It had the same effect as the shadow of a hawk on a lawn full of sparrows. Men, women and children scattered. The only people left in the muddy street were police. The noise of the rattle, familiar to many inside, penetrated the gloomy interior. Drinkers streamed out, reeking of gin, tobacco, fright. The raiders ignored them and charged into the tap room where panic spread amongst the crowded tables. Some bold souls jumped up pugnaciously, but the column of officers brushed them aside.

Dan pounded over fallen chairs and tables, broken glass, heard the crack of a truncheon on bone, the thud of a man falling, women screaming, dogs barking, shouts and curses. He shouldered open the door into the yard. His men streamed after him, Jones brandishing his pistol, his face flushed and eyes bright. Behind Dan, John Townsend yelled, "God save the King!"

From inside the skittles alley came the sounds of chairs scraping, cries of alarm, Metcalf calling for order. A chair flew through one of the windows at the side of the building. The rotten frame easily gave way and a head and shoulders appeared in the aperture. Dan waved at two of his men to seize the would-be escapee. He saw the constables rushing towards him and tried to wriggle back inside, but they caught hold of him and pulled him out. They snapped handcuffs on him, dragged him away and threw him against the far wall before returning to the fray.

Dan kicked open the door, strode into the room and fired one of his guns into the air. "Bow Street officer! You're all under arrest."

There was a shocked pause, then the constables waded in, truncheons swinging. Dan saw Isaac from Warren's tea shop dragged out by the arms, his shirt and jacket rucked up above his quivering belly. A massive constable ran past, hugging a diminutive, kicking, weeping Upton in his arms. The Irish shop assistant O'Brian, fighting with his back against a wall, was brought down by Jones with a bludgeon to the knee. MacGregor, who had vowed death to any who stood in his way, held out his hands in a gesture of surrender and Reeves snapped the cuffs on him. Captain Ellis had caught Simmons in an arm lock.

Dan pushed through the struggle, kicking chairs aside,

elbowing men out of his way. Ahead of him stood Metcalf. He had seen off one constable, who lay on the floor. The fallen man's eyes were open and he seemed more winded than hurt. Having done with him, Metcalf aimed his pistol at Ellis's back.

"Sam!" Dan shouted. He flung himself at Metcalf, brought his spent pistol down on the man's arm. Metcalf's aim veered, the gun went off, the bullet gouging a floorboard.

Metcalf wasted no time scrabbling for his gun. He rounded on Dan, fists at the ready. He stopped in his tracks.

"You! You're supposed to be dead."

"I'm not," Dan said. "Where's Broomhall?"

"I'll do for you this time," Metcalf yelled, and threw himself on Dan.

Dan raised his second pistol and fired. Metcalf staggered to his knees. Dan cursed and thrust his gun back into his belt. He had been saving the ball for Broomhall.

Metcalf clutched his arm, let the blood seep through his fingers. Realising it was only a flesh wound, he ignored it and tensed himself to spring at Dan. Dan aimed his boot at his jaw. The blow sent him spinning to the ground, out cold.

"Cuff him!" Dan yelled at Ellis.

The patrol captain nodded and crouched over the injured man. Dan caught sight of John Townsend standing over Warren. The tea grocer's face was covered in blood, his hands broken and bruised. He rolled back and forth, squealing beneath the blows of Townsend's cudgel.

"King killing no crime, eh?" Townsend yelled. "Liberty, equality and fraternity, is it?"

Dan grabbed Townsend's arm. "For God's sake, man, he's finished."

Townsend roared and whirled round, the cudgel raised. He recognised Dan and lowered his arm. "What's it to you? Traitors deserve all they get."

"Not without a trial, they don't."

Townsend's eyes narrowed. "So that's the way of it, is it?

You've spent too much time with this radical scum. You're beginning to sound like them."

Dan refused to grace this with an answer. He grabbed hold of the nearest constable. "Take this man away. Officer Townsend has finished with him."

"Damn you, Foster, I've called men out for less."

"Another time," said Dan, who had caught sight of a tall man in a green coat disappearing through the door at the top of the room.

He started after the fleeing figure. Someone lunged at him. With an impatient flick, Dan punched him in the mouth, sent him staggering away. The door closed behind the green coat. Dan drew his cutlass and snatched it open. The passageway was empty.

Dan pushed open the door to the lumber room where he had hidden on his first visit to the Chequers. Behind him the fight still raged, and from the yard came the sound of scuffles and voices, but here the cluttered darkness dulled the sounds. The tangle of broken furniture made black shapes that confused his eye. There was a rustling on his left. He turned, peered into the gloom, could make out nothing. He took a step forward.

He heard a scuffle in the shadows behind him and spun round. The broken skittle aimed at his head hit his arm instead. His cutlass clattered to the ground. A wild figure flung itself upon him, hands around his throat, eyes red, teeth bared.

Dan swung back his left arm, put all his might into a blow to the stomach. His right arm throbbed painfully but he used it anyway and delivered a blow to the kidney. The grip on his throat loosened, and Dan brought both hands up to knock the arms away. Without a pause he went after the staggering figure with a right, a left, a right, a left, and one final punch that sent him flying into a stack of chairs that collapsed beneath him. Dan dropped down to his knees, cleared away the debris from the unconscious man, and raised him into a sitting position.

It was not Broomhall.

# Chapter Twenty-Six

Dan gripped the man's collar and dragged him back to the main room, where the outnumbered United Patriots had at last surrendered. Captain Ellis and others were busy fitting cuffs on to their prisoners.

"Another one," said Dan, leaving his burden with two constables. "Ellis, have you seen Broomhall?"

The captain, who had a bloodied mouth but was otherwise unhurt, shook his head. "Just this ugly lot. No one of his description."

Dan ran out into the yard. There was a line of shackled men slumped against the wall now, and more joining them every minute. Some of the constables had brought lanterns to aid the search for weapons. Others had started leading Patriots out to the street, where a contingent of fresh officers had been brought up to escort them to Bow Street. Sir William and Sir Richard were ready to hold an all-night session to get the prisoners processed and taken to Newgate. The militia was on stand-by to help with the escorts and maintaining order.

Dan snatched one of the lanterns. A quick search confirmed that Broomhall was not amongst the arrested men in the yard or the tavern. He asked around, and finally one of the constables told him, "There was a man like that went out a while ago. Said he was from Hatton Garden office."

"You didn't ask to see identification?"

The young man bit his lip. "No, sir. Everything was so –"

Dan did not wait to hear his excuses. What mattered was finding Broomhall. But where could he have gone? He was not stupid enough to go back to his shop, which had been secured by a couple of constables. The Tooley Street tea shop had also been raided.

There would be no shortage of boatmen willing to take Broomhall out of town, for a price. Or he could go to one of the ships anchored in mid-river and secure himself a passage out of the country. But from where – Westminster Bridge? Hungerford Stairs? Wapping? Would he attempt to reach the waterside now, with the area swarming with police? He might: his escape from the Chequers had been brazen enough. On the other hand, he might decide to lie low until things had quietened down. If he did that, where would he hide?

There was Dawson's warehouse. Dan could check it out and be back in less than a quarter of an hour. He dumped the lantern and set off at a run.

Dan dropped from the wall into the yard and crouched in the shadows while he reloaded his pistol. The dog in the cooper's yard next door moved restlessly, his chain rattling. The watchman was drunk or asleep, though not snoring as loudly as the guard in the sentry box in St John's churchyard.

Dan was about to make his way to the window when the wicket door at the front of the warehouse swung open. Two men carrying lanterns emerged from the interior. They wore dark, mud-stained smocks over their clothes. They crossed the yard, entered one of the outhouses not far from where Dan was hiding, and after a bit of rummaging about came out, each pushing a handcart on which he had hung his lantern. They wheeled the carts back to the door and went inside. They were back in a moment, groaning under the weight of the shrouded burden they carried between them. When they had hauled it into one of the carts, they went back inside for another corpse they had left just inside the door. As they swung it onto the cart, one of them lost his grip and the body thudded against the side of the vehicle.

"Watch what you're fucking doing, Smith," his companion said.

Smith laughed. "He don't feel it."

They went back into the warehouse. After a few moments the door opened again, a light shone out, and another two men came out with a third body. Dawson appeared in the doorway behind them, his bare head shining red in the light from his lamp. He watched them add their load to the carts, then disappeared inside. They went in after him and shortly re-emerged with another cadaver.

When they had gone back inside, Dan pocketed his gun, darted across the yard and pressed his ear to the door. The body snatchers' heavy footsteps sounded dully as they made their way back to the room with the butcher's block. Dan slipped into the warehouse and as before hid amongst the crates outside the room. He heard voices and the grunting of men lifting heavy weights; the thud and drag of the disinterred bodies. The door swung open and the two pairs of men awkwardly manoeuvred their loads out of the room. Behind them stood Broomhall and Dawson.

"You'll get your money before the night is out, I tell you," Dawson said.

The door closed and Broomhall's answer was an angry murmur. The four men struggled past Dan's hiding place, their loads trailing unpleasant smells.

Dan drew out his pistol. The gang were still busy in the yard, preparing to set off on their rounds to the anatomy schools. All he had to do was wait for them to go, then he could go in and get Broomhall. Dawson too, if he was still there. He hunkered down in the shadows.

A flintlock cocked behind him. A cold circle of metal pressed into his skull.

"Drop it." The speaker was Smith.

Dan lowered his arm and placed the pistol on the ground.

"Stand. Slow now. No need to turn round."

Dan got up, felt the shove of Smith's gun in his back.

"In there."

Dan pushed the door open while behind him Smith stooped to pick up the gun from the floor. Dawson's startled face turned towards them. He whipped out his own pistol and sprang forward.

"What's all this?"

"Found him hiding out here," said Smith, and held out Dan's gun.

Dawson took the gun, squinted at the captive and burst out laughing. "Now that's what I call a fuckin' resurrection!"

Angrily, Broomhall shoved the red-headed man aside. "Bright? Metcalf said you were dead. How the hell did you get here?"

Dawson put Dan's gun down on the block. The door opened and the other three men came back into the room. Broomhall's look warned them to keep their surprise to themselves.

"Lucas, search him," Broomhall said.

A short, thin man with a face as sunken and waxy as those of the corpses he dealt in, nodded at Smith. "You and Trinder grab hold."

Smith and Trinder, a stocky man with strands of filthy, straggling hair encircling a bald spot on the top of his head, seized Dan's arms while Lucas riffled his pockets. He pulled out Dan's tipstaff and handed it to Broomhall.

"He's a Runner," he said.

"The devil!" Dawson cried. "You've only gone and let another bloody Runner in, Broomhall."

Broomhall planted himself in front of Dan. Dan refused to drop his own gaze. He stared his defiance at the murderer who now had him in his power.

"So Metcalf was right. You are a spy. But he said he'd dealt with you."

"He tried," Dan said.

"So who are you?"

"Dan Foster, Principal Officer of Bow Street. You killed

a fellow officer, and I'm here to see you hang for it."

"You were at the Chequers tonight?"

"You didn't see me because you were too busy running."

Lucas guffawed. Broomhall shot an ugly glance at him.

"We need to clear out of here," Dawson said. "What are you going to do about him?"

"What do you think?" Broomhall clicked his fingers. "Nipps."

The fourth resurrectionist, a hard-handed man whose knuckles bore the scars of countless fights and who was missing three of his front teeth, stepped up. He drew back his right fist and landed it in Dan's stomach. Dan crumpled, choking down his nausea. They dragged him upright and the knuckles drove again into the same spot. The pain brought him out in a cold sweat. Nipps grinned gummily and drew back his fist for a third blow.

"Hold hard!" Dawson said. "He looks to be in prime condition. I'd get a special price for such goods. Could be worth as much as six guineas. Can't you do him some other way?"

Broomhall, his gaze still fixed on Dan, said, "Very well. Pass me the pistol."

Dawson groaned. "Oh, come on. Surgeons won't pay so much if his innards is all blown out."

Broomhall wrenched his gaze from his victim and regarded the resurrection man with loathing. "What do you suggest?"

"Trinder?" Dawson said.

The stocky man drew a knife out of his pocket and let go of Dan's arm. Lucas took Trinder's place, tangled his fingers in Dan's hair and pulled his head back to expose his throat.

"Go on, then," said Broomhall. "Make it slow."

Dan struggled against the men's grip as Trinder's knife moved closer to his throat. Just like Kean, he thought, I'm going to die just like Kean, with a bunch of ugly lowlife jeering at me. He gasped his last, desperate words.

"If you kill me you'll never get out of here alive. The place is surrounded."

Trinder faltered.

Broomhall laughed. "I don't think so. You wouldn't have come in on your own if that was true. Carry on, Trinder."

Dan felt the hellish breath of Trinder's laughter in his face and braced himself for the final blow. Eleanor, Eleanor…

Outside a high, piping voice broke the night silence, accompanied by what sounded like someone hammering crazily on a saucepan. "Resurrection men! Here are resurrection men! Here are body snatchers!"

The dog in the cooper's yard set up a furious barking. From further down the street another joined in, then another and another, until it seemed that every hound in Southwark howled at the moon. The warning bell in St John's churchyard started to clang. The man in the sentry box had woken up.

"Resurrection men! Resurrection men!" he shouted sleepily.

"What the fuck's going on?" cried Dawson.

Dan took advantage of his captors' surprise and twisted himself free of Smith and Lucas. Smith lunged after him, but Dan met him full on with a fist in the face. The grave robber staggered away, his hand clutching at his mouth, blood spilling between his fingers. Dan and Broomhall made a grab for the gun on the butcher's block, but Dawson beat them to it. Dan flung himself to the ground and skidded on all fours to come up with a bang against one of the stout wooden legs of the block as Dawson's bullet passed over his head.

By now they could hear running feet, people yelling and hammering on the yard gates. Dawson's men began to grasp the danger of their situation: their clothes coated with grave mould, the corpses on their handcarts. The good people of Horsleydown might not have turned out to prevent a night-time stabbing, but grave robbing was another matter. Dawson shouted orders but no one listened to him. Smith turned and fled. Lucas, Nipps and Trinder were not far behind him. They pelted out into the yard just as the gates crashed open. Dawson swore and sprang after them.

Broomhall threw the tipstaff down and ran to the door. Dan rolled away from the block, grabbed his knees and brought him down hard on the stone floor. Broomhall tried to crawl off, kicking viciously at Dan's hands and arms. Dan threw himself on top of Broomhall and gripped his throat.

"Who killed Kean?"

"Who?"

"The man you knew as Scott. Who killed him?"

Broomhall laughed. "Not me. You'll have to ask Dawson."

"It was Dawson?"

"Ask him."

"Was he acting on your orders?"

Broomhall, still smirking, refused to answer. There was no time to get more out of him: Dawson was getting away. Dan would have to come back for Broomhall later. He delivered two crunching blows to the watchmaker's jaw. Broomhall sank back, unconscious. Dan left him where he lay, slammed the door and pushed the wooden bar back into place between the staples to lock him inside.

# Chapter Twenty-Seven

Smith had come to a dithering halt on the threshold of the warehouse door. Coming up behind him and Dawson, Dan saw that the yard had been taken over by a baying mob: prostitutes and their clients; apprentices and their masters; tradesmen and servants. Even the wretches who had only the gutter to sleep in had turned out, hating the thought that their bodies, starved and loathsome as they were, might end up in a surgeon's hands. Some carried torches, many were armed with household implements or tools, some with sticks and cudgels. One or two carried ancient pikes.

Dawson, pistol at the ready, hurtled into Smith, shoved him outside and yelled, "Here's one of the grabs!"

The crowd fell on the stumbling man. A hatchet caught him across the mouth, sending out a spray of blood. Lucas was down on his knees, surrounded by a group of screaming men and women, powerless to defend himself. Dan glimpsed Trinder disappearing around the side of the building. He could not see Nipps.

In the confusion Dawson backed away into the shadows. He swung himself onto the low roof of the lean-to and from there onto the wall. Dan raced after him.

A goblin figure brandishing a knife reared up in front of him. Dan drew back his fist and sent the fight-maddened man staggering away. Another, hunched and slavering, got the same treatment. Then Dan was in the shadows and the battle was behind him. He thought he saw something pale and imp-like scuttling after him, but lost sight of it and was too busy climbing after Dawson to give it any further thought. He swung his legs over the parapet and dropped down into the darkness, praying that he would not land on jagged glass or metal.

It was something soft and foul-smelling, a dead dog or cat. He rolled nimbly away and got to his feet. Ahead of him he saw Dawson's shadowy form picking its way over the dust heaps and rubbish towards the rubble of the ruined house. He saw a movement out of the corner of his eye, looked back and there was the imp again, straddling the wall. Dan shook his head: that beating was making him see things. He gritted his teeth and moved off. When he glanced over his shoulder, the apparition had gone.

Dawson ducked through an empty doorway. Dan was close enough to hear the man's feet crunching on the ruined floor. And something else: a crash, a curse, the thud of a body hitting the ground. At the same time something small and sly crept up behind Dan. He turned to meet it.

"Mr Bright! Are you all right?"

Dan gazed down at the boy. "Nick? Is that you?"

"Yers. How do you like your rescue?"

"It was you who started the alarm?"

"It was."

"But how – no, there isn't time. That man who was running away. I have to stop him."

"No you don't," said a modest voice from the doorway.

Ann stood on the broken doorstep. She moved aside to present her handiwork. Dawson lay on the debris-strewn floor, a deep gash across his white forehead.

Dan gasped. "What did you do?"

"I was hiding up there." She pointed to the upper floor, in the middle of which was a sagging hole. "I dropped a brick on his head."

"You've got a good aim, girl. But I didn't think you'd still be here."

"We knew you was gone but we stayed because it's a good place to hide," Nick said.

"Cos he thought you might come back," the girl said,

ignoring Nick's embarrassed attempt to silence her.

"Well, I'm glad to see you both again, and I shall see you rewarded for this night's work. Nick, do you think you could run to the Chequers and ask for Captain Ellis of Bow Street patrol? Tell him to bring some men with him."

The boy recoiled in dismay. "You're a Runner? I thought you was in another gang."

"I was what you are once," Dan said. "Now I'm a Runner."

Nick's eyes widened in wonder at the new possibility that opened before him. Even so, he hesitated.

"I promise you won't come to any harm," Dan said.

Nick nodded and ran off. Dan picked up Dawson's gun and used the prisoner's own scarf to tie his hands behind his back. He pushed him into a sitting position against a pile of bricks and crouched beside him. Dawson groaned and his eyes flickered open.

Dan cocked the pistol and pointed it at his chest. "I wouldn't struggle if I were you. Wouldn't want this going off."

Dawson sank back. "Bow Street pig."

"That's right. The man you knew as Scott was a friend of mine. Broomhall says he didn't kill him. He says I should ask you. I'm asking you. Did you kill him?"

"Broomhall? That whoreson! It wasn't me. I know nothing about it."

"My hand's getting tired holding this gun. A bit shaky. Hope I don't accidentally pull the trigger."

"It wasn't me, I tell you. Broomhall's lying. All I did was get rid of the body."

So that was why Broomhall had been smirking at him, Dan realised. He'd been sent on a false trail, and for no other purpose than to spite him. Broomhall had had nothing to gain from the lie: he knew he was going to hang. Dan didn't regret the second punch he'd given him. He wished he'd landed a third.

"You'd better tell me everything you know."

"That's it. Broomhall brought me the body and I got rid of it."

"What do you mean, he brought it to you?"

"What I said. He brought it to the warehouse. We cut it up for the schools."

"How did he die?"

"Stabbed. Several times."

"So it was Broomhall who did it?"

"Not he. He never lost control. This was too angry."

"So who then?"

"He didn't tell me."

Dan sank back on his heels. Assume Dawson was telling the truth and what did that leave? Broomhall had ordered someone, possibly Metcalf, to kill Kean when he discovered he was a law officer, and then he had ordered Dawson to dispose of the body. Or Metcalf, acting alone and from personal motives, had killed Kean because he felt he threatened his position in the organisation. Then Broomhall had ordered Dawson to get rid of the body as a favour to his second in command.

There was a loud roar, followed by a flash of light. Startled, Dan looked up. The night sky above the yard had turned an ugly red. The warehouse was on fire.

Dan listened to the mob's shouts and screams, the roar of the fire, the collapsing of charred and blistered beams. His stomach, already painful from his beating, roiled when he thought about Broomhall locked inside the warehouse. It was not the end he had intended for him. He hoped it would be quick.

It was then he noticed that Ann was not there. Perhaps she had gone after Nick. Or perhaps she had run away when she discovered he was a Bow Street Runner. Perhaps they both had, and there was no help coming. He'd have to get Dawson to Bow Street himself.

As he reached down to drag his prisoner to his feet, he heard a footstep behind him.

"Dan?"

Captain Ellis stood in the doorway, Nick beside him, both still panting from their run.

Dan got painfully to his feet. "We need the fire engines."

Ellis grinned. "For that big fire, do you mean? Already sent for."

"And there's a riot. You need to send some men."

"Already done. You look as if you need a doctor."

"It's nothing. Can you send a couple of men to Bow Street with Dawson?"

Ellis shouted an order over his shoulder and two patrolmen stepped into the ruin and dragged Dawson away.

"Where's Nick?"

The captain looked round in surprise. "He was here a minute ago."

No doubt he had gone to find Ann. Dan was not surprised. He would not have wanted to hang around law officers himself at their age. Nick had already done more than could be reasonably expected of him. Pity, though. Dan would have liked to thank him.

He picked his way over the uneven ground.

"Where are you going?" asked Ellis.

"To Metcalf's."

"Why?"

"Because he's the only suspect for Kean's death still alive. He's not likely to offer a confession though, not unless I can find some hard evidence to link him to the murder."

"Like what?"

"I don't know. There's probably nothing. But I won't know till I look."


It took Dan only a few minutes to reach Metcalf's rooms on Joyners Street. He banged on the door. A dim light appeared in the dusty glass above it, but no one came to let him in. He stopped knocking and listened to shuffling feet in the hall.

"Bow Street Officer! Open up or I'll have you arrested."

This provoked a sob, followed by the squeal of bolts and locks. A cross-eyed serving girl in a nightgown and heavily patched slippers stared out at him. Dan pushed his way inside.

"Which rooms are Metcalf's?"

"Mrs Carter! Mrs Carter!" the girl screeched. "There's a Runner here."

A door opened upstairs and the landlady, trailing tawdry lace and ribbons from her voluminous nightgown, appeared in the doorway. In one hand she held a candle, in the other a poker.

"Haven't I told you no one is to be let into the house after midnight?" she called.

Dan loped up the stairs. "I need to look at Metcalf's room."

"Mr Metcalf? Is he in trouble?"

"Just tell me where his room is."

"It's upstairs. But you can't –"

Dan snatched the candle and left her protesting on the landing. It was a large room, sparsely furnished. Only a jug of spills adorned the mantelpiece. The tabletop was bare, as was the table by the bed. There were no books, no letters, no London Corresponding Society magazines, pamphlets or papers. There was no shaving soap or razor on the wash stand; Dan found them stowed in a case in a drawer in the bedside table. He drew back a curtain over an alcove. Behind it were two pairs of polished boots and two identical suits of clothes. He searched the pockets: empty. There was nothing to suggest that Metcalf had recently been here, let alone link him to the London Corresponding Society, the United Patriots or Kean's death. Hardly anything to suggest he had ever lived here at all.

The mistress had gone back to her room to have hysterics, leaving the servant girl waiting in the cold hall to lock up after him. He thrust the candle at her, with a warning that some colleagues would call in later to take Metcalf's things and in the meantime no one was to go into the room.

The door of Broomhall's shop stood open and lights blazed from every window. Despite the lateness of the hour, the street was thronged with onlookers: neighbours who had left their warm beds; late-night revellers; market traders pausing on their way to work. At sight of Dan they all craned forward excitedly, hoping to see some new wonder.

He passed through the line of constables who were keeping back the crowd and asked the man on the door, "Who's in charge?"

"Officer Macmanus," he answered.

Inside, constables tramped about filling boxes and bags with papers. The massive locks on the strong box had been broken open, the trays emptied, the shop goods tipped into a sack. At the back of the building, men crashed around Broomhall's tiny workshop.

Dan ran upstairs. In the parlour the men had pulled out drawers, emptied cupboards, slashed cushions and dismantled furniture. They had even taken the prints off the walls and cut them out of their frames. Dan heard the racket of the same process going on next door. He pushed open the bedroom door.

Principal Officer Macmanus stood in the middle of the room, a pinch of snuff between his fingers, directing operations. He considered it beneath his rank to do the work himself. He had been a hatter before joining the force, though he had since reinvented himself as a gentleman investigator. He caught sight of Dan and with the air of a great man bestowing a favour he cried, "Foster! Let me shake your hand, man."

The men cheered as Macmanus pumped Dan's arm up and down, oblivious to his winces.

"Bloody good job, Foster," he boomed. "We've netted the lot of them."

"What have you found here?"

"The usual trash. Seditious books and pamphlets. Notes from their meetings."

"That'll be the London Corresponding Society. The United Patriots didn't keep notes."

"Correspondents, Patriots, it's all the same." Macmanus pointed at a roll of drawings on the stripped bed. "Found these plans of Warren House too. So that clinches it so far as Broomhall is concerned. All the proof we need to hang him."

"Broomhall is dead." Briefly, Dan told Macmanus what had happened at the warehouse. "I wondered if you could spare a couple of men to go through Metcalf's room. I think either he or Broomhall killed Kean. I've just been to his place but couldn't find anything. I also wondered if you'd object if I had a quick look round here too."

"Help yourself. We'll keep an eye out in here."

Dan went into the parlour and sorted through the mess. He found nothing and went back to the bedroom to let Macmanus know he had finished. The plans of Warren House and the surrounding area still lay on the bed. While he waited for Macmanus to finish overseeing some packing, Dan looked through them.

"These must have been supplied by an insider," he said. "A servant maybe. We need to get some officers over there before news of the raid on the Chequers reaches Wimbledon, else whoever it was will be gone."

"You're right. I'll get someone on to it. Find anything to help with the murder?"

"No. Didn't really expect to." Dan came to the last drawing. Someone had scribbled notes in the corner. It was a detailed description of the strength, route and routines of the horse patrol out of Wimbledon police depot. It too must have been supplied by someone on the inside. By a police officer. What was worse, Dan thought he recognised the handwriting.

"What's that you've got there?"

Dan looked up. "Nothing. I'll take these downstairs and put them in one of the crates."

"Right...you, man, lift down that hat box."

Macmanus was already refocussing on his search. Dan took the roll of papers and went out onto the landing, pulling the door to behind him. Here he stopped for a moment. There was no one on the stairs. He extracted the annotated plan from the bundle, put the rest on the floor and folded it up so the handwriting was uppermost. Then he opened his pocket book and took out the note he had taken from Kean's home: "14 B&C 1/9". It was not much to compare, and he only had a strip of light from the doorway, but he had seen larger samples of Kean's writing when he searched his desk. He was as certain as he could be that the writing was the same. Kean had been feeding information to Broomhall.

So Broomhall had known who Kean was. Did that make it less likely that he had killed Kean? Perhaps he got rid of him after he had the information he wanted, just as he had shot the sailor who brought him the message from France.

And why had Kean supplied the information anyway?

All he had were questions and the slender hope that he could get Metcalf to answer them. There was nothing else to try. He folded the sheet and shoved it into his pocket, picked up the rest of the roll and continued downstairs. He deposited the bulk of the plans in a container with the other confiscated papers and set off for Bow Street.

A row of covered wagons had drawn up outside the Magistrates' Office ready to convey the prisoners to Newgate. They were guarded by the militia, though the populace had so far shown no sympathy for the arrested radicals. If the United Patriots had not been involved in body snatching it might have been a different story. As it was, people stood around gaping with curiosity and swapping outlandish theories about the captured revolutionaries: they'd been rounded up after a battle at the gates of St James's Palace; they'd been taken off a French ship that had sailed up the Thames to Westminster; they'd been discovered performing Druidical rites in a cellar in Rotherhithe, stabbing an effigy of the King and casting spells against his life.

The corridor was so crowded Dan had difficulty opening the door. Inside prisoners huddled together, some already processed and waiting to go to Newgate, others still to be called into the courtroom for a preliminary examination by Sir William Addington and Sir Richard Ford. Dan saw Ellis in the main office and struggled over to him.

"Is Metcalf still here? I need to question him."

"Yes, he was in the last group taken before the magistrates. They should be coming out any moment now."

The clank of chain, tramp of feet, and cries of "Make way, there!" from the direction of the courtroom confirmed Ellis's prediction. Dan moved to intercept the prisoners' escort and request that Metcalf be released to him for questioning. He was a couple of feet away from the door when the tramping became a scuffle, the cries exclamations of alarm, the clank the clash of drawn cutlass.

"Look out there!" someone yelled.

The warning was immediately followed by a gunshot. Then there was silence. It lasted only a few seconds, time enough for Dan to push his way into the corridor.

The door on the courtyard was already filling with clerks and ushers who had rushed from the court room to see what had happened. The prisoners who had just been committed to gaol huddled against the wall, struggling to distance themselves from the catastrophe, though spattered with gore. A dark figure lay on the ground. It was surrounded by four guards, gazing down at the pool of red creeping across the filthy floorboards. Jones stood by uttering strange cries of distress.

And no wonder. The man on the floor had had his head blown off.

Dan grabbed the patrolman's arm and shook him out of his stupor. "What's happened here?"

Jones, unable to tear his gaze away from the body, answered, "He g...grabbed my p...pistol. I couldn't stop him. He shot himself."

Dan looked down at the corpse. In spite of the ravaged face, he recognised him. It was Metcalf.

# Chapter Twenty-Eight

Dan shrugged on his shirt as the doctor Sir William Addington had summoned to his office signalled that his examination was over.

"Don't think I've ever seen a man in such good condition," the doctor said. "Stomach like a plank. And that's what saved you from any serious damage as far as I can see. You're severely contused, as you don't need me to tell you. You need to rest and take it easy for a few days. But apart from that, you'll do."

"Excellent!" said Sir William. "Send me your bill."

The doctor snapped shut his bag, picked up his hat and coat and left.

It was late Friday morning, and peace and order had been restored to Bow Street. The Patriots were safely locked away and Sir Richard Ford had gone back to the Home Office to start building his case against them, after complaining at length about the deaths of the two key figures. Broomhall's body, or what was left of it, had been found lying face down on the threshold of the locked room in the warehouse. He had come round, crawled to the door, tried to get out...Dan pushed images of the man's last moments out of his mind.

Eight bodies had been found in the yard. Six of them were the shrouded corpses Dan had seen the resurrectionists load onto their carts. Of these, one had been caught in the fire; three had been so mauled about by the crowd they were unrecognisable; and the other two had been buried in a pauper's grave as no one had come forward to claim them.

The remaining bodies were those of Lucas and Smith,

whom Dan had seen fall into the hands of the mob. That left Nipps, who had used him as a punch bag, and Trinder, who had intended to cut his throat, unaccounted for.

"You've earned your reward, Foster," Sir William said. "And I shall take great pleasure in making sure that Sir Richard pays it."

"I don't know so much," Dan answered. "Both my suspects are dead and I still don't know for certain who killed Kean."

"I would have thought Metcalf's suicide was a fair indicator of his guilt."

"Maybe. I would much prefer to know."

"I think there's no doubt that it was one or other of them. And as they have both been served as they merit, we can be satisfied with the outcome of the case. And now, you should take the doctor's advice and go home and get some rest."

It was nearly mid-day when Dan left the office. He was halfway along Bow Street when church bells started to ring. From the east and west, north and south, the air reverberated with the sound. In every church in Southwark and beyond, the ringers woke the impressive notes of the great bells.

Men, women and children, already excited by the previous night's events, abandoned shop, workroom, tavern and house and rushed into the street. The news flew from mouth to mouth: the guns had gone off at Tower Hill, signalling that Admiral Duncan had defeated the Dutch fleet at Camperdown. With his ally smashed, Frenchie was in no doubt about who ruled the waves! For years the British had feared invasion; it would never happen now. Strangers hugged strangers, men and women seized one another and danced, children cheered, and the drink flowed.

So, Dan thought, everything could go on as it was before. There would be no invasion, no revolution, no change in the ministry, no aristocrats' heads on spikes. Children would still live on the streets, and fat magistrates would continue to hang them. Hard to see sometimes why people cheered.

Only the alternative was worse: imagine being governed by

men like Broomhall. All the same, perhaps it wasn't so difficult to see what drew men, good men, to causes like his. Men like Kean for example. What had happened to make him betray the King and Country he had served all his adult life, first as a soldier, then a law officer? It was not money troubles, as Dan knew from his search of Kean's bureau, which had turned up only settled and receipted bills. Perhaps he could find an answer if he could discover something of Kean's state of mind in the weeks before he died.

Dan pushed his way through the carousing couples in Long Acre and turned into a courtyard full of excited neighbours calling the news of Duncan's victory to one another. A frowsy woman opened Mrs Kean's door to him. Her name, he remembered, was Mrs Martin. The room was full of packing cases, books and knick-knacks wrapped in paper, and much of the furniture had already gone. Dan glanced over to where the bureau had stood. The tomahawks had been taken from the wall.

Mrs Kean stood by a chair covered in a pile of bed linens, folding them up and putting them into a box with sprigs of dried lavender.

"Officer Foster, isn't it?" she said. "I'm sorry I can't offer you any refreshment."

"Where are you going?" he asked, taking off his hat.

"Back to my father's farm in Kent. Here, Mrs Martin, would you like this coverlet? I've already packed one."

"You really don't want it? Well, if you're sure, dearie." Mrs Martin added it to the pile of gifts she had already accumulated.

Mrs Kean looked around helplessly then moved to clear the chair.

"I'm fine standing," Dan said. "I just came to tell you that the men responsible for your husband's death were killed last night when we tried to arrest them." There was no need to inflict the details on her.

Her hand flew up to her mouth and she tottered. Dan

caught her, swept the linen off the chair and lowered her into it. He fanned her with his hat.

"Is there any brandy in the house?" he asked Mrs Martin.

Mrs Martin, who stood flapping her hand in front of her face and gasping, "La! La!", calmed herself long enough to remember that she had seen a half-full bottle somewhere and went unerringly to the basket where it was stowed. She unwrapped a couple of glasses, poured out the spirit and held them out to Dan. Dan refused the one for himself and, while Mrs Martin happily guzzled it, held the other to Mrs Kean's lips. She took a sip, coughed and pushed it away.

"Thank you. It's just the surprise…I hadn't heard anything from Sir William."

"He'll be writing to you officially," Dan said. "But I wanted you to know as soon as possible."

"Thank you." A thought struck her. "Was it you that arrested them?"

"I was there, yes."

"I'd rather they had hanged, but I'm glad they paid for what they did."

"La! La!" said Mrs Martin, just to remind them she was still there, and poured herself another measure of brandy.

"Do you know why they killed him?" Mrs Kean asked.

"They were planning to assassinate the King and his ministers. Your husband infiltrated their gang and found out what they were up to."

Mrs Kean straightened her back proudly. "So he died defending his sovereign?"

With the real purpose of his visit yet to be achieved, Dan was reluctant to reveal the truth. He "hummed" non-committally.

"When are you leaving?" he asked.

"My father is coming for me in two days."

"You should get Sir William's official letter before then, but I'll take a note of your new address just in case there's any delay."

She gave it to him and he wrote it in his notebook.

"He told me about you," she added. "He said you were a fighting man, one of the best he'd ever seen."

"That was generous of him. And he was a good police officer. Never gave up on a case."

She smiled. "Yes, he sometimes made it something of a crusade."

"I remember you told me he talked to you about his work."

"Yes."

"But then he stopped. Do you remember when that was?"

"Why, is it important?"

"I'm just trying to get some dates clear in my mind. For the trials. Kean hadn't had time to write up his notes." If he had ever intended to.

Mrs Martin quietly sloshed another brandy into her glass. Mrs Kean's brow puckered, thinking.

"It was the start of August, just after the Hobbs case. You know it?"

"I can't say that I do," Dan lied. He wanted Mrs Kean to keep talking.

"Esther Hobbs. She was raped and murdered. She was only a child. George saw the body. He said it reminded him of something he had seen when he was in the Army, he would never tell me what it was. He started having nightmares and drinking too much. Then he hardly slept; he worked all day and night on the investigation. They charged a young man for it, but he got off. George said it was because the judge knew the young man's father. He was so angry, as much with himself as anything. He said he should have made a stronger case, one no one could ignore, not even a corrupt judge."

Every officer had a case like that, Dan thought, the one that got under your skin; the one where justice failed; the one you remembered to your dying day. And now he thought he understood what had turned Kean into a traitor. One horrific case too many; one slapdash trial too many; one hasty judge too many. Kean had given years of honest service to the job before he had cracked under the strain. He had looked square at the rottenness at the heart of the system, and he had decided that only sweeping the whole lot away would make any difference.

At least that was how Dan imagined it. He would never know for certain what had been in Kean's mind when he went to Broomhall with information that would help him start a revolution. Now Dan had to decide what to do about it. He could hand in the plan with Kean's handwriting on it. It would destroy the dead man's reputation, and the good work he had done would be forgotten. His widow would lose the solace of thinking her husband had died a hero. She would also lose any reward monies owing to him from the service.

Dan could do that, but he had seen the girl's body too.

# Chapter Twenty-Nine

Home for Dan was the rooms in Newport Street which he had taken over from Walter when he returned to Barcombe. He had only been back to Russell Street to collect a few things, and neither Caroline nor Eleanor had spoken to him. Their mother had stood in front of the kitchen door like a benevolent guard dog, but a determined one. He could have put his foot down, reminded the women that this was his house, Caroline was his wife, that the rights of ownership were all his. But what would have been the point? He did not want to live in the sight of the women he had hurt.

It was a temporary arrangement, but he had no idea what might be a more permanent one. And there had hardly been much time to think about it. He wondered what Caroline and Eleanor would think of him when they read the news that the United Patriots' plot to overthrow the Government had been crushed. Would Eleanor remember the day they had talked about it, her concern for the danger he was in? Would Caroline forget her jealous rage if only for a moment, and feel even the slightest bit of pride in him for the part he had played?

He could have gone home, played the conquering hero. Being a hero was easier than being a husband. He should never have married Caroline, never have admitted his feelings for Eleanor, never lain with Anna Halling, never have had Davy... No. He refused to regret that. He had no idea why or how it had happened; it was the strangest falling in love he had ever known. In only a week the child had wrapped himself around his heart, bound him tight with love. How did they do that with their wailing and puling and kicking and laughing and gurgling? He had no idea. All he knew was that where Davy was, home was.

Yet he did not want to go there just yet. For one thing, he would never sleep with the uproar of the Camperdown celebrations going on. For another, he had promised Rosie that he would hire a servant to look after her. He set off for Southwark to search for Nick.

It was dark by the time he found the boy, scavenging in Honey Lane Market. The hall was an empty, echoing space of shuttered stalls, scraps and mangy dogs. It did not take long to strike their bargain: Nick would get his food and lodging in return for helping Rosie about the house.

"There's a place for Ann too, if she wants to come," Dan said.

Nick wiped his sleeve across his nose. "Her and the others've gone. Said I brung the Runners on 'em." The boy sniffed again. "Shan't miss 'em."

To save the boy's dignity, Dan took the declaration at face value. He took Nick to the gymnasium. Noah had experience of dealing with a verminous, filthy child. Between them they shaved the boy's head and burned his clothes, along with the lice that had made their home in them. Then Noah marched the boy round to the baths for a long soak and scrub while Dan dug out some of his old clothes.

Paul had gone out to join the street party and there was no one in the gymnasium. It was quiet save for the occasional cheers and shouts that drifted in. Dan sat down by the fire. He reached into his pocket and drew out Broomhall's plan with Kean's notes on it. He looked at it for a moment, then slowly tore it in pieces and fed the fragments into the flames.

When it was all gone he sat back in the chair. By the time Noah and Nick returned he was fast asleep. Noah threw a blanket over him and sent Nick to spend the night in Dan's bed.

Dan let himself into the house in Newport Street one Monday evening towards the end of October after spending the day in the office writing up reports and putting in a good word with

Sir William Addington for Patrolman Jones. It was the first opportunity Sir William had had to consider how to deal with the young man, who had been suspended from duty pending his decision. Dan agreed that Jones was not the brightest spark, but pointed out that he was eager to do his duty and with time would improve. In the end the magistrate agreed to give him another chance: he had three months to prove himself capable, and any more mistakes in that time would see him out of the service.

The landlady was in the hall before Dan had taken two steps towards the staircase.

"Oh, Mr Foster, something dreadful! As I was coming back from doing my shopping this afternoon, I came upon two low fellows conferring outside the area railings. I am sure the villains are planning to break in and rob us."

Yesterday it had been beggars sitting on the doorstep and creating a nuisance; the day before she had had him checking the locks on the downstairs windows.

"They were probably just two men meeting in the street."

"Oh, no, they were up to no good. I could tell from the way they talked."

"What did they say?"

"I couldn't understand it. It was a vile, gypsy language such as rogues speak."

"Arey sneaks touting the case, eh?"

"Why, that's exactly what I heard them say! I daresay you must have to know their manner of speaking in your line of work."

Dan, who had been brought up by thieves, said, "I've picked up a bit here and there. But, Mrs Hampton, I can't arrest men for talking."

"But they were conspiring, Mr Foster, conspiring. Shouldn't you put a constable outside the house?"

"It's too desperate a case for that, Mrs Hampton. What I need from you is a detailed description of the men that I can take into Bow Street tomorrow."

"One of them had wicked, bulging eyes –"

"It would be better if you could write it out. Then I can get it copied and mobilise the force to go out looking for them. Do you think you could do that for me, Mrs Hampton?"

"I'll do it straight away, Mr Foster. Shall I bring it up to you later?"

"Perhaps you could give it to me in the morning before I set off for work, Mrs Hampton?"

"I will."

With that she flounced off to her spotless parlour where, Dan presumed, she spent the evening drawing up her account of the burglars. He continued up the stairs. Outside the door he paused. There was a voice he had not heard here before. Wondering what new trouble awaited him, he turned the handle and went inside.

Caroline sat on the armchair near the fire with Davy on her lap. Rosie sat opposite her, and Nick occupied a stool between them. He jumped up to take Dan's coat and hat. The clothes that had hung off him when he was first put into them were already a better fit. Rosie had also started dosing him for his ringworm, and after only a week of eating well and sleeping in safety he was beginning to look more civilised, though he had not yet got used to wearing shoes.

Warily, Dan kept an eye on his wife as he let the boy help him.

Caroline returned his gaze with a mocking smile. "I'm not going to dash the baby's brains out on the fender if that's what you're worried about."

Rosie gasped.

"I would like to talk to Mr Foster in private," Caroline continued.

Dan nodded at Rosie and Nick. The girl moved to take Davy from Caroline, but she held on to him. He did not seem to mind: he slept contentedly in her arms. With a lingering look at the infant, Rosie carried her work and a candle into the bedroom. Nick took the opportunity to indulge his lingering passion for wandering the streets and slipped outside.

"Sit down," Caroline said. "Or am I to break my neck craning up at you?"

Dan pulled up a wooden chair and placed it opposite her.

"I wasn't expecting you."

"That's because I didn't tell you I was coming...So this is where you've been hiding, is it?"

He followed her gaze to a pile of bedding in the corner.

"Rosie and Davy have the bedroom."

She arched an eyebrow. "I'm glad to hear you're keeping it in your breeches now."

"She's just a girl, for God's sake. What do you want?"

She ignored the question. "Where did you pick up the ugly boy?"

"In Southwark. He saved my life. Why are you here, Caroline?"

She ignored him for a moment and made cooing noises at the baby. "He's got your eyes, Dan. Watchful. And you can't tell what's going on behind them."

Dan put out his hand and touched his son gently on the head before frowning at his wife. "What is it you want?"

She looked at him for a moment, then with an impatient gesture looked away. "I didn't mean it to be like this. We haven't got off to a very good start, have we?"

Dan made no answer.

"You ask what I want? I want my husband back. Oh, not to be like we were before," she hurried on before he could speak. "I want you to come home, Dan, you and the baby. He's your son, after all. A part of you." She smiled sadly. "That gives me half of what I wanted. And look on the bright side. I get a baby without having to go through the agonies of giving birth to him myself."

"You want us to live together as a family?"

"I don't want to have the neighbours looking at me pityingly because my husband prefers to live with a milk-faced girl and an ugly boy," she said sharply. She checked herself. "No, that's not what I mean. I rehearsed it over and over in my head on the way here and now it's coming out all wrong. But it is what I want. You, me and the baby. The way things should have been."

"Did it mean so much to you, to have one of our own?"

"I thought things would be better if we did. Didn't you?"

"Sometimes."

"Then will you come home, Dan? Can't we try again?"

He hesitated.

She looked away from him. "Eleanor isn't there. She's gone to Aunt Mary's."

Mrs Harper's sister lived in Leeds. "Is she coming back?" he asked after a moment.

"Captain Ellis certainly hopes so. He's called to ask after her nearly every day."

What else could he have expected? He had never had anything to offer Eleanor but illicit love and he had led her to believe he was above that. And then he had lain with another woman. She had every right to find happiness with someone else. It was time for him to face up to the fact of his marriage, stop pretending things could be any other than what they were. Caroline did not forgive him, and he did not ask her to. But if they both tried harder they could make something out of the wreckage. Neither of them would get exactly what they wanted. But it was something.

He felt Caroline's hand on his arm. "Dan?"

"Rosie will be happy to go back to Barcombe, but I've offered Nick a home. I can't abandon him now."

She pouted distastefully. "Then I suppose he'll have to come with you. But in return."

"Yes?"

"I don't like Davy. I want to choose a different name for the boy."

"Like what?"

"Alexander."

"Alexander? Who do we know called Alexander?"

"No one. I just like the name."

Dan glanced down at his son. It seemed a small price to pay for his safety and security. And if he was honest, he had never cared much for his name either. So here was something for them to agree on. A good omen, surely.

"Alexander it is."

# Chapter Thirty

By the time the King's carriage emerged from St James's Park and passed through Storey's Gate, the approach to Westminster Bridge was almost blocked by the festive crowds. Dan, one of a line of officers and constables whose task was to clear a path for the royal progress, ushered the excited men, women and children back. They took the shoving in good part, as eager to see the King pass them as he was to go by.

King George was on his way to Greenwich to join the *Royal Charlotte* which would take him to the Nore to visit his victorious fleet. There, with much firing of salutes, he would present Admiral Duncan with a sword, hand out titles to officers who had distinguished themselves at Camperdown, and allow the sailors in their best uniforms to cheer him. The vessels in the Thames were a gay spectacle of flag and pennant, and many of the onlookers sported plaid scarves, belts and neckerchiefs in a variety of patterns and colours in honour of the Scottish Admiral.

Dan glanced over his shoulder and caught his first sight of the carriage which had brought its royal occupant from Windsor. Every now and again the King waved, sending his subjects into paroxysms of delight. Dan saw a flash of yellow inside the vehicle and recognised John Townsend's canary waistcoat. The Bow Street officer sat beside his royal charge, smirking proudly. Dan wondered that he didn't give a regal wave out of the other window.

As the people pressed forward for a better view, Dan and his men had a hard time to keep them from tumbling into the path of the vehicle. Crushing one of his loyal subjects to death under his carriage wheels would prove something of a dampener on the King's royal celebrations. Luckily, the bottleneck forced it to go at a walking pace.

"Make way, there!" Dan shouted. "Keep a tight hold of your child, missus."

The woman addressed shot him an indignant glance but did look around for her little boy, who clung nervously to her skirts.

"Step away!" Dan pushed back a young, well-dressed man, a medical student from the drunken look of him.

On his left he glimpsed a woman in a dark cloak. Her face was pale, her eyes wide, her lips pressed shut in a white line. Dan thought he recognised her, but as she disappeared behind a fat merchant did not have time to place her. He was distracted by some foolishness on his right, and when he looked back again the woman in the dark cloak had made her way to the front of the crowd. Suddenly she slipped under the linked arms of the constables, ran towards the carriage and raised her right arm.

"Gun!" someone yelled.

There was a panicky scramble away from danger, the disorder spreading and made worse because no one knew what they were running from. The row of constables fragmented, the men unsure which way to go. Dan elbowed aside the officer nearest to him and lunged towards the carriage, put himself in the woman's line of sight. He was dimly aware of Townsend's contorted face in the window, one hand pressed on His Majesty's chest pushing him back in his seat, the other reaching towards his yellow waistcoat for his gun.

The woman faltered as the new target presented itself to her aim. "You!" she hissed. "You killed him!"

Dan hardly had time to realise that it was Mrs Chambers before the bullet hit him.

When he woke it was broad daylight and he was lying in his own bed. A strong, eye-watering smell hung in the air: someone must be frying beef and onions.

Why had they left him to sleep in? He should be up and doing...he pushed aside the bedclothes, raised himself into a sitting position, swung his legs over the edge of the bed. To his surprise, he was left feeling as weak as if he had been in a ten-round fight with England champion John Jackson. He could not bend his right arm. He looked down and saw it was bandaged.

"Lie back, lovey."

He felt strong, warm hands on his shoulders pushing him back onto the pillows.

"Mother? What are you doing here?"

Mrs Harper pulled the covers back over him, poured a glass of water and put it to his lips. "Caroline's gone downstairs for a rest."

"But why am I here?"

"You don't remember?"

All that came at first was tumult and blare: shouting, screaming, horses whinnying, weapons rattling, a flash of light and an explosion. There had been a sensation of falling from a great height, his head striking something hard, then a feeling as if he lay at the bottom of a river looking up at arms and legs flailing through the water above him.

"She shot me. Mrs Chambers."

Mrs Harper nodded. "The wicked, adulterous thing!"

He passed his left hand over his chest. "Where?"

"Your arm. The bullet missed the bone, thank goodness. You would have been well days ago if that fool of a doctor hadn't let it get infected."

He looked at her in dismay. "Will I be able to use it again?"

"Onions."

He looked at her uncomprehendingly. Perhaps he was delirious.

"Onions," Mrs Harper repeated. "None of those new-fangled pastes and powders. A bit of onion on the wound and it came up right as rain."

"So that's what I could smell. I thought it was someone

221

frying something." A new thought struck him. "I could eat."

She beamed at him. "That's a good sign. I'll go and fetch you a bit of broth."

The next time he woke, Caroline was standing by the bed holding Alexander.

"Look, Alex," she said. "Daddy's awake."

She swung the baby down so that Dan could press his lips to a fat little cheek. Then she sat on the side of the bed and plumped the child into Dan's lap. He shifted position to make the child comfortable, wincing at the pain of moving his arm. He and Caroline leaned over the baby, heads almost touching. Her face was clear and bright, her eyes shining, and she was smiling. She looked up, saw he was gazing at her and in confusion busied herself adjusting the child's dress.

"We thought we'd lost you, Danny," she said, without lifting her head.

He laid his hand over hers. "I'm still here."

She raised her face, full of anxious appeal. "It will be all right now, won't it?"

"It will."

Alex began to cry. The door opened and Mrs Harper bustled in carrying a pile of clean bed linen. "Caroline! Dan's not up to having the babe crawling all over him!"

Dan and Caroline exchanged a conspiratorial smile.

"But I am," he said.

"Are you awake, son?"

Dan opened his eyes and sat up. Moving about came easily now, and his arm was more stiff than painful.

"I could get up," he said.

"That's the way," Noah answered.

This time when Dan put his feet on the floor, he felt he could trust them to bear his weight. He was still unsteady, but that was only because he had not used his muscles enough.

"I need to do some training," he said, lowering himself into the chair by the hearth.

Noah sat down next to him and reached into a bag he had brought with him. "I thought it was time. I brought you this." He handed Dan a pair of wooden bottle-shaped weights.

"Thanks, Dad. I'll start with them straight away."

"Do a few stretches too. And get that shoulder moving." Noah gave him the familiar appraising look, as if assessing his injuries after a bout in the ring. He nodded to himself, satisfied with what he saw, then pulled a folded newspaper from his pocket. "Have you seen this?"

"No. What is it?"

Noah held it out.

"You read it to me, Dad."

"It's a few days old, you understand," Noah said. He followed the lines with his finger, pronounced the words carefully.

*Attempt on the King's life foiled by courage of Bow Street Officer. Yesterday morning as the King was approaching Westminster Bridge en route to Greenwich to join the royal yacht, a mad woman leapt out of the crowd and attempted to fire a gun into His Majesty's carriage. His Majesty's life was saved by the quick action of the Bow Street officer in attendance upon him. Mr John Townsend is well known about the town –*

"Townsend!" Dan exclaimed. "Well, I'll be damned!"

*– well known about the town as an officer of courage and resourcefulness. Without a thought for his own safety, he sprang to His Majesty's defence and by his quick response enabled the constables to seize and disarm the deranged creature. We understand that one of the constables was slightly injured in the affray.*

"Constable!" Dan cried indignantly.

*His loyal subjects apprehended that the King had
come to no harm with expressions of the most lively joy.
His Majesty continued his engagement, and arrived
at Lord Hood's apartments in Greenwich Hospital at
nine o'clock. The West London Militia was drawn up
at the entrance to the Hospital and played during the
whole time the King remained there. The Princess of
Wales had arrived moments before and their meeting
was cordial on both sides. The King was conducted on
board the Royal Charlotte yacht in a six-oared barge.*

"This bit's not very interesting." Noah skipped on to the end.

*The woman, who gave her name as 'A Friend of Liberty',
was taken to Newgate where she was examined by the
prison doctor, who pronounced it as his opinion that
the woman's senses were disordered, but whether the
disorder is permanent or temporary has yet to be seen.*

Noah lowered the paper.

"The blasted conceited puppy!" Dan said.

"He's that and more, is John Townsend," Noah agreed. "And
it's said the King has given him a handsome reward. Ought to
be yours by rights."

"That it ought. But what can I do? I can't call the man
a liar. Not in public, anyway."

"What about talking to Sir William?"

"Won't do me any good to go bleating to the magistrate.
No, Dad, the best thing to do is let it drop. If kissing the King's
boots means so much to Townsend, wish him joy of it! What
has become of Mrs Chambers?"

"Tried last week and found guilty, but on account of her sex
and the state of her mind, the King commuted her sentence to
transportation."

"A hard sentence enough for a woman like her," Dan said.

"She did try to kill you."

"She thinks I'm to blame for her lover's death. And in truth, it is thanks to me that Broomhall died."

"He wouldn't have died if he hadn't pursued a criminal course, and no fault lies with you."

"If you say so…now, what did you say I should do with those weights?"

# Chapter Thirty-One

Dan waited until he heard the front door close before he got out of bed. The cheerful chatter of his wife and mother-in-law drifted up to the window, quickly faded away. Nick had been sent to the coal dealer's to chase up a late delivery. The house was empty. Dan opened the closet and selected some clothes: a good, long jacket, clean shirt and stockings, waistcoat and breeches, and his favourite boots. He took his time; no one would be home for ages and he would be gone by then.

A few minutes later he stepped outside. It was good to be back on the street amongst the noise and movement, to breathe the cold air, suck in the smells of horses, drains, fried food, cheap perfume, filthy beggars, smoking chimneys, rotting refuse, and more: all the nasty, squalid, familiar odours of London. For days he had sat in the house fretting to be out, but Caroline had insisted he was not ready to return to work. Yet his mind had given him no rest. Either Broomhall or Metcalf had killed Kean, and now both were dead.

That should have been enough to satisfy him. But it wasn't. Dawson had disposed of the body at Broomhall's command, but according to him it was not Broomhall who killed Kean. Metcalf may have had a motive for the murder, and his suicide was suggestive of guilt. That it was one or other or both of them together was likely. But Dan didn't know, and that irked him. None of the United Patriots they'd arrested knew anything, and there was no reason not to believe them. Who was there left to ask?

There was one person who had been close to Broomhall: Mrs Chambers. But whether she would talk to him was another matter. Still, he had to try, or never rest satisfied with himself.

The entrance to Newgate was busy as usual. Visiting friends and relatives passed in and out. Tradesmen brought supplies; constables and turnkeys went about their business; street women and beggars vied for attention. Dan walked through the archway, paused to announce his arrival to the porter. He stopped at the sight of the well-dressed woman sitting primly on a chair behind the porter's desk. She had a book open in front of her, and seemed unaware of the jangle and dirt of her surroundings.

"Miss Chambers!"

She looked up, a rebuff on her lips. When she saw who it was she snapped the book shut, dropped it into her bag and jumped up to meet him.

"Mr Bright!"

"Foster."

"Yes, of course. Principal Officer Foster of Bow Street. I heard you had been injured. I hope you are well now?"

"I'm well, thank you. I thought you would be in Liverpool by this time."

"Oh, Liverpool is quite out. Father and I have opened a bookshop on the Strand. Chambers and Daughter. It sounds well, does it not?"

"So no more bawdy pictures?"

"As a matter of fact, I…we have decided to continue that part of the business, in a separate workshop. It is the only way we can finance the shop at the moment."

She at least had the decency to blush. Dan suspected that "at the moment" was likely to turn into "a very long time". Miss Chambers was a young woman determined to make her way in the world. She would go where the money was.

"What are you doing here? Won't they let you in to visit your mother?"

"I can go in if I choose, but I don't choose. I'm waiting for Father."

"Don't you visit her?"

"Not I! I hope never to see the woman again. She's broken Father's heart."

"Which is surely a matter between her and your Father. And if he can see her –"

"Then why won't I? I won't. That is all."

"She's your mother, and for the best part of your life she's looked after you. And your Father loves her."

"And look where that's got us. No, Mr Foster, the sooner she's gone, the better."

"For you, do you mean?"

"And for Father and the girls. But you have no right to speak to me like this. It is not your place."

"You're right. But I tell you this, Miss Chambers. Whatever crimes your mother committed, she's about to pay a terrible price for them. You may have very few chances to see her in this world again. And one day you're going to wake up and be sorry that you never said a kind word to her in her time of trouble – never said any word at all."

"How dare you! You – you –"

Dan interrupted her. "Mr Chambers, sir! Your daughter was just telling me about your new venture."

Chambers shuffled towards them. He stooped more than Dan remembered, and his face was more lined, his eyes red, and he was thin and gaunt. The hand he placed in Dan's trembled.

"Mr Foster, how can I ever expect you to forgive us? But my wife – she was not in her right mind. If you could see her now, how guilt torments her, hear her beg me to abandon her, to let them send her to the hulk as soon as possible."

"I assure you I have not come to add to her torments," Dan answered. "I only wish to ask her a few questions that are still unanswered. Details only."

Chambers grasped Dan's hand in both of his. "Bless you, Mr Foster, bless you!"

Dan awkwardly freed himself. "You don't have to thank me."

"It was a kind of madness, you know," Chambers said. "A kind of madness."

"Come along, Father," Evelyn said. "It won't do you any good to linger in this unhealthy spot."

"Of course, my dear. Perhaps you will call on us at the new shop, Mr Foster?"

"Yes, I will." Dan tipped his hat. "Good day, Miss Chambers."

She took her father's arm and nodded coldly.

Dan walked through the court to the women's block. A turnkey met him and led him into the building. They went up a couple of flights of stairs where the man unlocked the door to a long chamber crowded with beds. Women of all ages clustered on and around them, smoking, drinking, talking, arguing, weeping, nursing babies.

The gaoler pointed. "She's over there."

Dan thanked him and slipped some coins into his outstretched hand. He made his way along the filthy room, ignoring the whistles and catcalls. The air was pungent with the smell of bodies, piss pots, foul breath.

Mrs Chambers sat on her narrow bed, her hands in her lap, gazing vacantly into space. With an effort she tore herself away from whatever gloomy visions occupied her and looked up at him.

"It's you," she said dully.

Thanks to her husband's care, her appearance was clean, though she was no longer the image of the busy, prosperous shopkeeper. Her dress hung off her thin body and her hair was carelessly arranged. The parcel of food Mr Chambers had left her was already nearly empty, most of it taken from under her apathetic nose by her neighbours who sat in a huddle, gobbling the pies and cake.

"Can I sit down?"

She shrugged and swung her legs over the side of the iron bedstead. He sat down beside her, removed his hat, took a minute to put into words what he had come to say.

"I'm sorry it ended how it did. I didn't mean Broomhall to die like that."

"But he did."

"There was nothing else I could do. I had to stop him. You know what he was planning."

"He was planning to overthrow a corrupt regime."

"He was planning to unleash violence and anarchy."

"In order to put a stop to the greater violence inflicted on the people by the King and his bloodthirsty ministers." She turned her face towards him. "Are you proud of what you do?"

"Not always, no."

"Nor should you be."

"I'm a police officer. It's my job to bring criminals to justice."

"You're a spy and an informer, the upholder of a rotten cause, the servant of a cruel and vicious government."

"Dress it up how you like, murder is murder. I saw Broomhall kill one man, order the death of another, and I know he was involved in Kean's death."

"Edward had nothing to do with it."

"Then it was Metcalf did the deed, but Broomhall helped him."

"It wasn't Metcalf. It was me."

"What?"

"I killed George Kean."

A shrill voice broke in on them. "Is he bothering you, love?"

Dan looked up. A pair of young, slatternly women with heavily painted faces had stopped at the foot of the bed.

"He can bother me any time," the other girl cried.

"Go away," he snapped.

"Hoity-toity! Enjoy your bag o' bones then!"

Screeching with laughter at their own wit, the women promenaded away arm in arm.

Dan turned back to Mrs Chambers. She showed not the least sign of emotion. He could hardly believe that the confession had passed her lips.

"What reason would you have to kill him?"

"He was my husband." She stared ahead of her, her voice toneless. "He was a soldier. We married just before he was sent to fight in America. He said he'd come back, but he never did. I thought he was dead. And then one day he walked into the shop with Edward. I was so angry to discover he'd been alive all the time, that he'd abandoned me, left me with nothing. He came back to the shop on his own afterwards, maudlin with drink."

Evelyn Chambers had told Dan that Kean, calling himself Scott, had called at the shop. When Dan had mentioned this to her father, Mr Chambers said he came to buy a book. Since that had been sufficient to explain his visit, Dan had thought no more about it. Why would he, when he had two strong suspects in Broomhall and Metcalf, and no reason to connect Kean and Mrs Chambers?

"He said he was sick of everything – of his wife, his job. His job above all. He'd thought waging war on the old laws and stringing up the lawyers and judges was the only way to change things. But now he'd seen me again after all these years, he realised what it was he wanted. He said he'd never had a day's happiness since he lost me. Lost me! We'd go away, start afresh...the only way I could get rid of him before Mr Chambers discovered us was to agree to meet him again. I said I'd come to him at his lodgings, we'd talk properly, make plans. He was going to destroy my marriage, make my daughters illegitimate. I couldn't let him do that."

"But he had as much to lose as you did. You could have threatened him with gaol for bigamy."

"How would it have helped to have the truth come out in court? No, there was only one way to be safe."

"What happened?"

"He took a room in a lodging house on Gainsford Street, one of those you hire by the hour, so we could meet. The next evening I went to see him as we'd arranged. I hid a knife in my pocket. When I got there he was in his shirtsleeves. He was drinking. I told him it was too late for us, begged

231

him to leave me alone, but he wouldn't listen. He just kept slobbering and pawing at me. Oh, he drove me to distraction. So I stabbed him. It was only a scratch and he was more surprised than hurt. He stood there staring at me, clutching his stomach, the blood seeping on to his shirt. I stabbed him again, harder this time, and I just kept going until he fell. My arms ached and my hands were wet with his blood. I didn't know what to do. I ran to Edward's shop and he came and sorted everything out."

"Is that when Broomhall found out who Scott really was?"

"Edward always knew he was a Runner, but he kept it from the others. He didn't know we'd been married until after George died. Then he said he'd just found out he was a police spy and that was why he had him killed. Of course, they all thought he'd done it himself."

Dan guessed that, knowing Broomhall's temper as they did, no one had dared ask too much about Kean's disappearance. "How did Broomhall know Kean?"

"They first met, if you can call it that, during a raid at the London Corresponding Society committee rooms in Wych Street a couple of years ago. George was afraid that if he went to meetings close to home, he'd be recognised. When he found out Edward was in charge in Southwark, he tracked him down and told him he wanted to join the fight against tyranny."

"And convinced him of his change of heart? But how did he know about the United Patriots?"

"He didn't at first, but Edward soon realised he could be useful and recruited him."

Dan could see how useful Kean, a serving police officer and ex-soldier, must have seemed to Broomhall. But did Mrs Chambers know anything more specific than that? Did she know about the map with Kean's notes on it?

"How did Kean make himself useful?"

She shrugged. "Made bombs, I suppose. It's a pity that Edward didn't get the chance to use them."

"To blow up half of London."

"And build it up again."

"If you say so." Dan picked up his hat and stood up.

"Will I hang now?"

"Not because of me, you won't."

"You won't arrest me for the murder?"

"You've already been tried and sentenced. You can make a confession to someone else if it's the rope you're after. But if you've any feelings left for your family, you'll spare them that. I shan't say a word."

# Chapter Thirty-Two

Dan was in the Bow Street office one afternoon a couple of weeks later writing up an arrest report when John Townsend sauntered in. Inky Tom jumped up to fetch him a chair, which he took in pompous style. He removed his hat, placed the tip of his cane on the floor and folded his hands over the handle. Lavender, Principal Officers Taylor and Miller, and a small crowd of gaolers and clerks gathered around him, eager for royal gossip.

A few days earlier, Mrs Chambers had been taken down to Portsmouth to join a women's convict ship bound for Botany Bay. She had not shared her confession with anyone else, for which Dan was glad.

He wasn't the only one with something to be happy about. For the last few days Captain Ellis had been walking around with a huge smile on his face: Eleanor had written to say she would be home next week. She was bringing her aunt with her. The distraction of having a visitor should make the homecoming easier for all of them.

And Caroline was more contented than Dan had seen her for a long time. The novelty of a baby had not worn off and she still seemed enchanted by Alexander. On his way out of the house that morning, Dan had been thrilled to see his boy clench his fists, though Caroline said it was only what all babies did.

Dan, back on a training regime himself, had taken Nick to Noah's gym and introduced him to the fistic arts. The lad had taken to the sport with gusto. Though not an elegant fighter, he showed signs of being a plucky one.

"You've seen the news today, no doubt?" Townsend said. "The arrests in Scotland?"

The answer was a chorus of "no's", so Townsend explained. "A number of rebellious Caledonians calling themselves the United Scotsmen have been arrested. That'll pull 'em up short, eh? Give the Irish rebels and the English radicals something to think about." He leaned forward with a confidential air and said loudly, "I have it on good authority that there's going to be a similar operation against the London Corresponding Society. I played my part in the downfall of the United Patriots, and I'll do the same against the LCS, until every enemy of His Most Gracious Majesty is put down. Why, only yesterday the Prince of Wales said to me, 'Townsend,' he said, 'Townsend, I am relying on you to protect the Queen and the Princesses from these damned levellers and dissenters!' 'Why, Your Highness,' says I, 'you can rely on John Townsend for that. I won't rest until every one of your enemies is burning in the pit of hell.'"

Inky Tom's mouth fell open in admiration. The others declared their determination to support Townsend. Dan said nothing, scribbled his signature at the bottom of a sheet of paper and reached for a fresh piece.

Townsend looked at him. "What do you say to that, Foster? Time to see the rogues on the run properly this time, eh?"

"If they've committed a crime, yes," Dan answered without looking up from his writing.

"What, you don't think it a crime to wish to overthrow the wisest, the most benevolent, the most enlightened constitution on the globe?"

"I'd think the wish a crime if there was such a thing to overthrow."

Townsend's eyebrows shot up towards his hairline. "That is a strange opinion for an officer of the law to hold. The best thing to do with these treacherous, malcontented rats is to ferret 'em out and nail 'em to the gibbet."

Dan shrugged and went back to his report. He was not interested in pursuing the argument.

Townsend winked at his audience. "I do believe our friend

here has caught the levelling contagion himself."

"Oh, no, sir!" Inky Tom cried. "I heard Sir William say that without Mr Foster we'd never have brought down the United Patriots."

Townsend frowned. "I don't think Foster was all on his own, though?"

"He was when he risked his life to join 'em, the murdering gang of body snatchers."

"That's enough, Tom," Dan said. "The case is closed and no more is to be said about it." For some minutes he had been aware of a commotion outside and he changed the subject by asking, "What's that noise?"

Tom went to the window and looked out. "There's a crowd gathered."

"What, a riot?" asked Officer Taylor, his hand moving to the handle of his pistol.

"It looks like you might get a chance to quell a rebellious mob this very day, Townsend," Dan said.

"I don't think they're rioting," Tom called over his shoulder.

Lavender, who was standing behind him, nodded. "They look as if they've found something vastly entertaining about the police office all of a sudden. And the officers who have come out of the Brown Bear seem to be sharing the joke. Macmanus is almost bursting with laughing."

Reassured by this, Townsend and the rest crowded into the passageway to get a closer look. Dan stayed at his desk. A minute later Macmanus appeared in the doorway.

"Hey, Foster, something here for you!"

"What?"

Macmanus had already gone. Dan got up and followed him into the passage. He could just see over the tops of his colleagues' heads to the laughing, cheering crowd outside. From somewhere in its midst poured a stream of obscenities.

"What's going on?" he asked.

"See for yourself," chuckled Macmanus, stepping aside to make room for Dan on the doorstep.

Officers Taylor and Miller had gone down into the crowd. It had parted to let them through, revealing two men sitting on the pavement, tied together back to back. They were red in the face with rage, spitting, kicking and cursing. One of them had a large sheet of paper pinned to his coat.

The officers dragged the captives to their feet and Taylor tore off the note.

"Here, Foster!" he called.

Inky Tom grabbed the paper and passed it back to Dan, who read out the words scrawled on the sheet.

"*Officer Foster. A token of my gratitude. BH.* It's from Ben Hardyman, the resurrectionist."

He put the note in his pocket and looked down at the battered and mired figures of Nipps and Trinder, the missing members of Dawson's body-snatching gang.

"You have some unsavoury friends, Foster," said John Townsend.

Dan ignored the remark. "Bring them inside," he said.

Taylor and Miller marched the hapless pair into the building. The crowd, seeing the fun was over, dispersed quietly. Dan remained on the doorstep and watched Townsend strut off after them, his cane tapping irritably on the pavement. As if aware of Dan's gaze, the Prince of Wales's friend turned and looked back at him.

It was a look of pure animosity. Still, Dan told himself, their mutual dislike was unlikely to make much difference to either of them. Their paths did not often cross. The centre of Townsend's life was Buckingham House, Dan's Bow Street. Dan put it out of his mind and followed the others back into the police office.

THE END

# Notes

**Arey sneaks touting the case**
Thieves who specialise in robbing basements (arey sneaks) observing (touting) the house (case).

**Broughton's Rules**
In 1743, undefeated pugilist Jack Broughton (c.1703–1789), who ran a boxing academy for the gentry in London (the amphitheatre on Oxford Road), formulated the first set of rules for the sport. Amongst other things, the rules banned hitting a man when he was down, or grabbing him below the waist or by the hair or breeches. Originally intended only for use in his academy, Broughton's Rules were widely adopted and were not replaced until the introduction of the "New Rules" in 1838.

**Bully**
A man who protects prostitutes; often employed in a brothel.

**Clouts**
Cloths, rags.

**Dive**
To pick a pocket.

**Flat**
Someone easily cheated.

**Gagging Acts (The Seditious Meetings Act and The Treasonable and Seditious Practices Act) (Also known as the Two Acts)**
The Seditious Meetings Act and The Treasonable and Seditious Practices Act, known as the Gagging Acts, were passed in 1795 in an effort to suppress radical political societies, in particular the London Corresponding Society. The Seditious Meetings Act banned public meetings of more than fifty attendees unless a Magistrate's Licence had first been obtained. The Act also gave magistrates the power to close a licensed meeting if they deemed speeches were likely to bring the King or constitution into contempt.

The Treasonable Practices Act extended the meaning of "high treason" to include any who "compassed or devised" the death, imprisonment, harm or deposition of the King, or who pressured him to change his policies. Where formerly treason had been defined as acts taken or plotted against the monarch, it now incorporated speaking or writing where no act had been carried out.

| | |
|---|---|
| **Grabs** | Body snatchers. |
| **Jerry Sneak** | A sneak or informer (also a henpecked husband). |
| **London Corresponding Society** | A radical men's organisation founded by shoemaker Thomas Hardy (1752–1832) in 1792. The LCS called for universal male suffrage and annual parliaments, and welcomed the French Revolution. As its name suggests, it was in constant contact with radicals in other parts of the country. However, the Government took increasingly repressive measures against it, finally outlawing it in 1799. |
| **Lumper** | Labourer who loads or unloads ships' cargoes. |
| **Madge** | A woman's genitals. |
| **Molly house** | A brothel for homosexual men. |
| **Mufflers** | Padded boxing gloves. |
| **Nabman** | Police officer, constable. |
| **Nattomy** | A skeleton or body for dissection. |
| **Pigeon** | A man who is easily tricked. |
| **Pock-fretten** | Marked with smallpox. |
| **Quartered** | Divided into parts fewer or more than four (old usage; more familiar to us as meaning divided into four). |
| **Resurrection Men** | Men who steal bodies from graveyards in order to sell them to doctors and medical students for dissection. |
| **Rhino** | Money. |
| **The Fancy** | Followers of boxing. (Also used of other sports, e.g. pigeon fanciers.) |
| **Thing** | A corpse. |

# Acknowledgements

I would like to thank all the people who have helped me in the writing of this book. I am grateful to Sanjida O'Connell of ARC Editorial for reading an early draft; to my beta readers David Penny, Debbie Young, Richard Tearle and Alison Morton for their thoughtful comments; to Alison Jack for her editorial services; and to Helen Hart and the team at SilverWood Books for being so lovely to work with. Special thanks to my sister and formidable editor, Glynis van Uden, who never misses a thing, and to Helen French for advice on forensic pathology. As ever, I can't thank my husband, Gerard, enough for his support, enthusiasm and optimism. And above all, thank you to the readers who were kind enough to ask, "When will there be another Dan Foster Mystery?" I hope you have enjoyed this one!

Bow Street Runners and bare-knuckle fighters, radicals and pickpockets, resurrection men and bluestockings...

Find out more about Dan Foster's world at
www.lucienneboyce.com